big
NATE
REVENGE OF THE
CREAM PUFFS

More

big NATE

adventures from

LINCOLN PEIRCE

Big Nate From the Top

Big Nate Out Loud

Big Nate and Friends

Big Nate Makes the Grade

Big Nate All Work and No Play

Big Nate: Game On!

Big Nate: I Can't Take It!

Big Nate: Great Minds Think Alike

Big Nate: The Crowd Goes Wild!

Big Nate's Greatest Hits

Big Nate: Say Good-bye to Dork City

Big Nate: Welcome to My World

Big Nate: Thunka, Thunka, Thunka

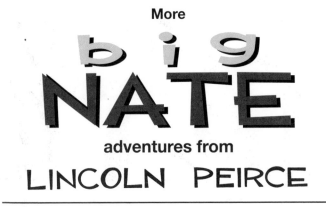

big NATE
REVENGE OF THE CREAM PUFFS

by LINCOLN PEIRCE

Andrews McMeel
PUBLISHING®

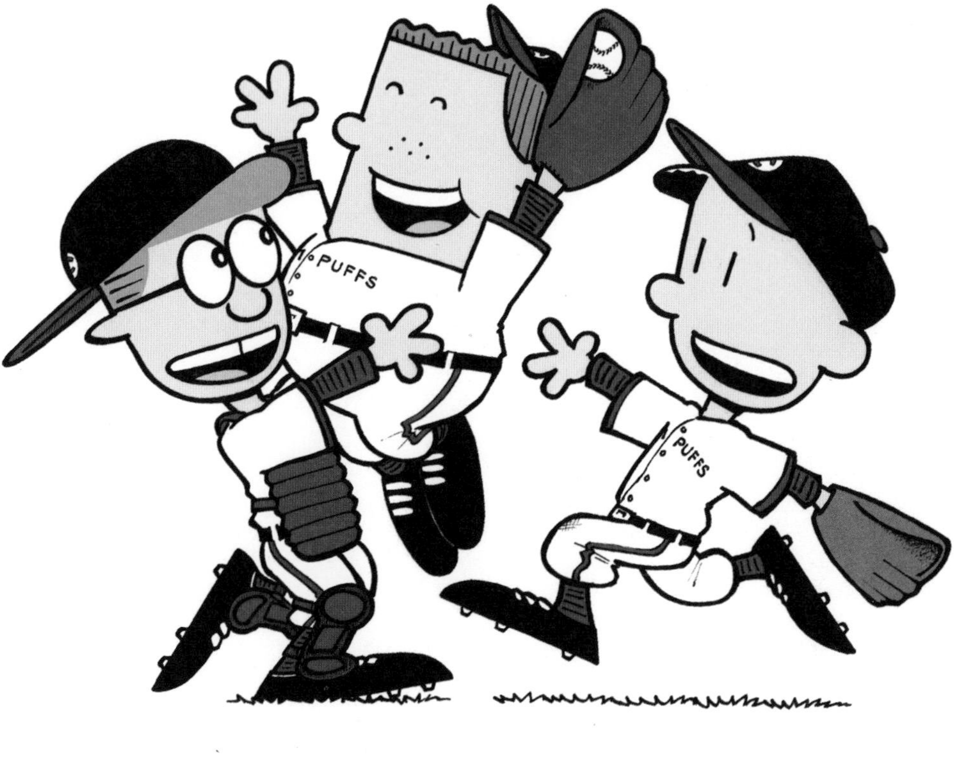
PUFFS
PUFFS

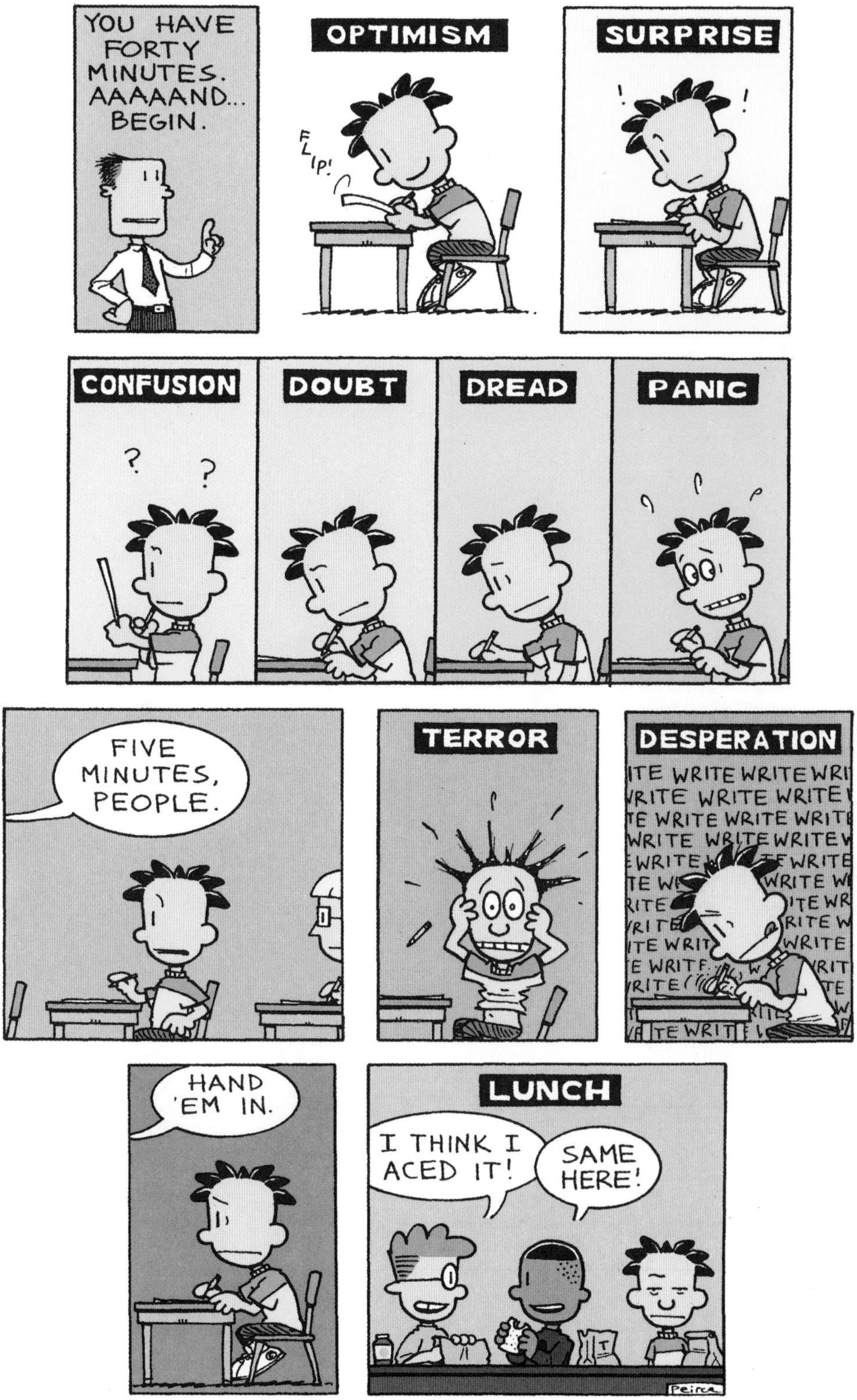
YOU HAVE FORTY MINUTES. AAAAAND... BEGIN.
OPTIMISM
FLIP!
SURPRISE
CONFUSION
DOUBT
DREAD
PANIC
FIVE MINUTES, PEOPLE.
TERROR
DESPERATION
HAND 'EM IN.
LUNCH
I THINK I ACED IT!
SAME HERE!
Peirce

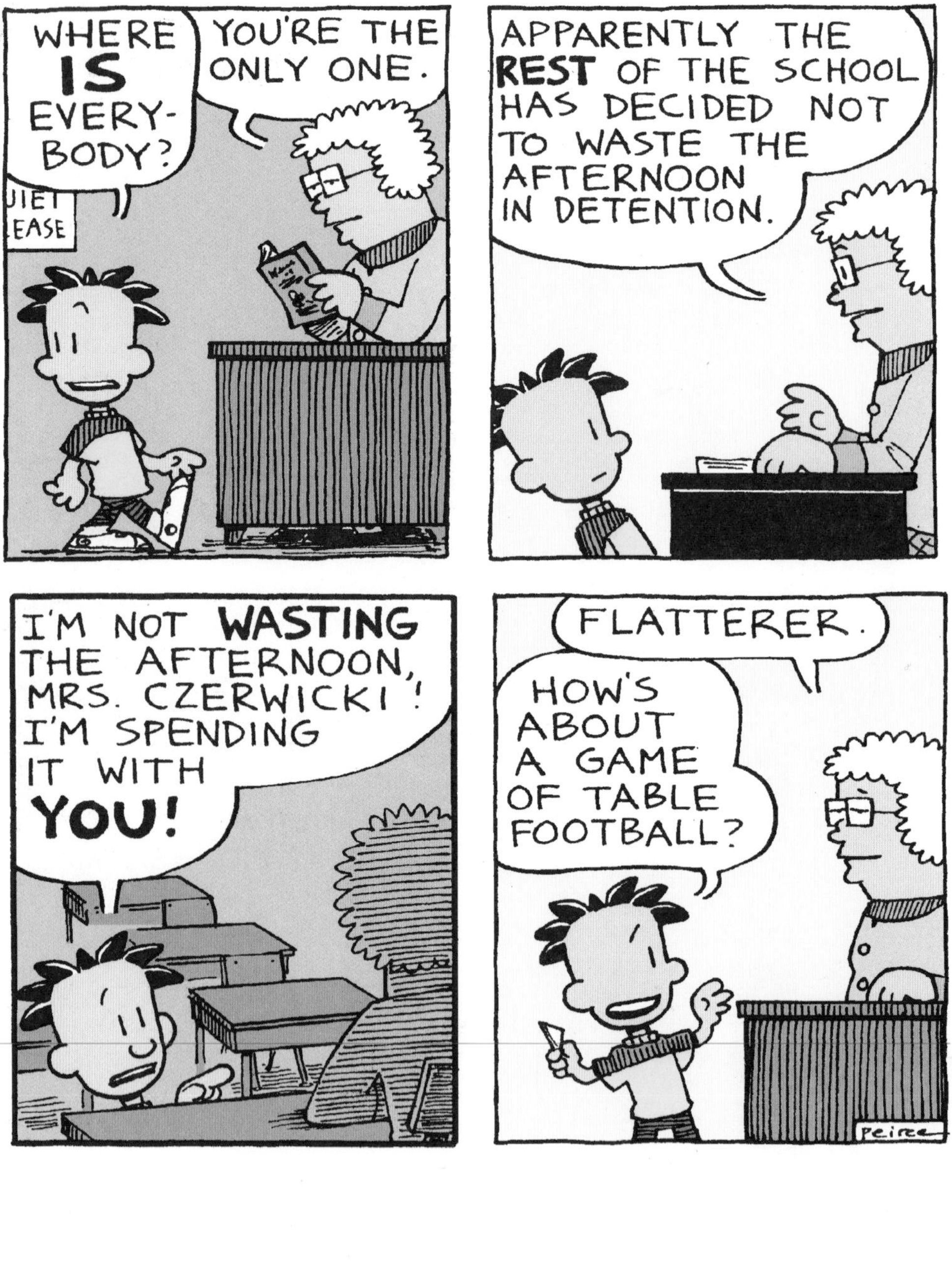
WHERE IS EVERY-BODY?
YOU'RE THE ONLY ONE.
APPARENTLY THE REST OF THE SCHOOL HAS DECIDED NOT TO WASTE THE AFTERNOON IN DETENTION.
I'M NOT WASTING THE AFTERNOON, MRS. CZERWICKI! I'M SPENDING IT WITH YOU!
HOW'S ABOUT A GAME OF TABLE FOOTBALL?
FLATTERER.
peirce

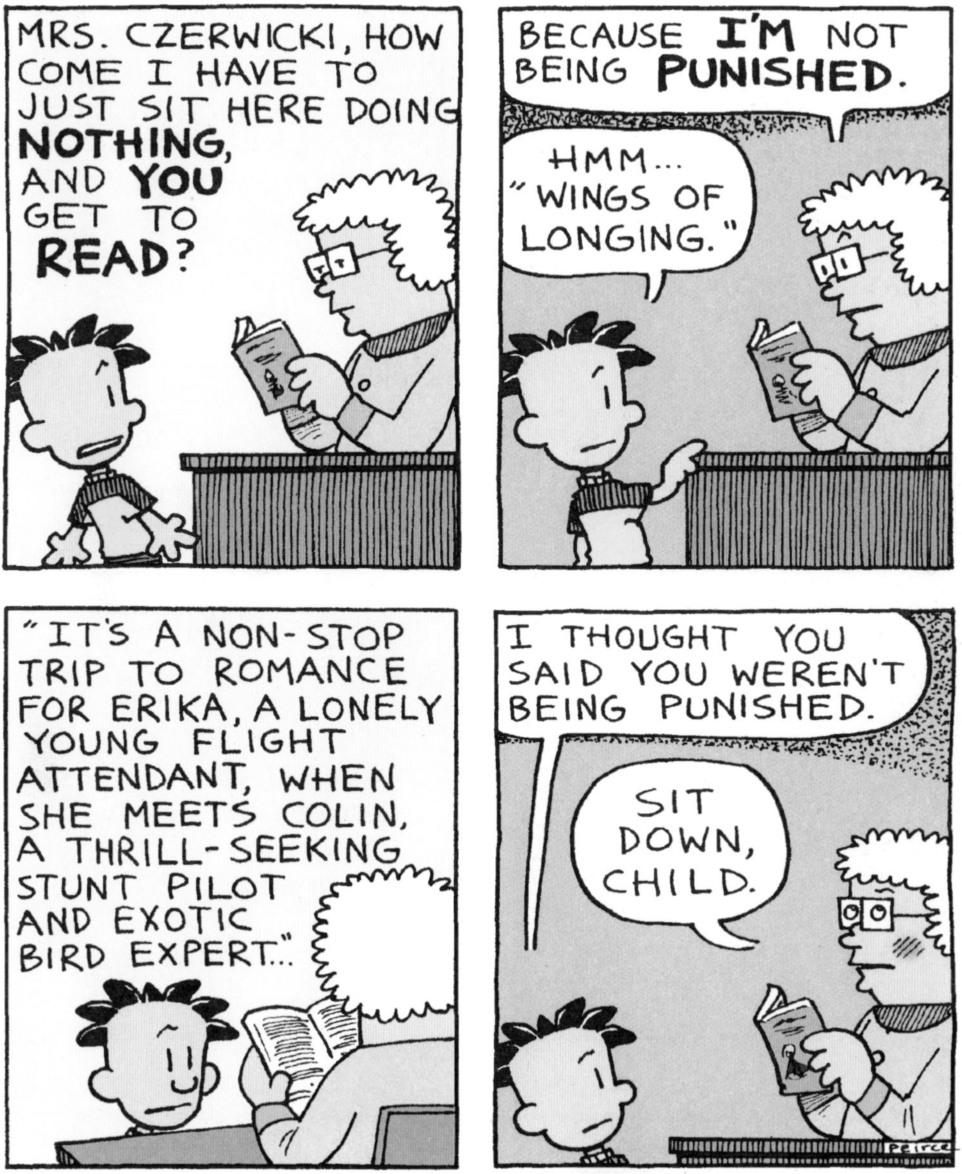
MRS. CZERWICKI, HOW COME I HAVE TO JUST SIT HERE DOING NOTHING, AND YOU GET TO READ?
BECAUSE I'M NOT BEING PUNISHED.
HMM... "WINGS OF LONGING."
"IT'S A NON-STOP TRIP TO ROMANCE FOR ERIKA, A LONELY YOUNG FLIGHT ATTENDANT, WHEN SHE MEETS COLIN, A THRILL-SEEKING STUNT PILOT AND EXOTIC BIRD EXPERT..."
I THOUGHT YOU SAID YOU WEREN'T BEING PUNISHED.
SIT DOWN, CHILD.
PEIRCE

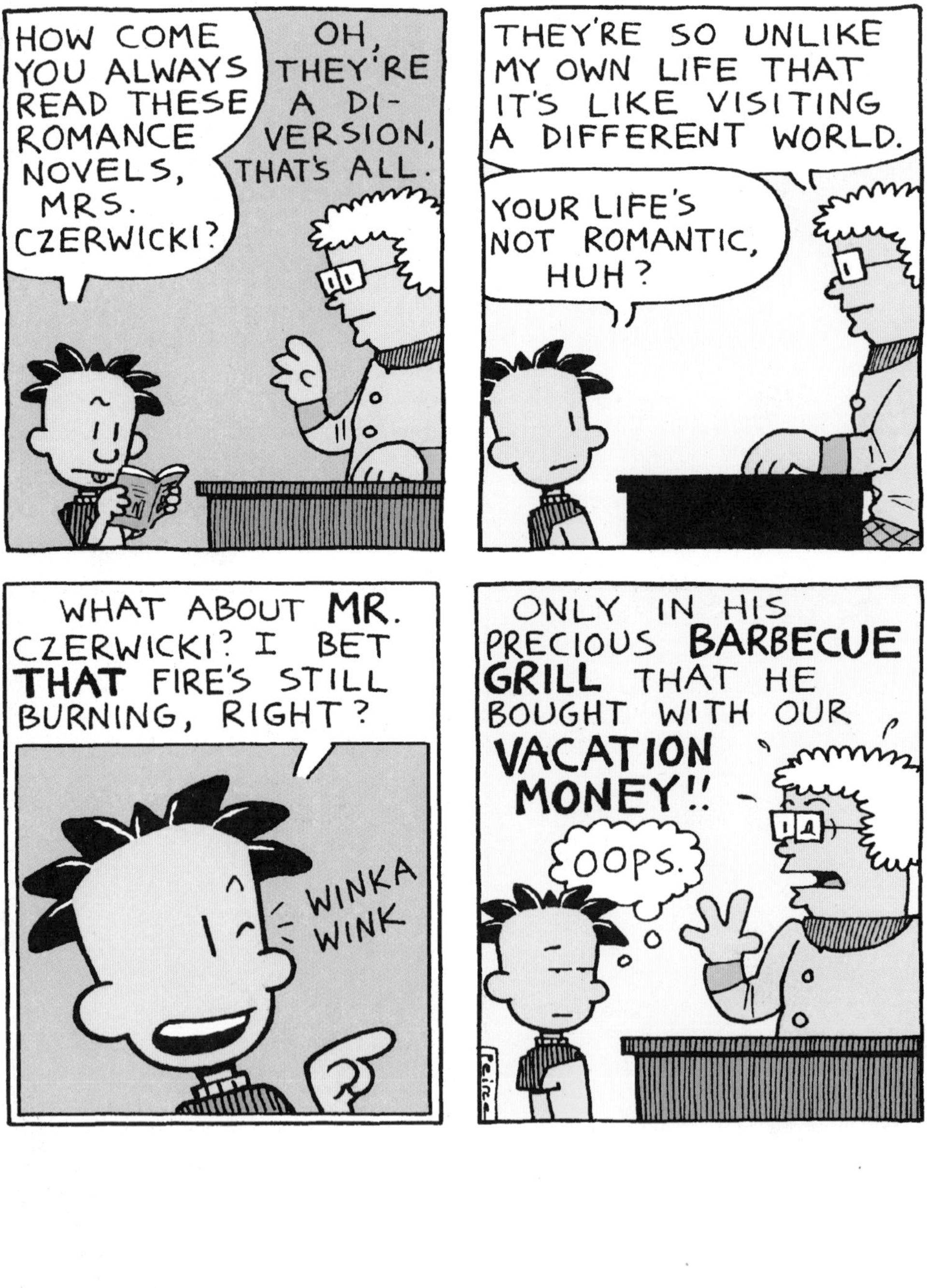
HOW COME YOU ALWAYS READ THESE ROMANCE NOVELS, MRS. CZERWICKI?
OH, THEY'RE A DI-VERSION, THAT'S ALL.
THEY'RE SO UNLIKE MY OWN LIFE THAT IT'S LIKE VISITING A DIFFERENT WORLD.
YOUR LIFE'S NOT ROMANTIC, HUH?
WHAT ABOUT **MR.** CZERWICKI? I BET **THAT** FIRE'S STILL BURNING, RIGHT?
WINKA WINK
ONLY IN HIS PRECIOUS **BARBECUE GRILL** THAT HE BOUGHT WITH OUR **VACATION MONEY!!**
OOPS.
Peirce

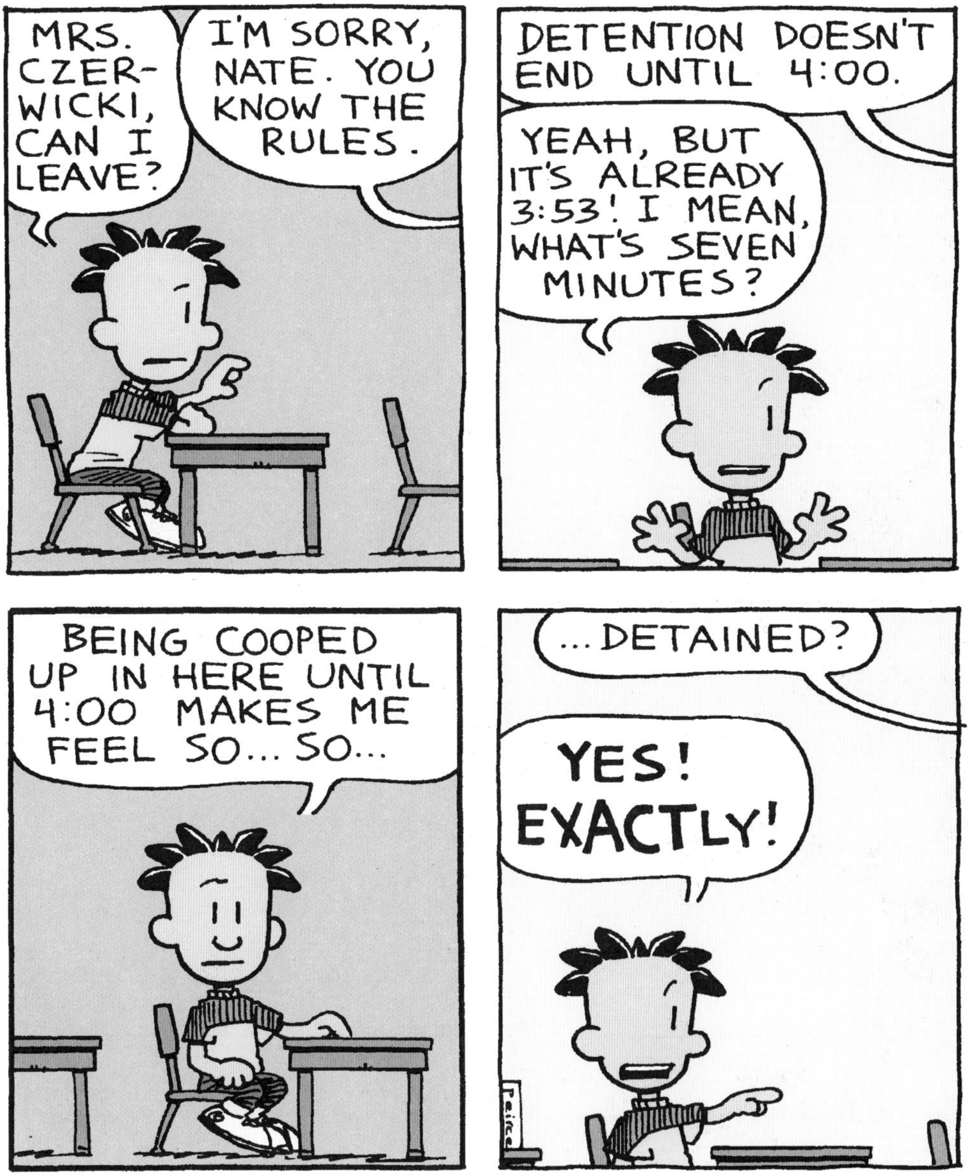
MRS. CZER-WICKI, CAN I LEAVE?
I'M SORRY, NATE. YOU KNOW THE RULES.
DETENTION DOESN'T END UNTIL 4:00.
YEAH, BUT IT'S ALREADY 3:53! I MEAN, WHAT'S SEVEN MINUTES?
BEING COOPED UP IN HERE UNTIL 4:00 MAKES ME FEEL SO... SO...
...DETAINED?
YES! EXACTLY!
Peirce

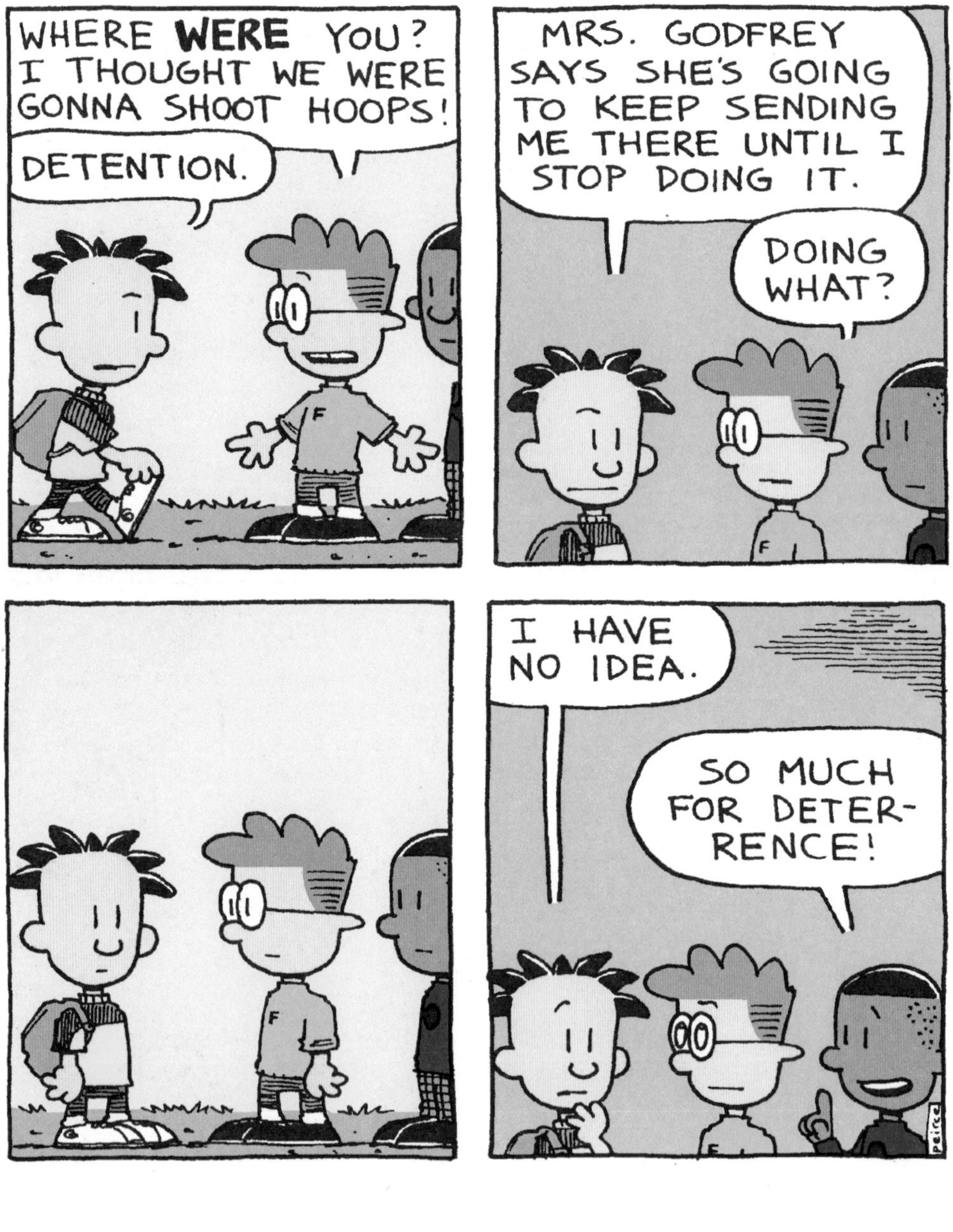
WHERE **WERE** YOU? I THOUGHT WE WERE GONNA SHOOT HOOPS!
DETENTION.
MRS. GODFREY SAYS SHE'S GOING TO KEEP SENDING ME THERE UNTIL I STOP DOING IT.
DOING WHAT?
I HAVE NO IDEA.
SO MUCH FOR DETER-RENCE!
peirce

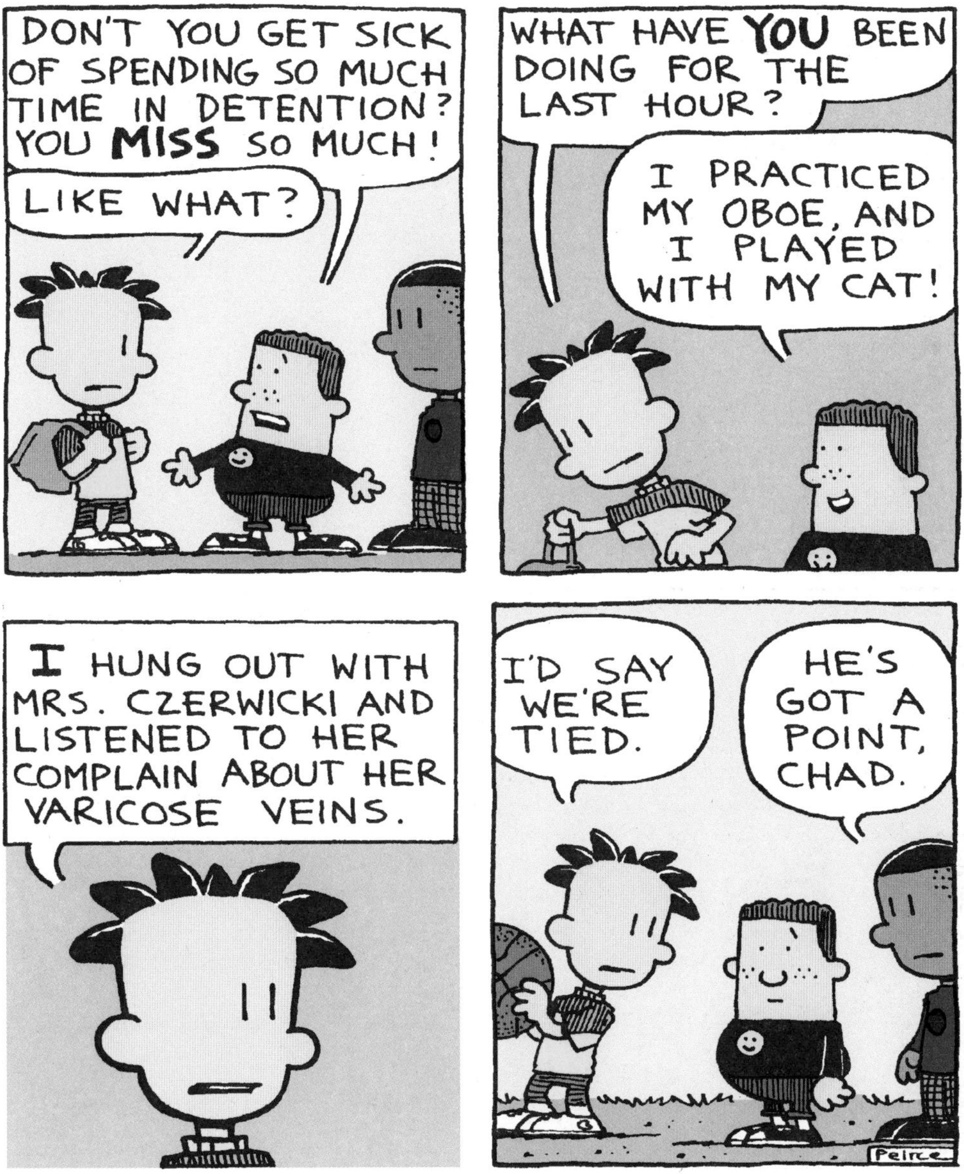
DON'T YOU GET SICK OF SPENDING SO MUCH TIME IN DETENTION? YOU MISS SO MUCH!
LIKE WHAT?
WHAT HAVE YOU BEEN DOING FOR THE LAST HOUR?
I PRACTICED MY OBOE, AND I PLAYED WITH MY CAT!
I HUNG OUT WITH MRS. CZERWICKI AND LISTENED TO HER COMPLAIN ABOUT HER VARICOSE VEINS.
I'D SAY WE'RE TIED.
HE'S GOT A POINT, CHAD.
Peirce

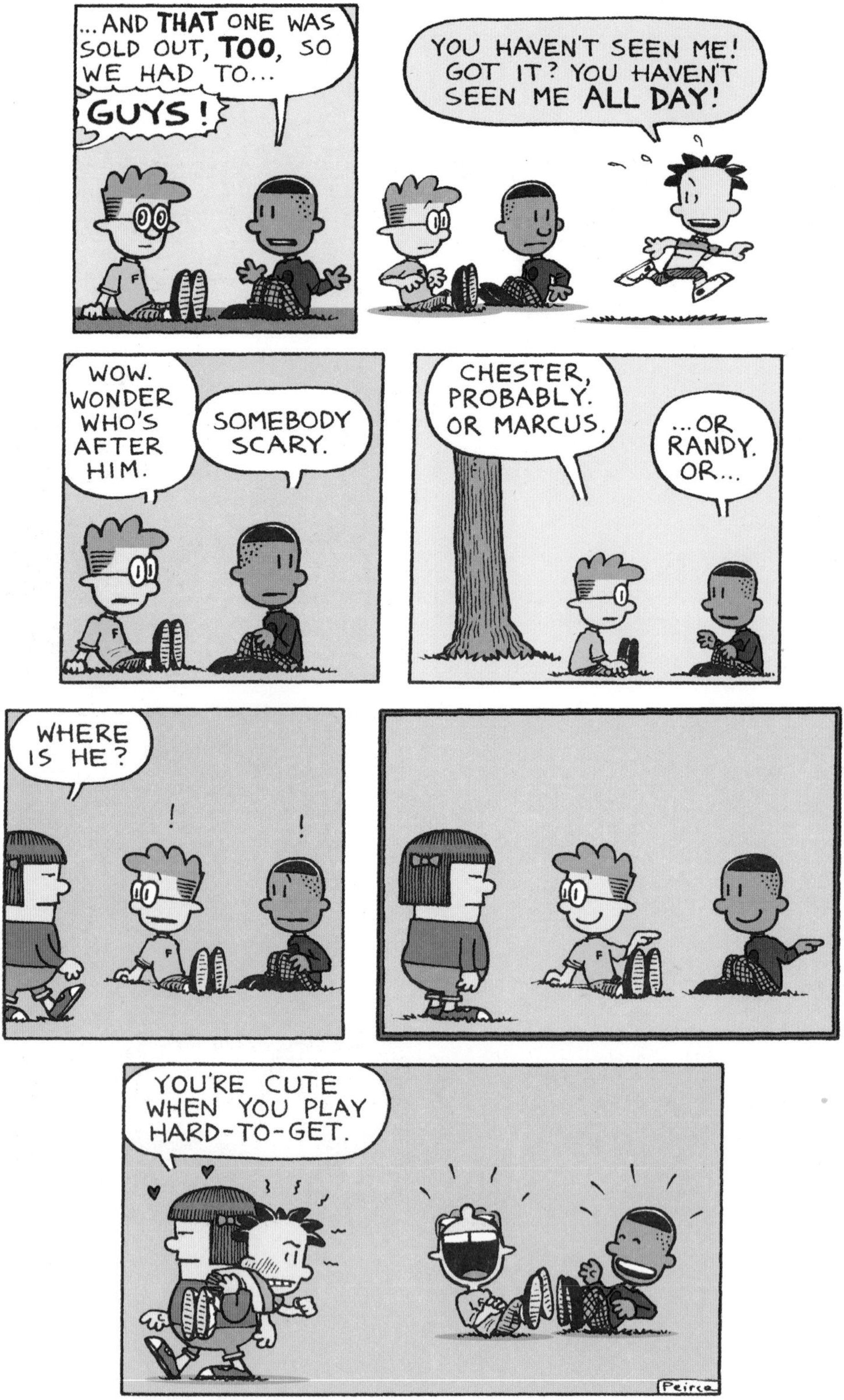
...AND THAT ONE WAS SOLD OUT, TOO, SO WE HAD TO...
GUYS!
YOU HAVEN'T SEEN ME! GOT IT? YOU HAVEN'T SEEN ME ALL DAY!
WOW. WONDER WHO'S AFTER HIM.
SOMEBODY SCARY.
CHESTER, PROBABLY. OR MARCUS.
...OR RANDY. OR...
WHERE IS HE?
!
!
YOU'RE CUTE WHEN YOU PLAY HARD-TO-GET.
Peirce

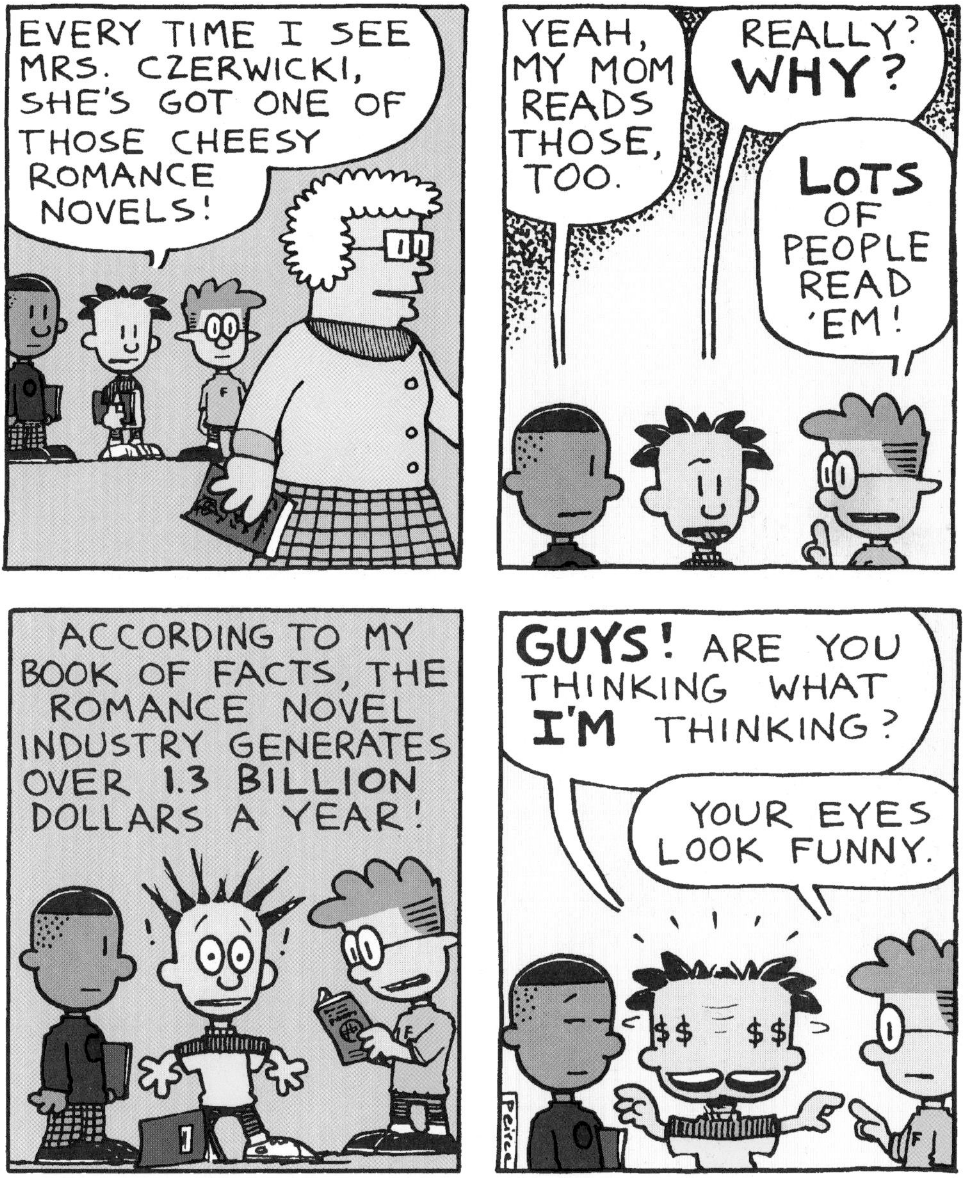
EVERY TIME I SEE MRS. CZERWICKI, SHE'S GOT ONE OF THOSE CHEESY ROMANCE NOVELS!
YEAH, MY MOM READS THOSE, TOO.
REALLY? WHY?
LOTS OF PEOPLE READ 'EM!
ACCORDING TO MY BOOK OF FACTS, THE ROMANCE NOVEL INDUSTRY GENERATES OVER 1.3 BILLION DOLLARS A YEAR!
GUYS! ARE YOU THINKING WHAT I'M THINKING?
YOUR EYES LOOK FUNNY.
PEIRCE

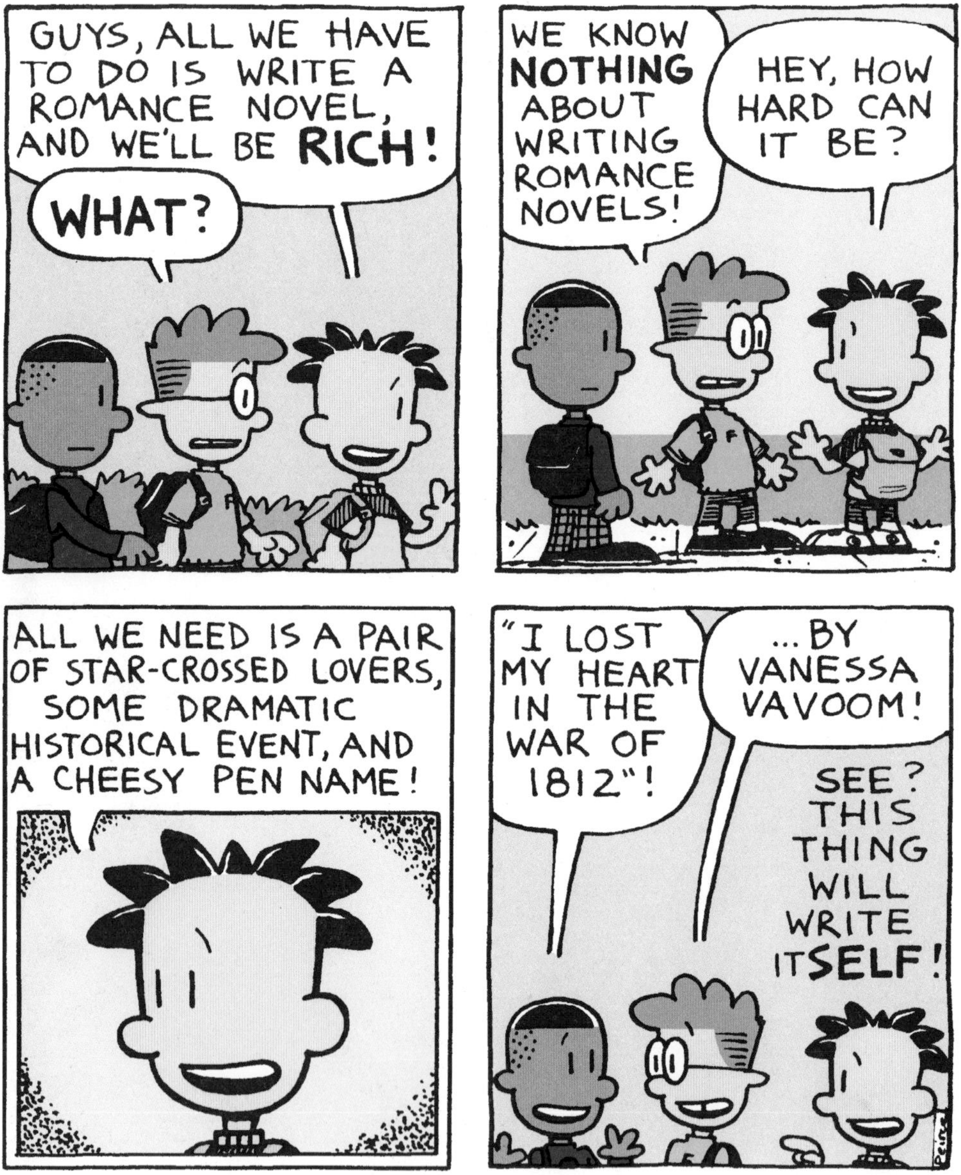
GUYS, ALL WE HAVE TO DO IS WRITE A ROMANCE NOVEL, AND WE'LL BE RICH!
WHAT?
WE KNOW NOTHING ABOUT WRITING ROMANCE NOVELS!
HEY, HOW HARD CAN IT BE?
ALL WE NEED IS A PAIR OF STAR-CROSSED LOVERS, SOME DRAMATIC HISTORICAL EVENT, AND A CHEESY PEN NAME!
"I LOST MY HEART IN THE WAR OF 1812"!
...BY VANESSA VAVOOM!
SEE? THIS THING WILL WRITE ITSELF!

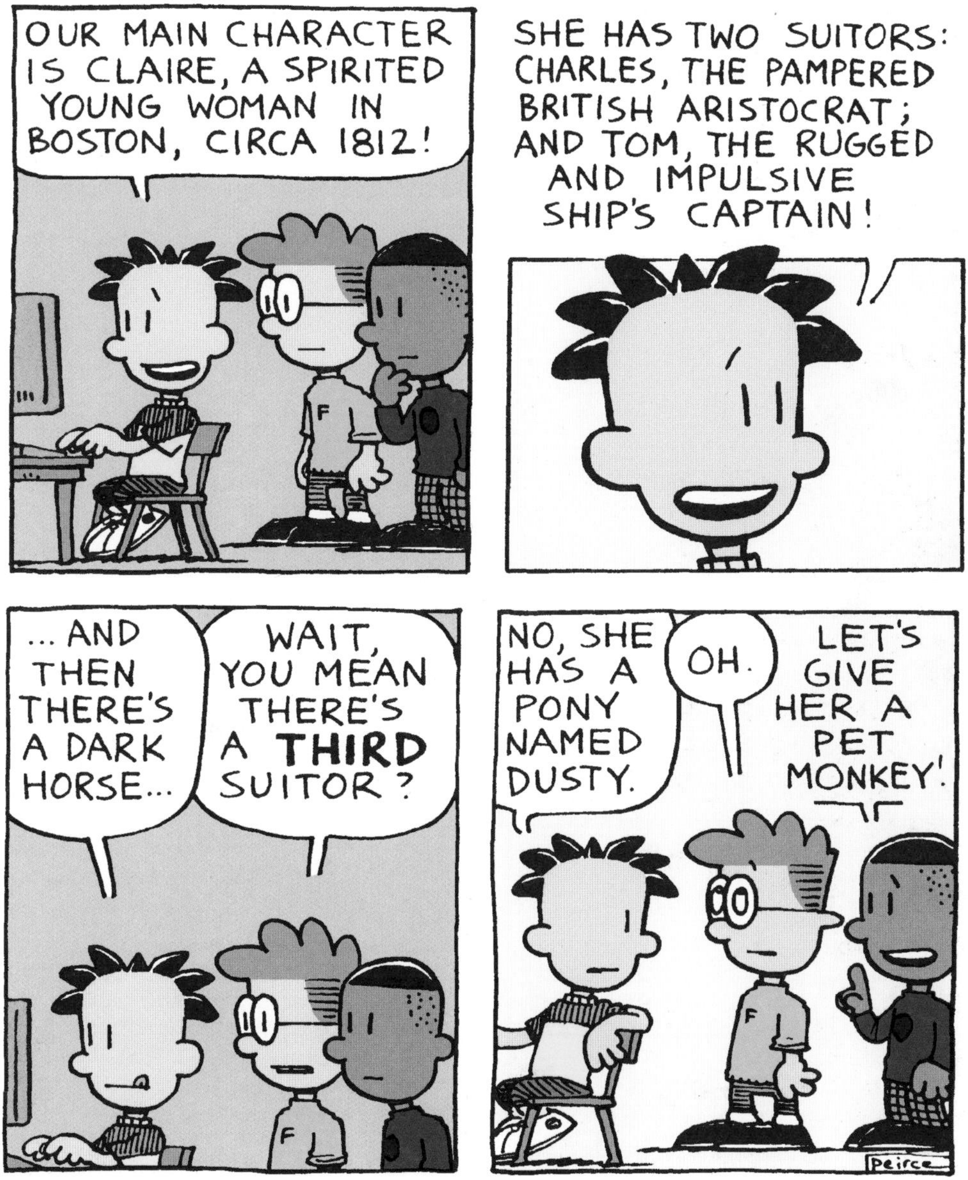
OUR MAIN CHARACTER IS CLAIRE, A SPIRITED YOUNG WOMAN IN BOSTON, CIRCA 1812!
SHE HAS TWO SUITORS: CHARLES, THE PAMPERED BRITISH ARISTOCRAT; AND TOM, THE RUGGED AND IMPULSIVE SHIP'S CAPTAIN!
... AND THEN THERE'S A DARK HORSE...
WAIT, YOU MEAN THERE'S A **THIRD** SUITOR?
NO, SHE HAS A PONY NAMED DUSTY.
OH.
LET'S GIVE HER A PET MONKEY!
Peirce

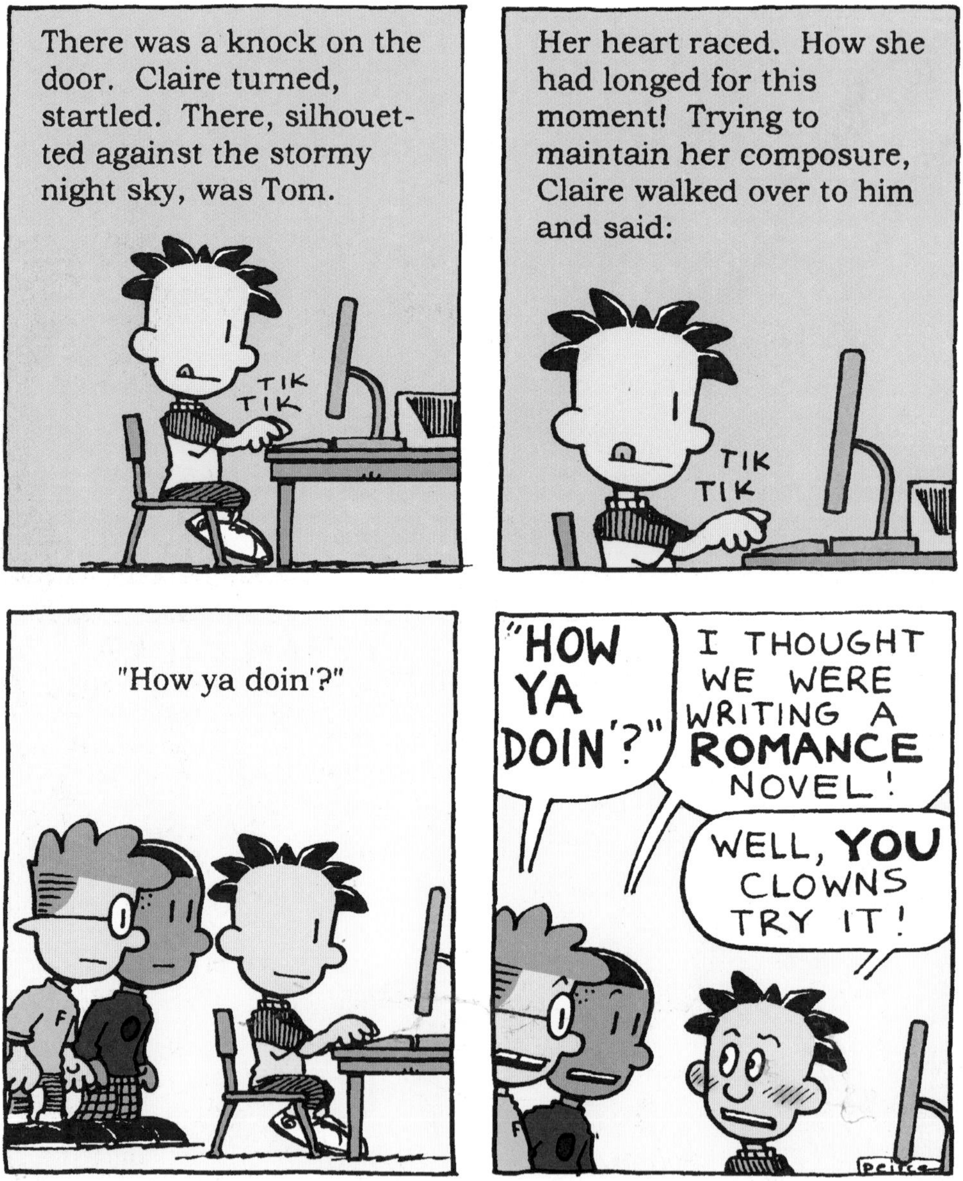
There was a knock on the door. Claire turned, startled. There, silhouetted against the stormy night sky, was Tom.
TIK TIK
Her heart raced. How she had longed for this moment! Trying to maintain her composure, Claire walked over to him and said:
TIK TIK
"How ya doin'?"
"HOW YA DOIN'?"
I THOUGHT WE WERE WRITING A ROMANCE NOVEL!
WELL, YOU CLOWNS TRY IT!

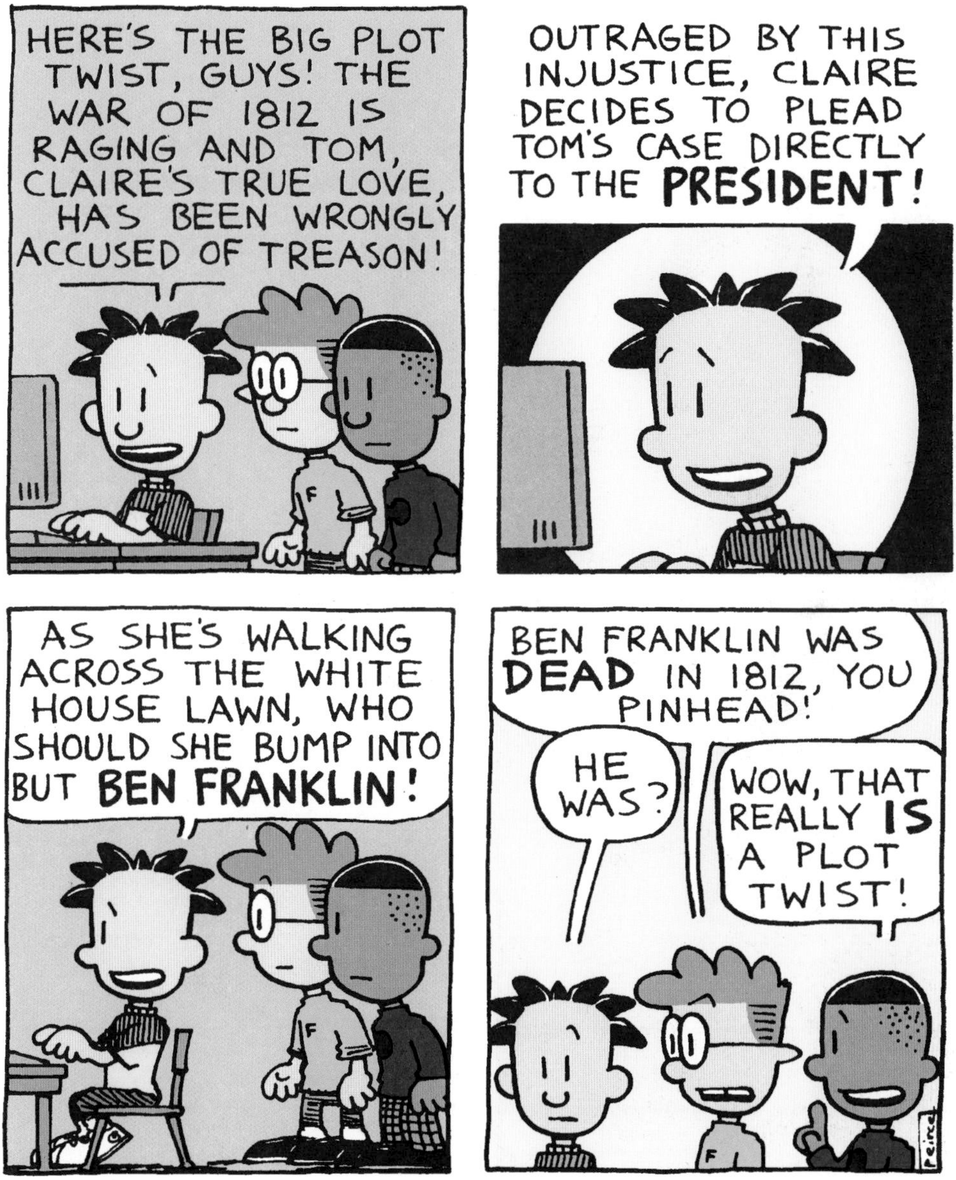
HERE'S THE BIG PLOT TWIST, GUYS! THE WAR OF 1812 IS RAGING AND TOM, CLAIRE'S TRUE LOVE, HAS BEEN WRONGLY ACCUSED OF TREASON!
OUTRAGED BY THIS INJUSTICE, CLAIRE DECIDES TO PLEAD TOM'S CASE DIRECTLY TO THE **PRESIDENT**!
AS SHE'S WALKING ACROSS THE WHITE HOUSE LAWN, WHO SHOULD SHE BUMP INTO BUT **BEN FRANKLIN**!
BEN FRANKLIN WAS **DEAD** IN 1812, YOU PINHEAD!
HE WAS?
WOW, THAT REALLY **IS** A PLOT TWIST!

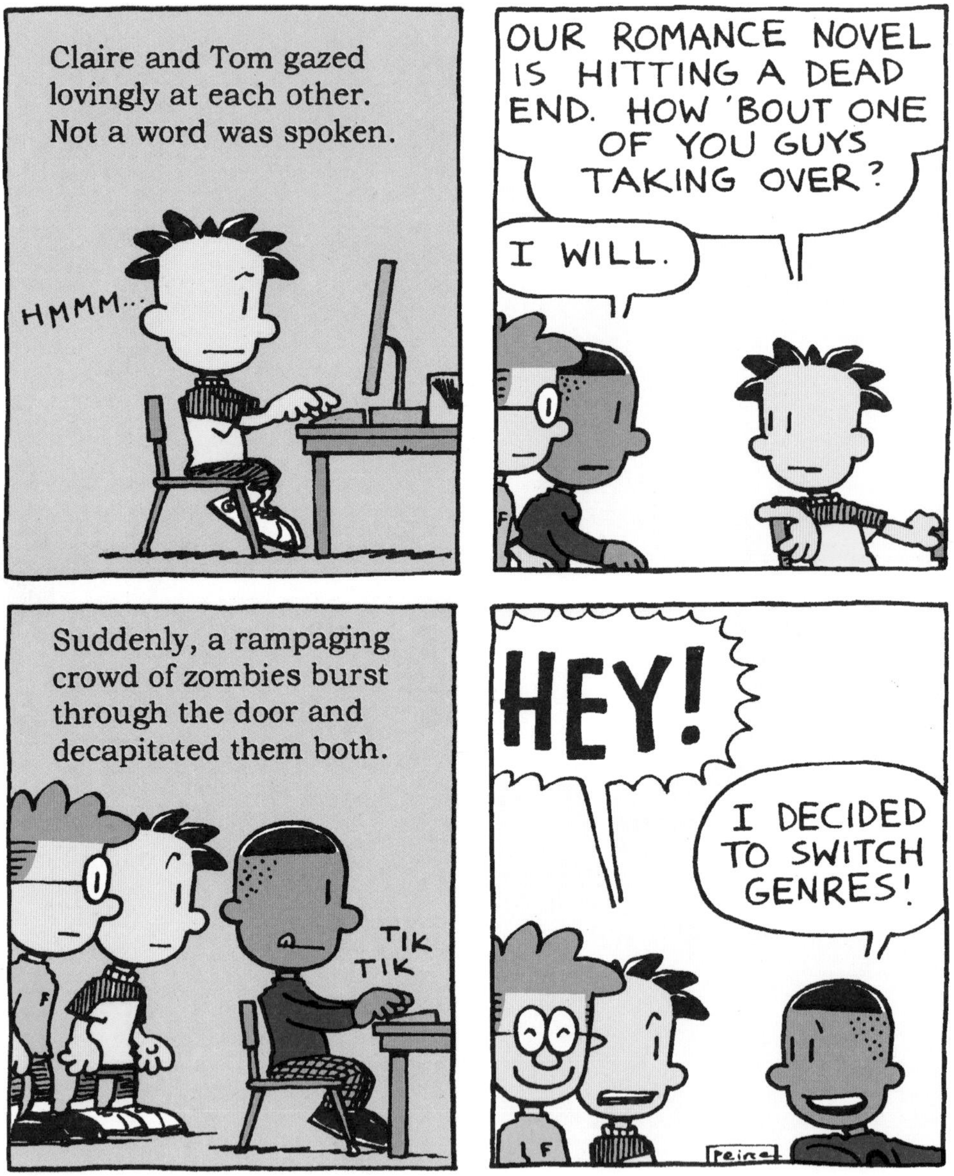
Claire and Tom gazed lovingly at each other. Not a word was spoken.
HMMM...
OUR ROMANCE NOVEL IS HITTING A DEAD END. HOW 'BOUT ONE OF YOU GUYS TAKING OVER?
I WILL.
Suddenly, a rampaging crowd of zombies burst through the door and decapitated them both.
TIK TIK
HEY!
I DECIDED TO SWITCH GENRES!
peirce

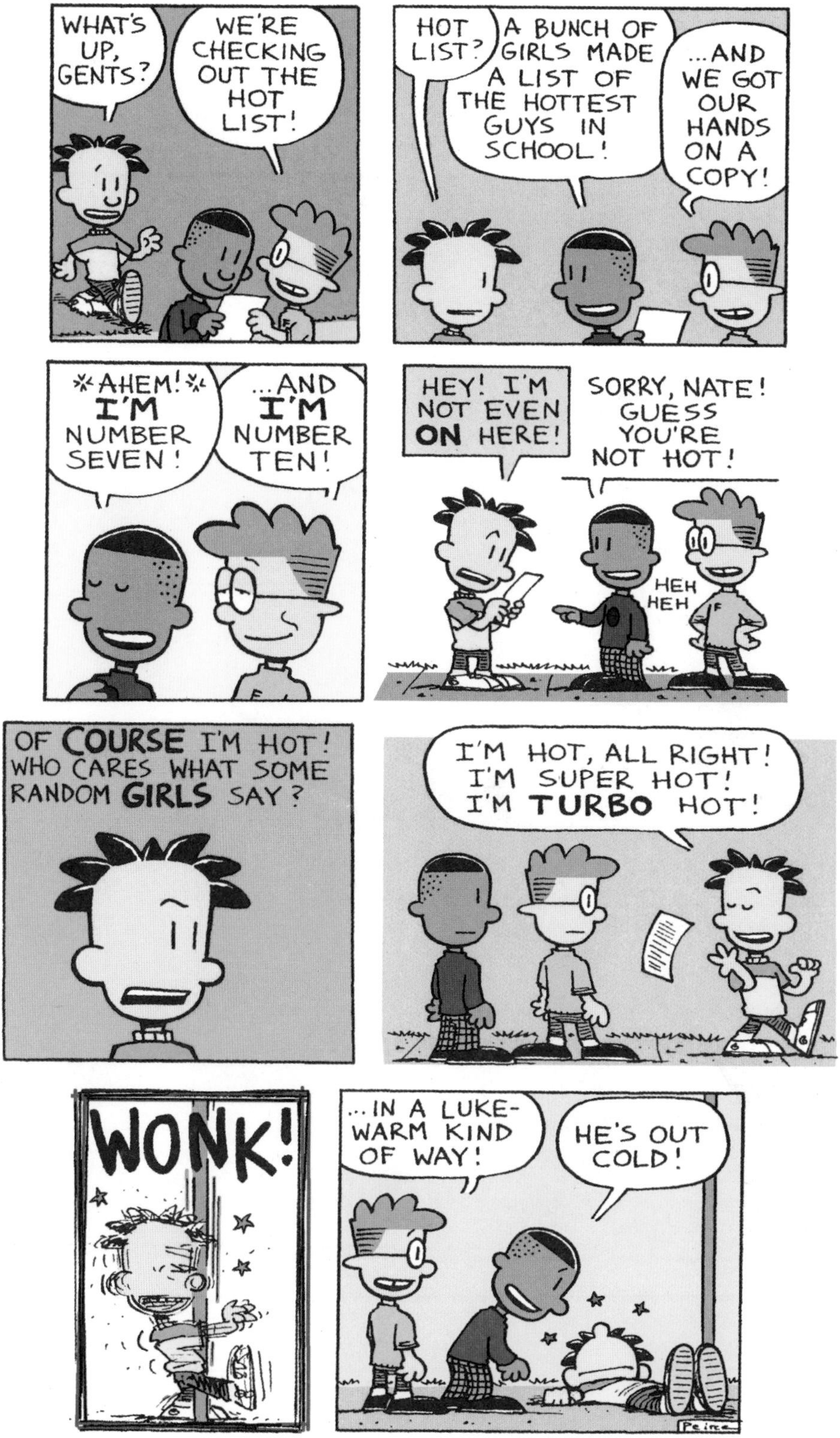
WHAT'S UP, GENTS?
WE'RE CHECKING OUT THE HOT LIST!
HOT LIST?
A BUNCH OF GIRLS MADE A LIST OF THE HOTTEST GUYS IN SCHOOL!
...AND WE GOT OUR HANDS ON A COPY!
AHEM! I'M NUMBER SEVEN!
...AND I'M NUMBER TEN!
HEY! I'M NOT EVEN ON HERE!
SORRY, NATE! GUESS YOU'RE NOT HOT!
HEH HEH
OF COURSE I'M HOT! WHO CARES WHAT SOME RANDOM GIRLS SAY?
I'M HOT, ALL RIGHT! I'M SUPER HOT! I'M TURBO HOT!
WONK!
...IN A LUKE-WARM KIND OF WAY!
HE'S OUT COLD!
Peirce

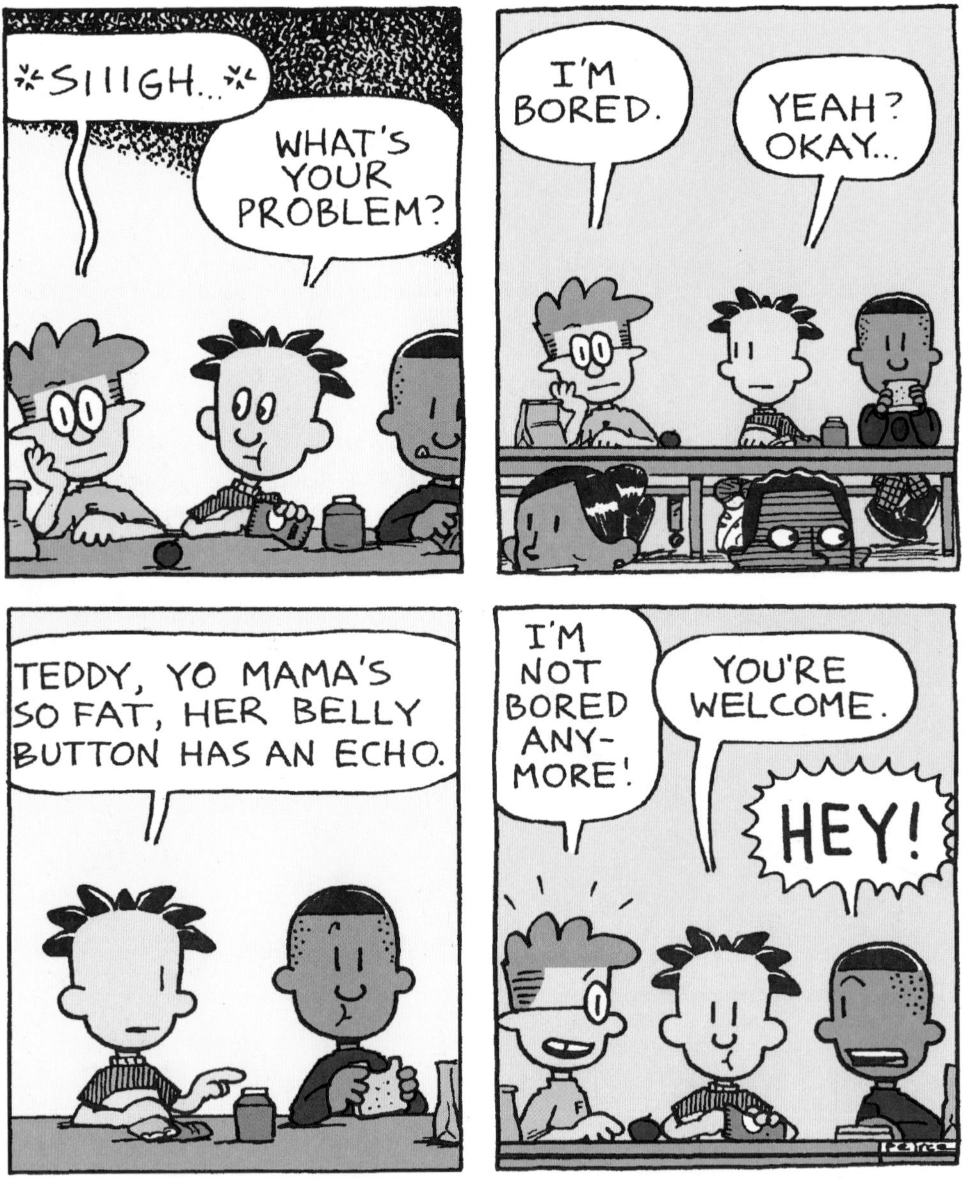
SIIIGH...
WHAT'S YOUR PROBLEM?
I'M BORED.
YEAH? OKAY...
TEDDY, YO MAMA'S SO FAT, HER BELLY BUTTON HAS AN ECHO.
I'M NOT BORED ANY-MORE!
YOU'RE WELCOME.
HEY!

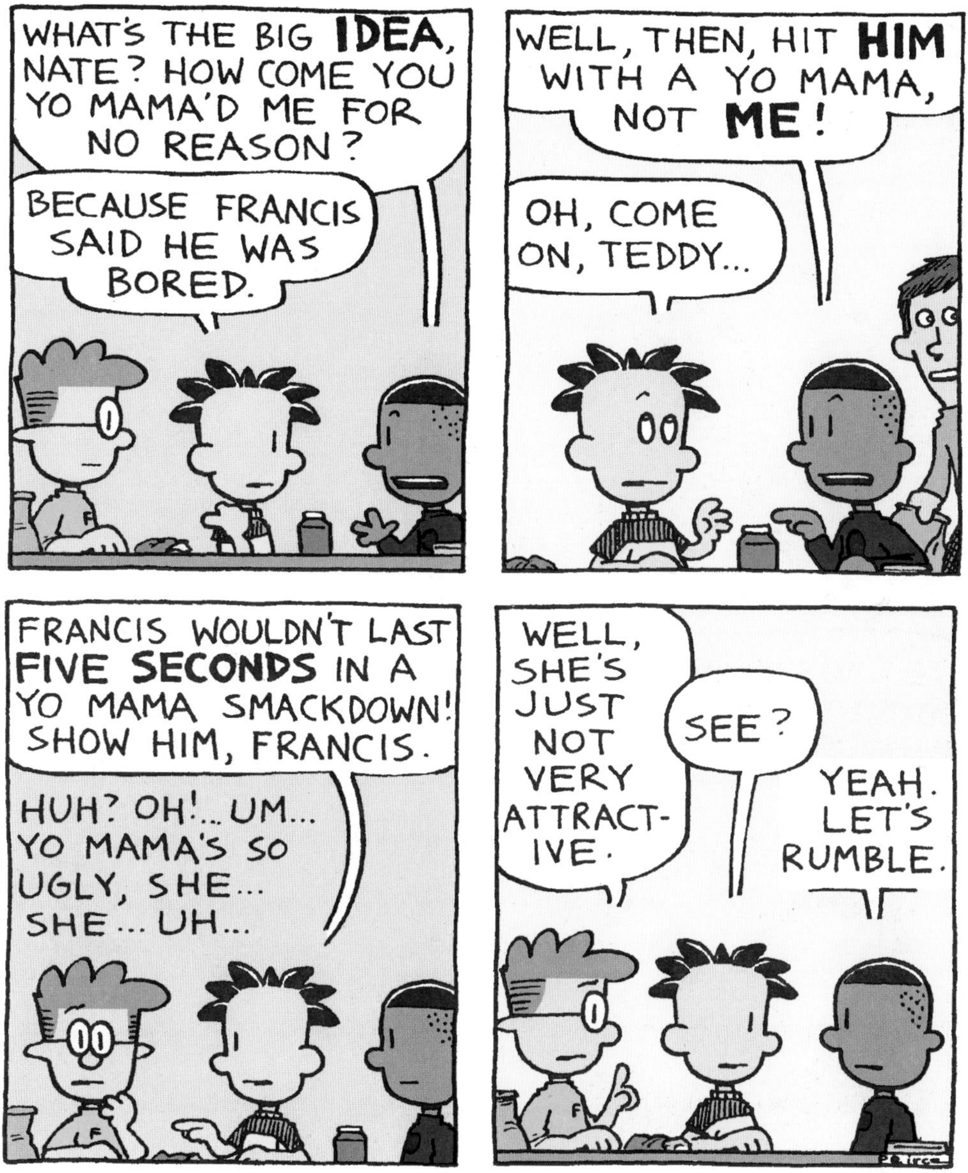
WHAT'S THE BIG IDEA, NATE? HOW COME YOU YO MAMA'D ME FOR NO REASON?
BECAUSE FRANCIS SAID HE WAS BORED.
WELL, THEN, HIT HIM WITH A YO MAMA, NOT ME!
OH, COME ON, TEDDY...
FRANCIS WOULDN'T LAST FIVE SECONDS IN A YO MAMA SMACKDOWN! SHOW HIM, FRANCIS.
HUH? OH!... UM... YO MAMA'S SO UGLY, SHE... SHE... UH...
WELL, SHE'S JUST NOT VERY ATTRACT-IVE.
SEE?
YEAH. LET'S RUMBLE.

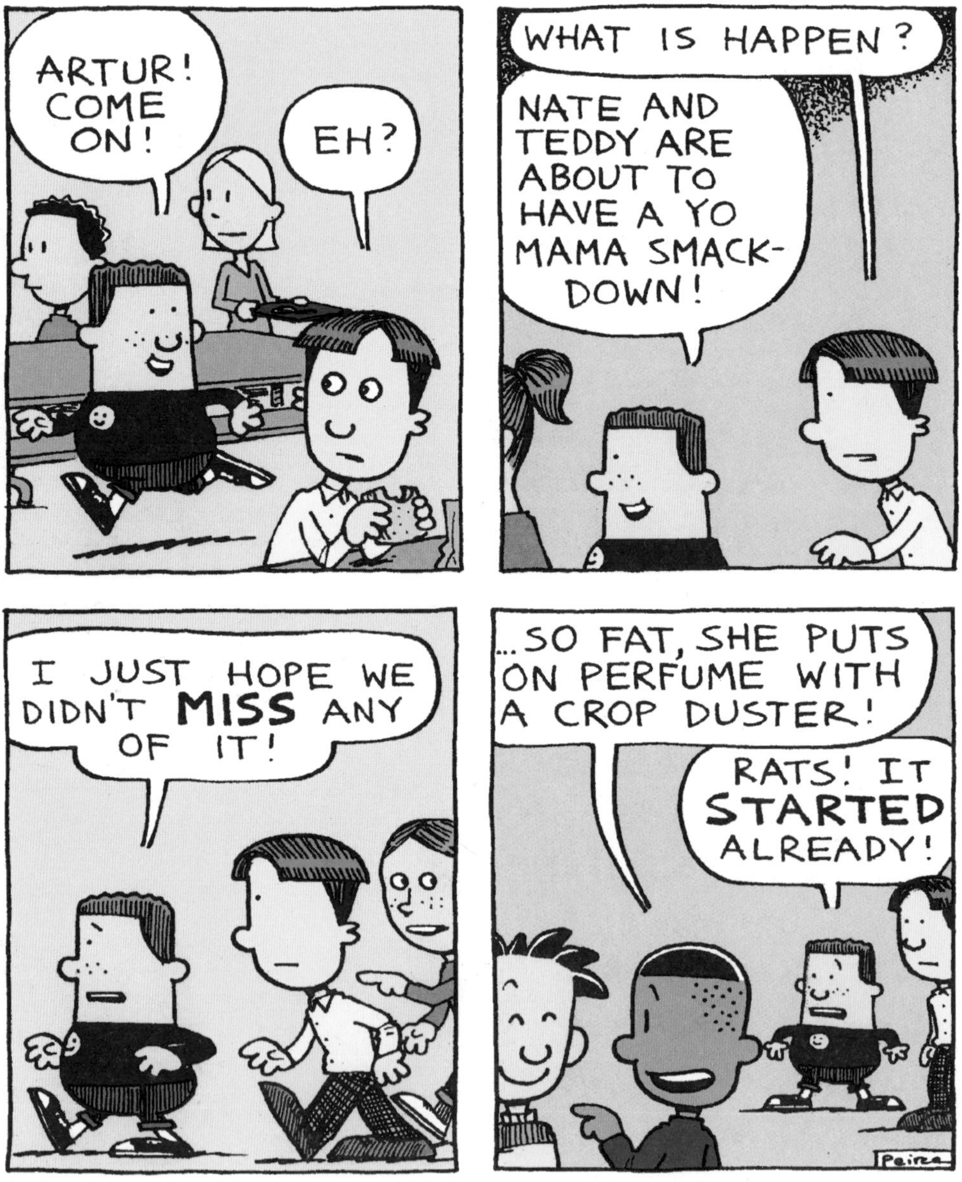
ARTUR! COME ON!
EH?
WHAT IS HAPPEN?
NATE AND TEDDY ARE ABOUT TO HAVE A YO MAMA SMACK-DOWN!
I JUST HOPE WE DIDN'T MISS ANY OF IT!
...SO FAT, SHE PUTS ON PERFUME WITH A CROP DUSTER!
RATS! IT STARTED ALREADY!
Peirce

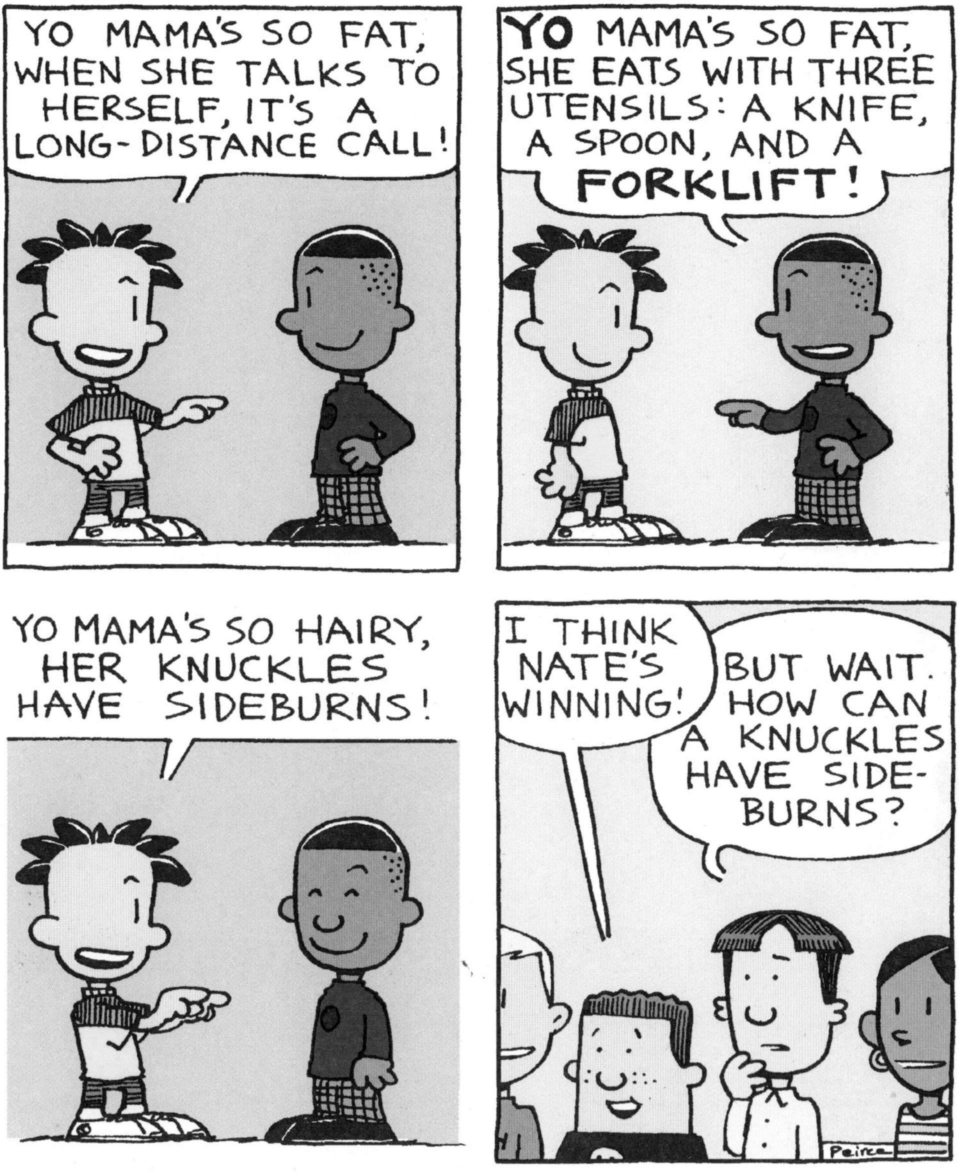
YO MAMA'S SO FAT, WHEN SHE TALKS TO HERSELF, IT'S A LONG-DISTANCE CALL!
YO MAMA'S SO FAT, SHE EATS WITH THREE UTENSILS: A KNIFE, A SPOON, AND A FORKLIFT!
YO MAMA'S SO HAIRY, HER KNUCKLES HAVE SIDEBURNS!
I THINK NATE'S WINNING!
BUT WAIT. HOW CAN A KNUCKLES HAVE SIDE-BURNS?
Peirce

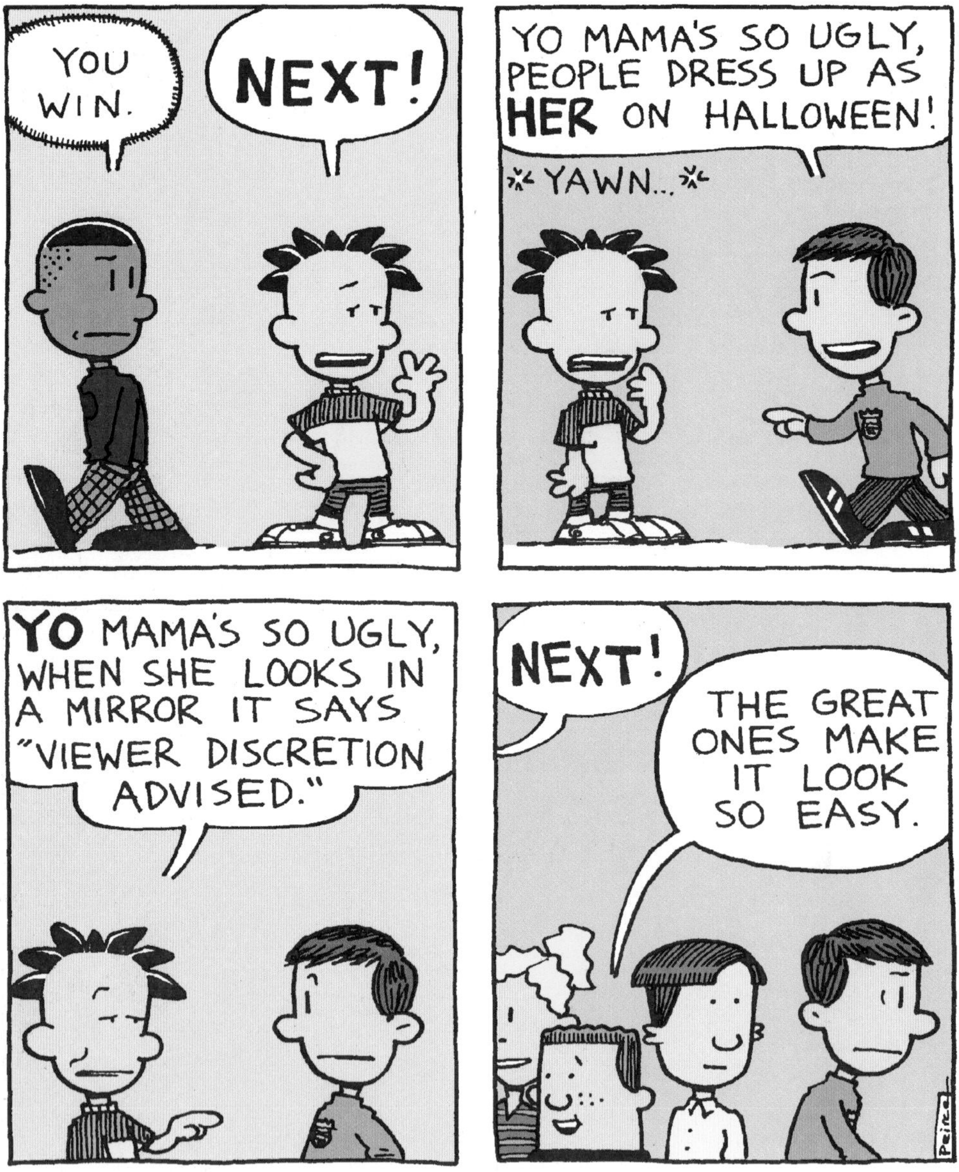
YOU WIN.
NEXT!
YO MAMA'S SO UGLY, PEOPLE DRESS UP AS HER ON HALLOWEEN!
YAWN...
YO MAMA'S SO UGLY, WHEN SHE LOOKS IN A MIRROR IT SAYS "VIEWER DISCRETION ADVISED."
NEXT!
THE GREAT ONES MAKE IT LOOK SO EASY.

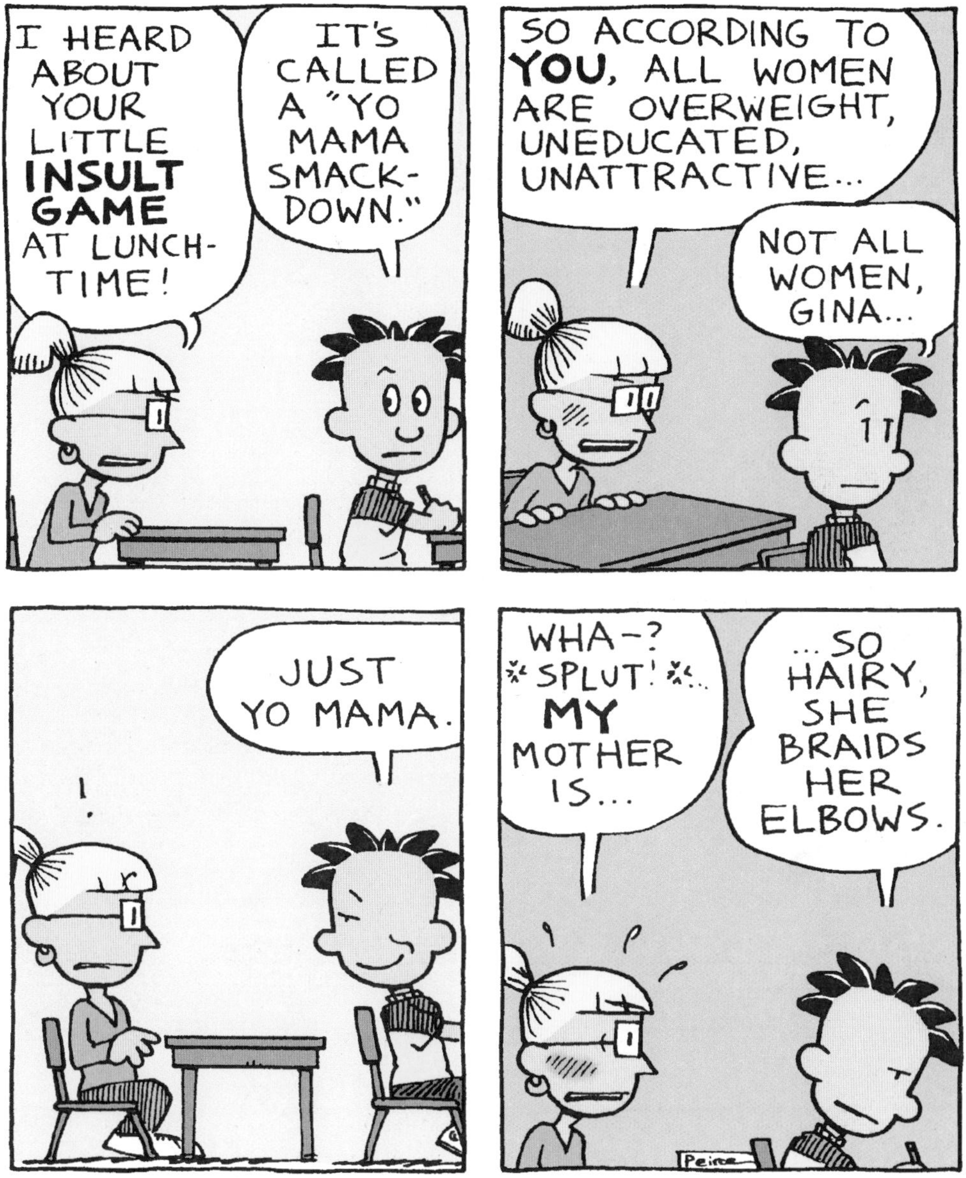
I HEARD ABOUT YOUR LITTLE **INSULT GAME** AT LUNCHTIME!
IT'S CALLED A "YO MAMA SMACKDOWN."
SO ACCORDING TO **YOU**, ALL WOMEN ARE OVERWEIGHT, UNEDUCATED, UNATTRACTIVE...
NOT ALL WOMEN, GINA...
JUST YO MAMA.
!
WHA-? SPLUT! **MY** MOTHER IS...
...SO HAIRY, SHE BRAIDS HER ELBOWS.
Peirce

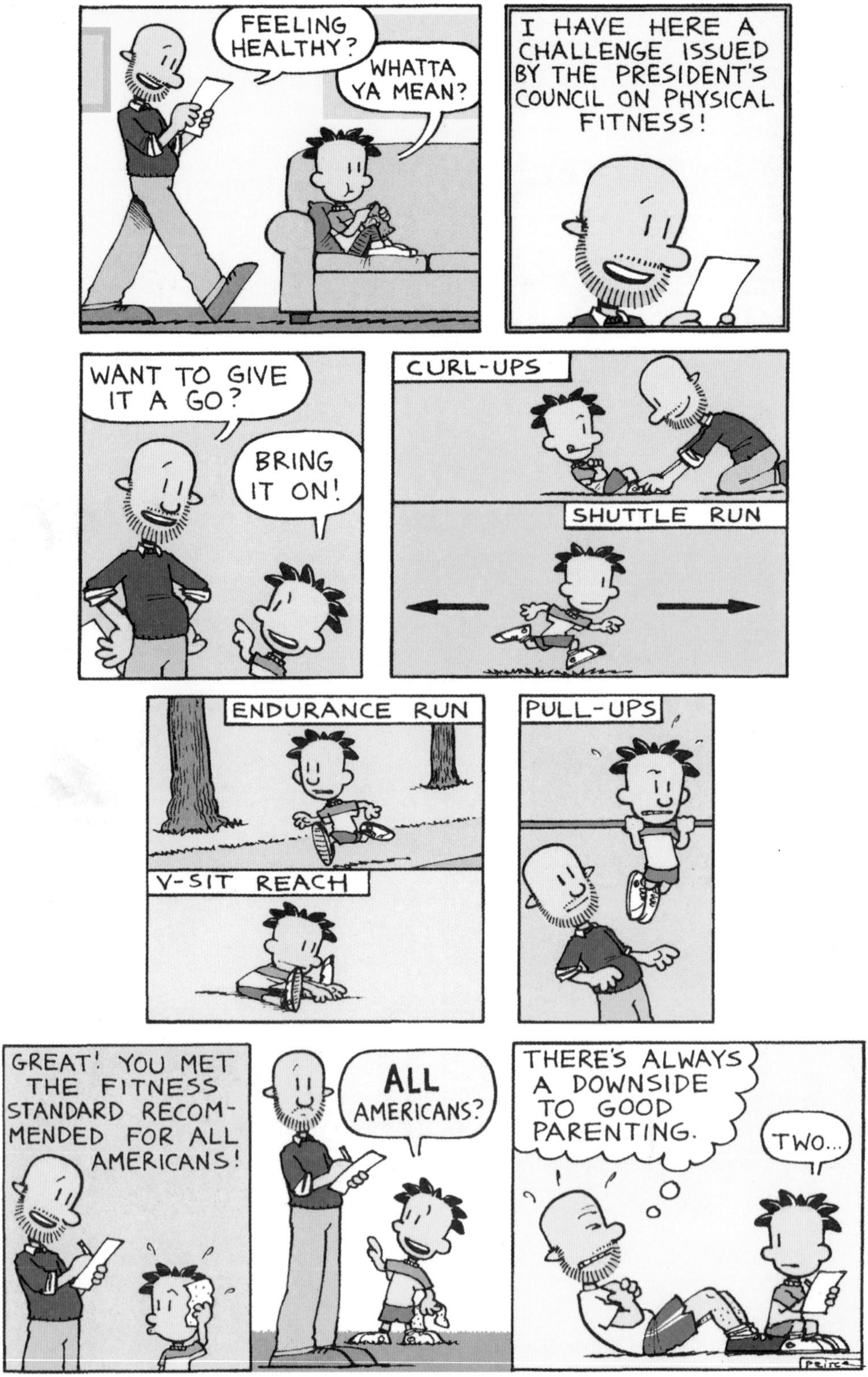
FEELING HEALTHY?
WHATTA YA MEAN?
I HAVE HERE A CHALLENGE ISSUED BY THE PRESIDENT'S COUNCIL ON PHYSICAL FITNESS!
WANT TO GIVE IT A GO?
BRING IT ON!
CURL-UPS
SHUTTLE RUN
ENDURANCE RUN
PULL-UPS
V-SIT REACH
GREAT! YOU MET THE FITNESS STANDARD RECOMMENDED FOR ALL AMERICANS!
ALL AMERICANS?
THERE'S ALWAYS A DOWNSIDE TO GOOD PARENTING.
TWO...
peirce

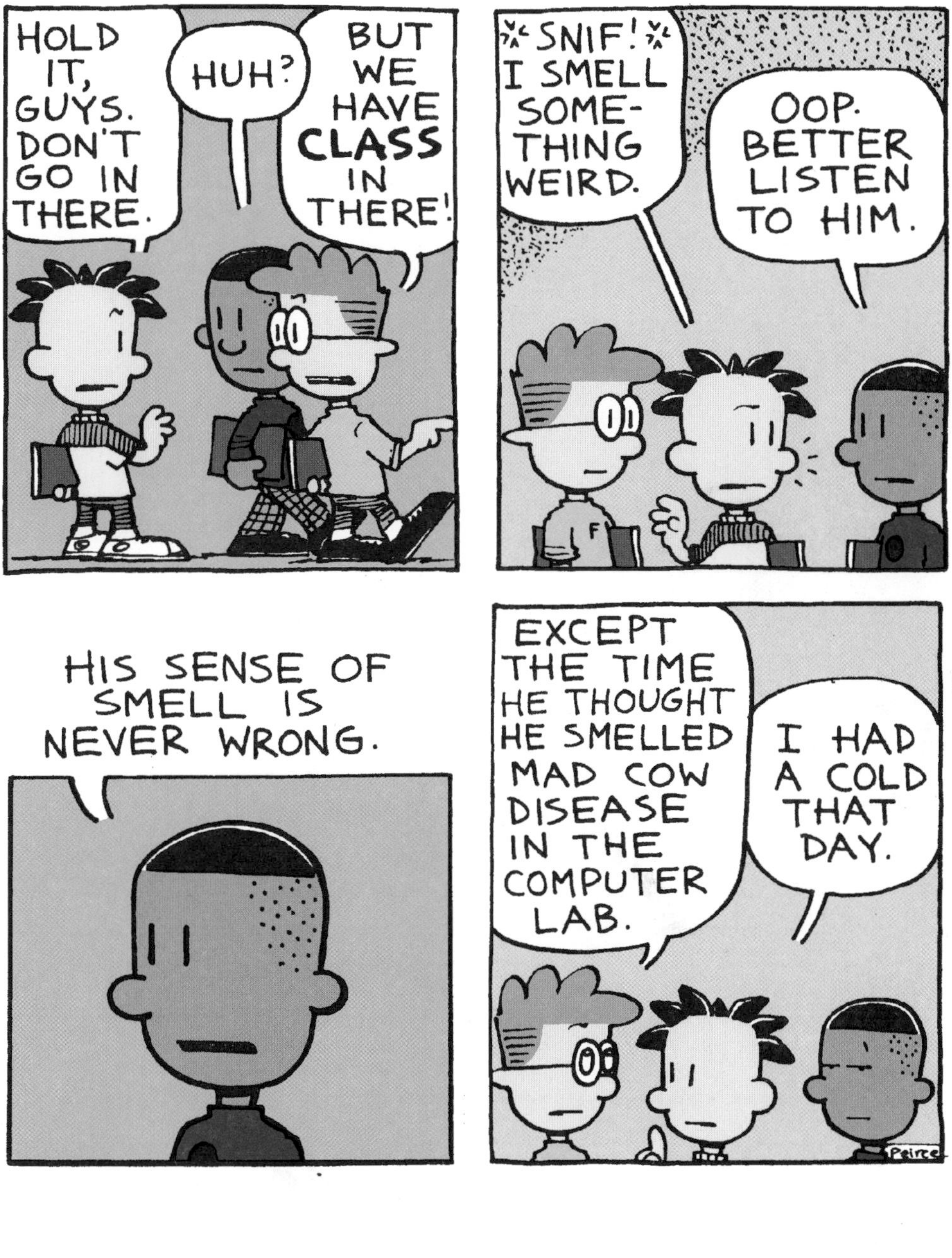
HOLD IT, GUYS. DON'T GO IN THERE.
HUH?
BUT WE HAVE **CLASS** IN THERE!
SNIF! I SMELL SOMETHING WEIRD.
OOP. BETTER LISTEN TO HIM.
HIS SENSE OF SMELL IS NEVER WRONG.
EXCEPT THE TIME HE THOUGHT HE SMELLED MAD COW DISEASE IN THE COMPUTER LAB.
I HAD A COLD THAT DAY.
Peirce

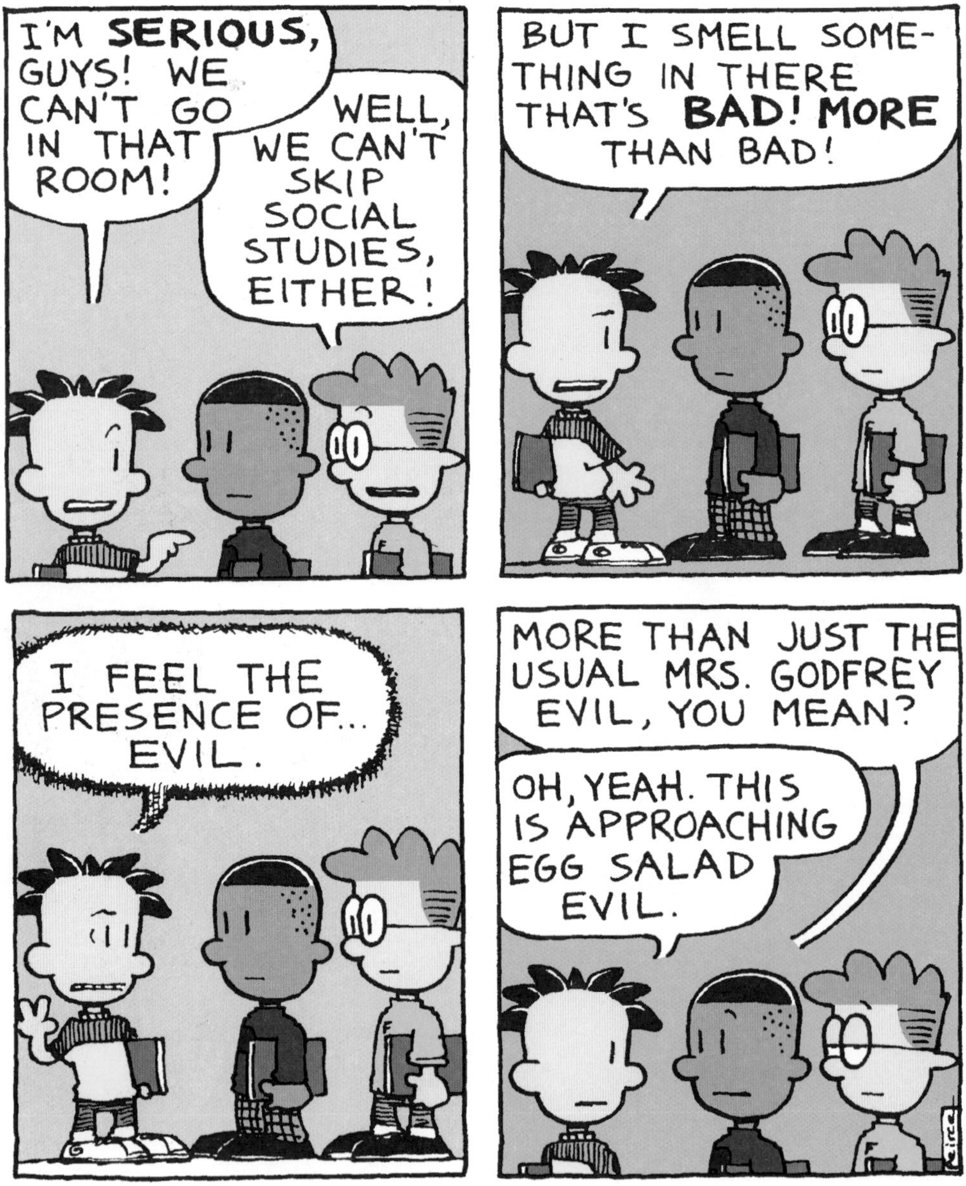
I'M **SERIOUS,** GUYS! WE CAN'T GO IN THAT ROOM!
WELL, WE CAN'T SKIP SOCIAL STUDIES, EITHER!
BUT I SMELL SOMETHING IN THERE THAT'S **BAD! MORE** THAN BAD!
I FEEL THE PRESENCE OF... EVIL.
MORE THAN JUST THE USUAL MRS. GODFREY EVIL, YOU MEAN?
OH, YEAH. THIS IS APPROACHING EGG SALAD EVIL.
Peirce

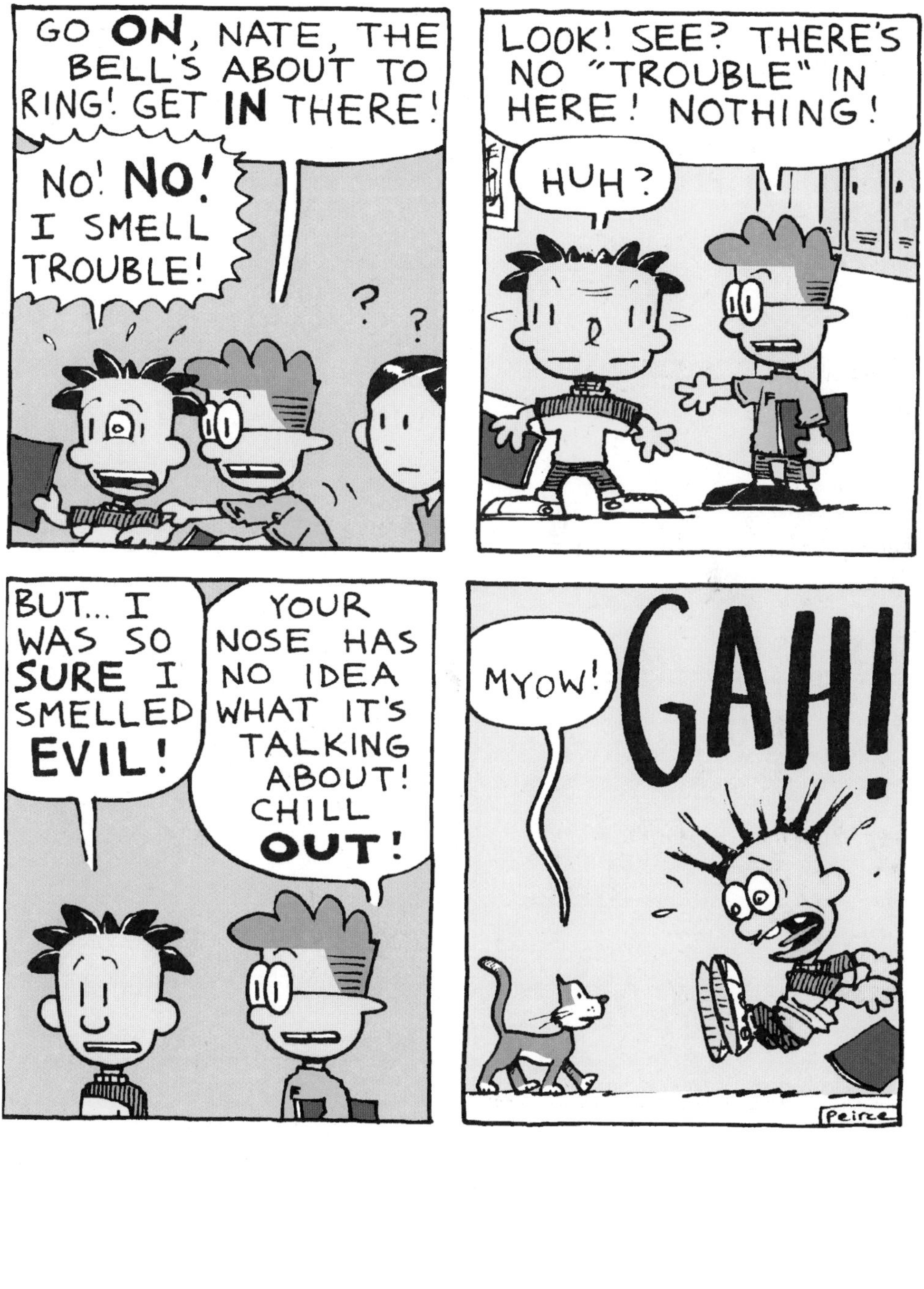
GO ON, NATE, THE BELL'S ABOUT TO RING! GET IN THERE!
NO! NO! I SMELL TROUBLE!
?
?
LOOK! SEE? THERE'S NO "TROUBLE" IN HERE! NOTHING!
HUH?
BUT... I WAS SO SURE I SMELLED EVIL!
YOUR NOSE HAS NO IDEA WHAT IT'S TALKING ABOUT! CHILL OUT!
MYOW!
GAH!
Peirce

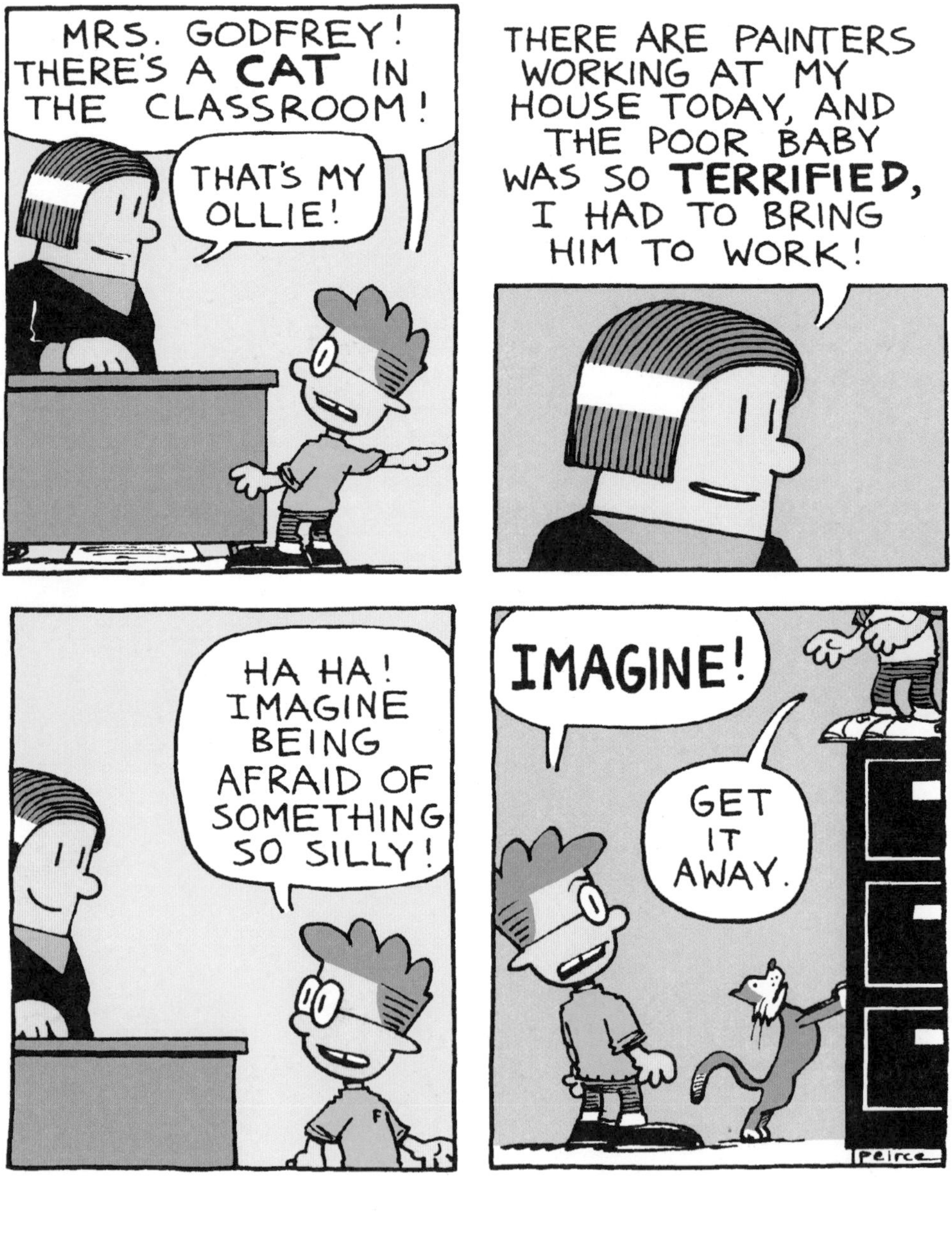
MRS. GODFREY! THERE'S A CAT IN THE CLASSROOM!
THAT'S MY OLLIE!
THERE ARE PAINTERS WORKING AT MY HOUSE TODAY, AND THE POOR BABY WAS SO TERRIFIED, I HAD TO BRING HIM TO WORK!
HA HA! IMAGINE BEING AFRAID OF SOMETHING SO SILLY!
IMAGINE!
GET IT AWAY.
peirce

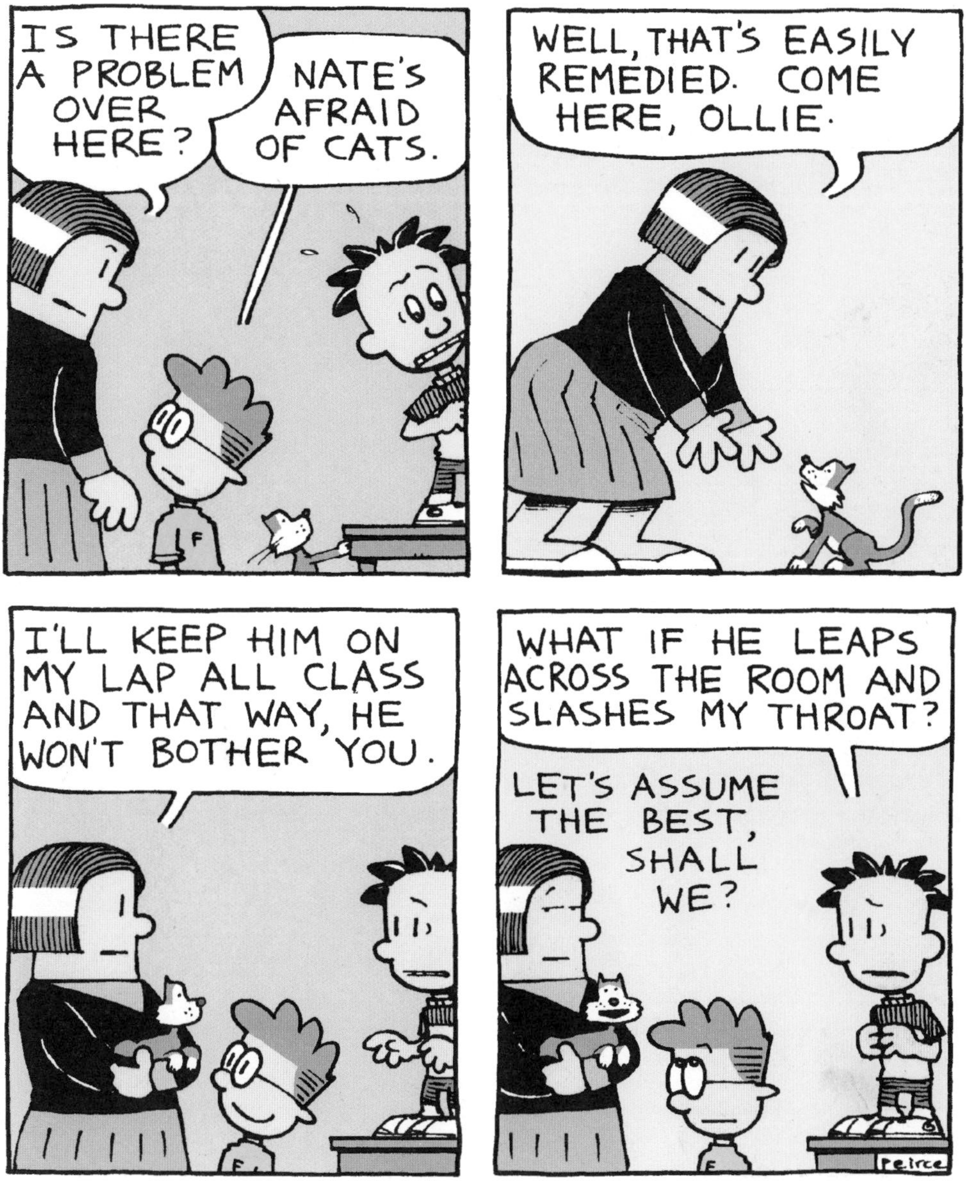
IS THERE A PROBLEM OVER HERE?
NATE'S AFRAID OF CATS.
WELL, THAT'S EASILY REMEDIED. COME HERE, OLLIE.
I'LL KEEP HIM ON MY LAP ALL CLASS AND THAT WAY, HE WON'T BOTHER YOU.
WHAT IF HE LEAPS ACROSS THE ROOM AND SLASHES MY THROAT?
LET'S ASSUME THE BEST, SHALL WE?
peirce

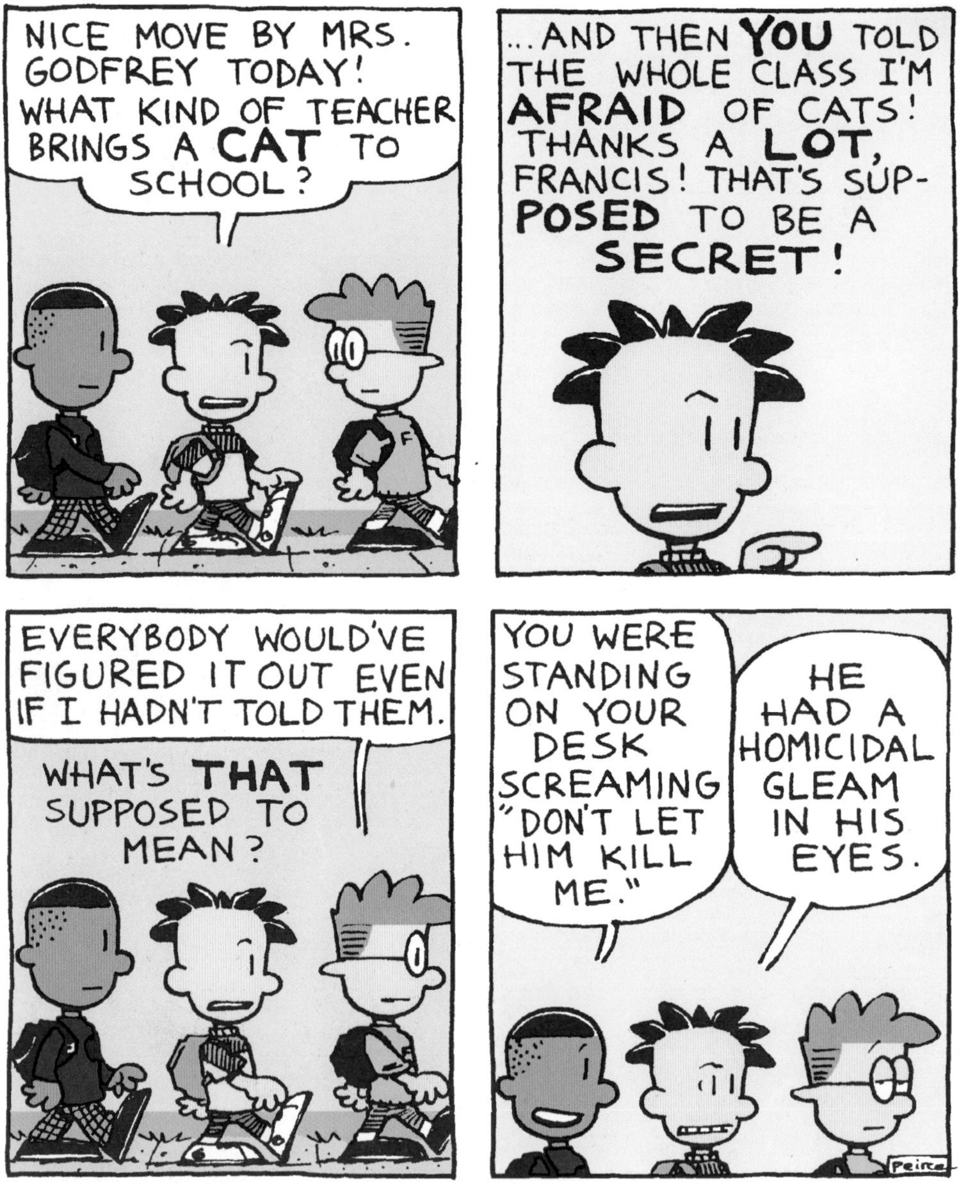
NICE MOVE BY MRS. GODFREY TODAY! WHAT KIND OF TEACHER BRINGS A CAT TO SCHOOL?
...AND THEN YOU TOLD THE WHOLE CLASS I'M AFRAID OF CATS! THANKS A LOT, FRANCIS! THAT'S SUPPOSED TO BE A SECRET!
EVERYBODY WOULD'VE FIGURED IT OUT EVEN IF I HADN'T TOLD THEM.
WHAT'S THAT SUPPOSED TO MEAN?
YOU WERE STANDING ON YOUR DESK SCREAMING "DON'T LET HIM KILL ME."
HE HAD A HOMICIDAL GLEAM IN HIS EYES.
Peirce

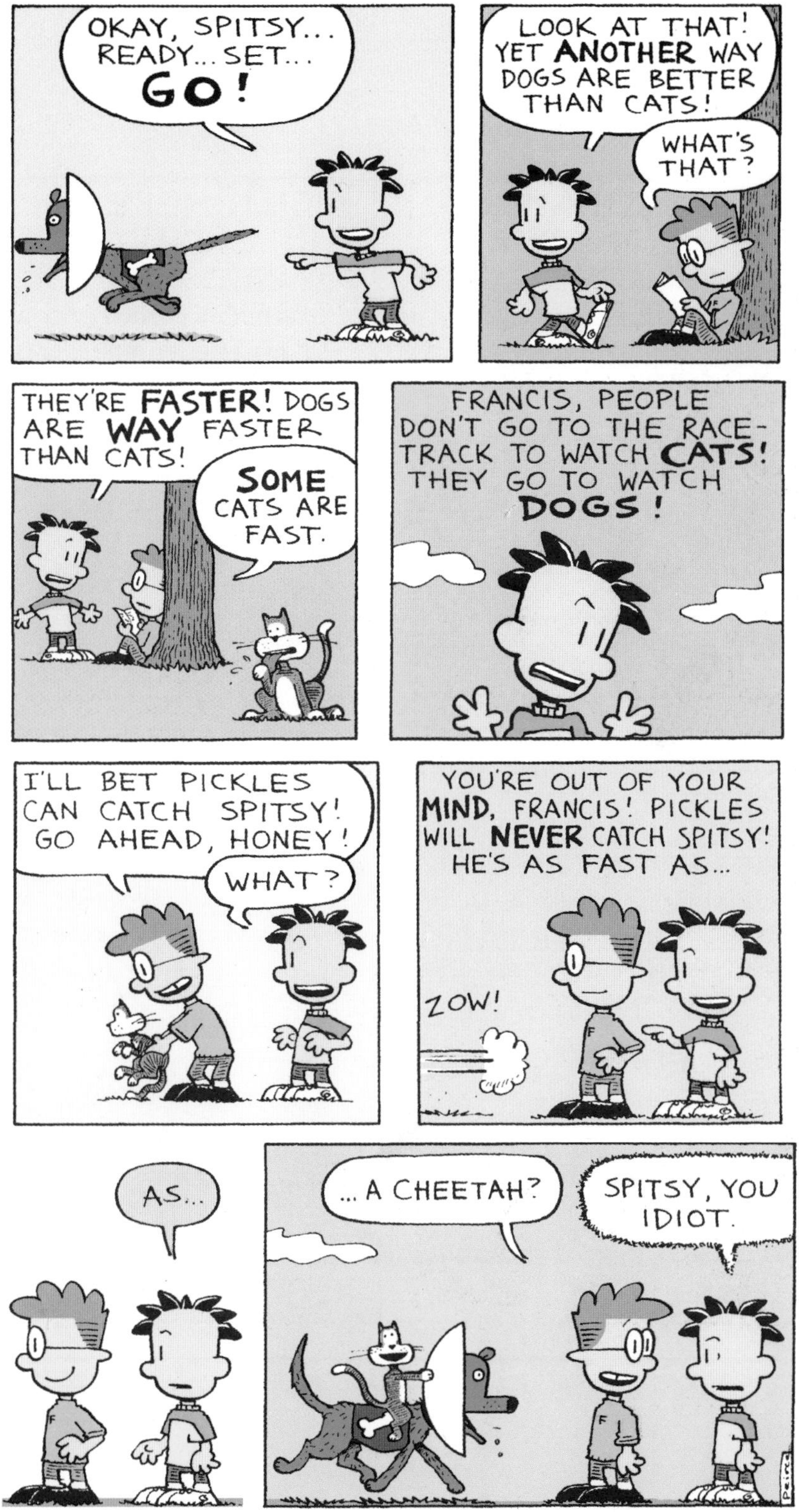
OKAY, SPITSY... READY... SET... GO!
LOOK AT THAT! YET ANOTHER WAY DOGS ARE BETTER THAN CATS!
WHAT'S THAT?
THEY'RE FASTER! DOGS ARE WAY FASTER THAN CATS!
SOME CATS ARE FAST.
FRANCIS, PEOPLE DON'T GO TO THE RACE-TRACK TO WATCH CATS! THEY GO TO WATCH DOGS!
I'LL BET PICKLES CAN CATCH SPITSY! GO AHEAD, HONEY!
WHAT?
YOU'RE OUT OF YOUR MIND, FRANCIS! PICKLES WILL NEVER CATCH SPITSY! HE'S AS FAST AS...
ZOW!
AS...
... A CHEETAH?
SPITSY, YOU IDIOT.
Peirce

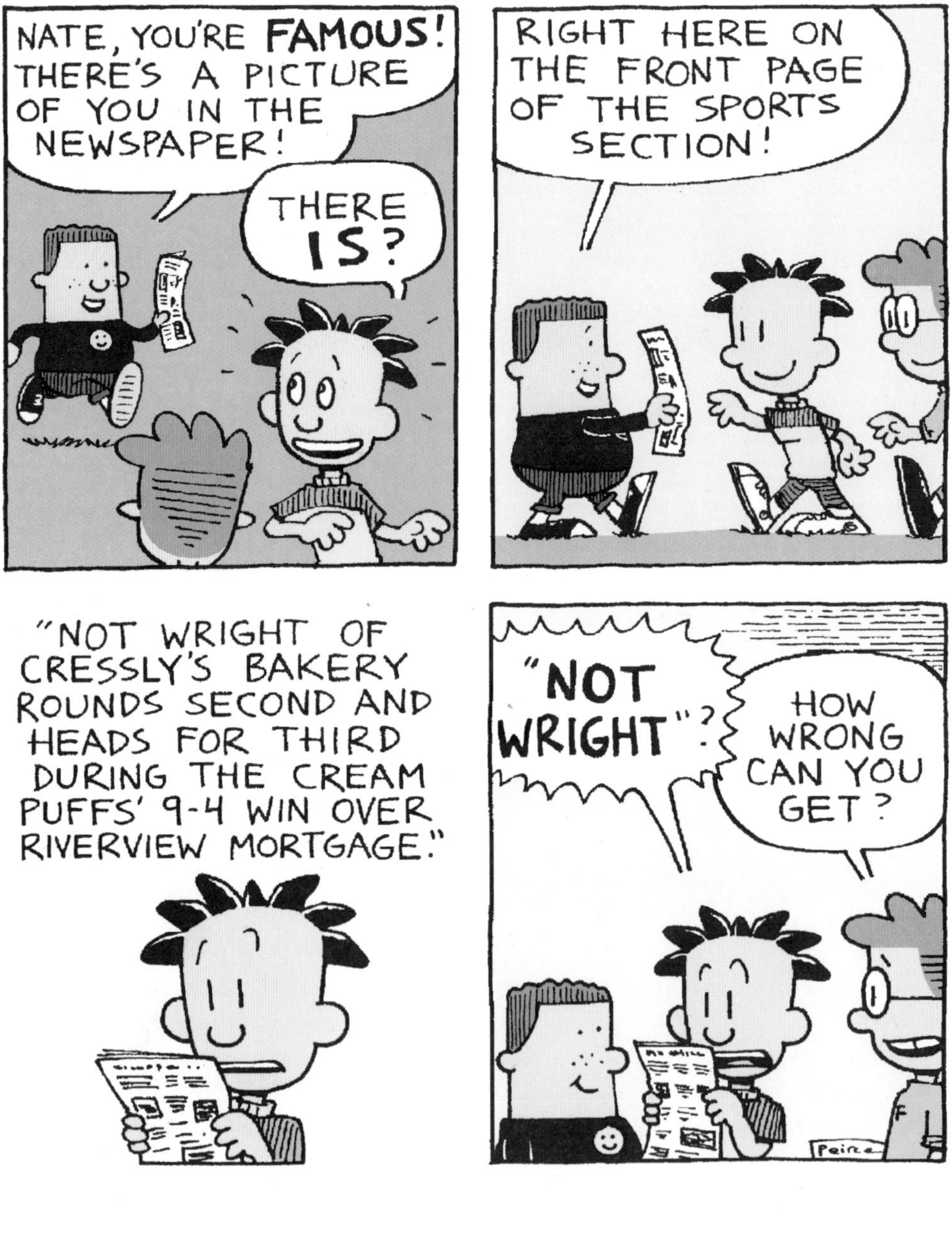
NATE, YOU'RE **FAMOUS**! THERE'S A PICTURE OF YOU IN THE NEWSPAPER!
THERE **IS**?
RIGHT HERE ON THE FRONT PAGE OF THE SPORTS SECTION!
"NOT WRIGHT OF CRESSLY'S BAKERY ROUNDS SECOND AND HEADS FOR THIRD DURING THE CREAM PUFFS' 9-4 WIN OVER RIVERVIEW MORTGAGE."
"**NOT WRIGHT**"?
HOW WRONG CAN YOU GET?
Peirce

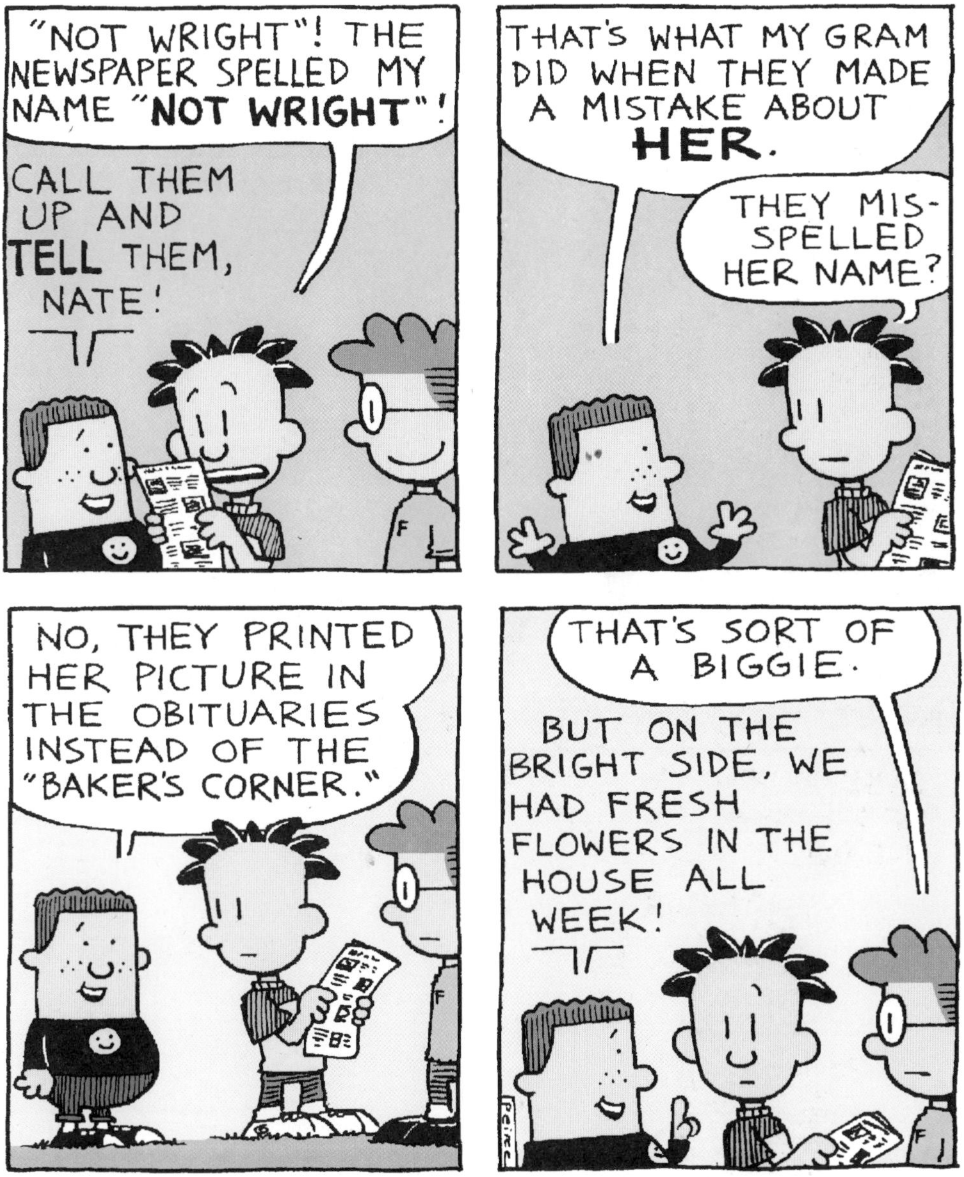
"NOT WRIGHT"! THE NEWSPAPER SPELLED MY NAME "**NOT WRIGHT**"!
CALL THEM UP AND **TELL** THEM, NATE!
THAT'S WHAT MY GRAM DID WHEN THEY MADE A MISTAKE ABOUT **HER**.
THEY MIS-SPELLED HER NAME?
NO, THEY PRINTED HER PICTURE IN THE OBITUARIES INSTEAD OF THE "BAKER'S CORNER."
THAT'S SORT OF A BIGGIE.
BUT ON THE BRIGHT SIDE, WE HAD FRESH FLOWERS IN THE HOUSE ALL WEEK!
PEIRCE

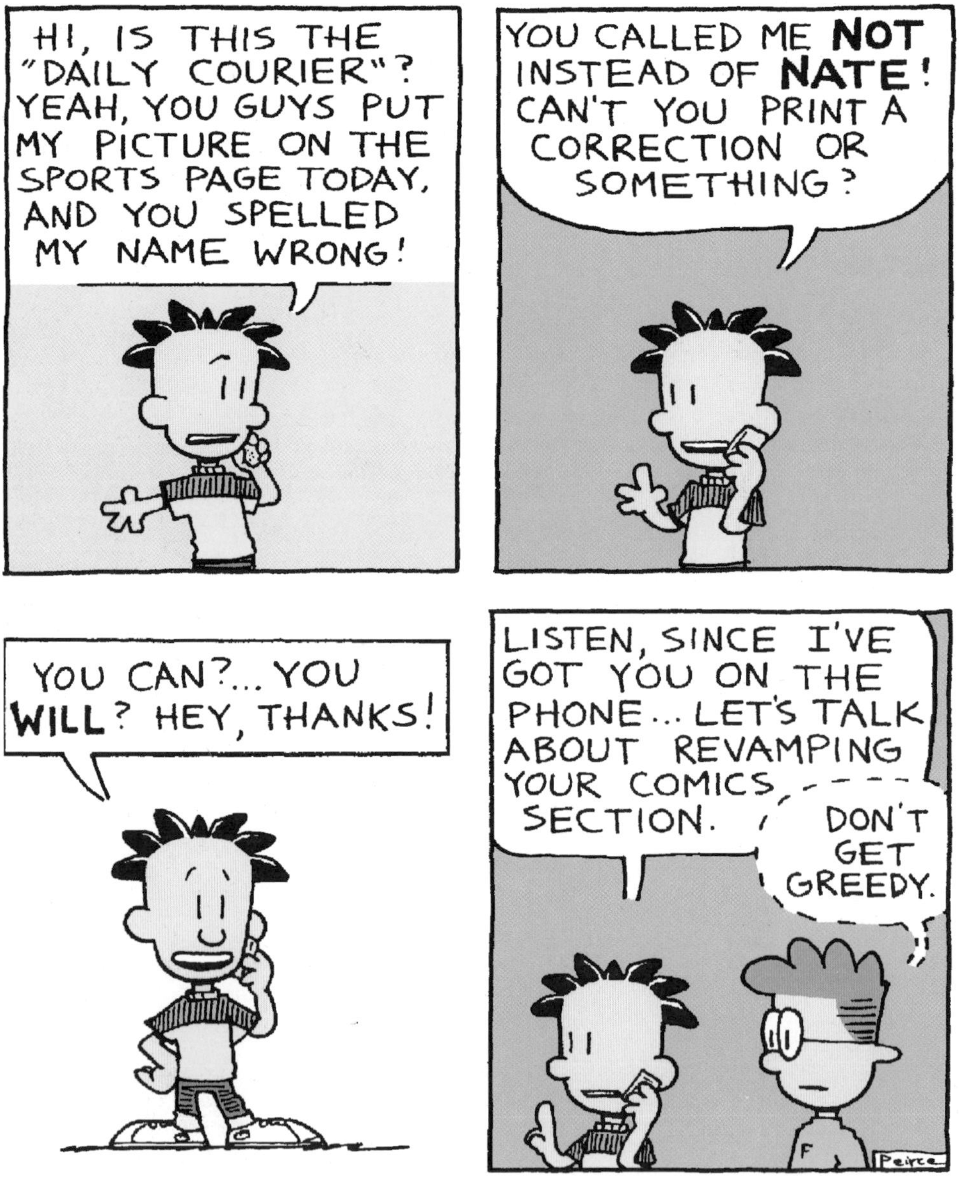
HI, IS THIS THE "DAILY COURIER"? YEAH, YOU GUYS PUT MY PICTURE ON THE SPORTS PAGE TODAY, AND YOU SPELLED MY NAME WRONG!
YOU CALLED ME NOT INSTEAD OF NATE! CAN'T YOU PRINT A CORRECTION OR SOMETHING?
YOU CAN?... YOU WILL? HEY, THANKS!
LISTEN, SINCE I'VE GOT YOU ON THE PHONE... LET'S TALK ABOUT REVAMPING YOUR COMICS SECTION.
DON'T GET GREEDY.
Peirce

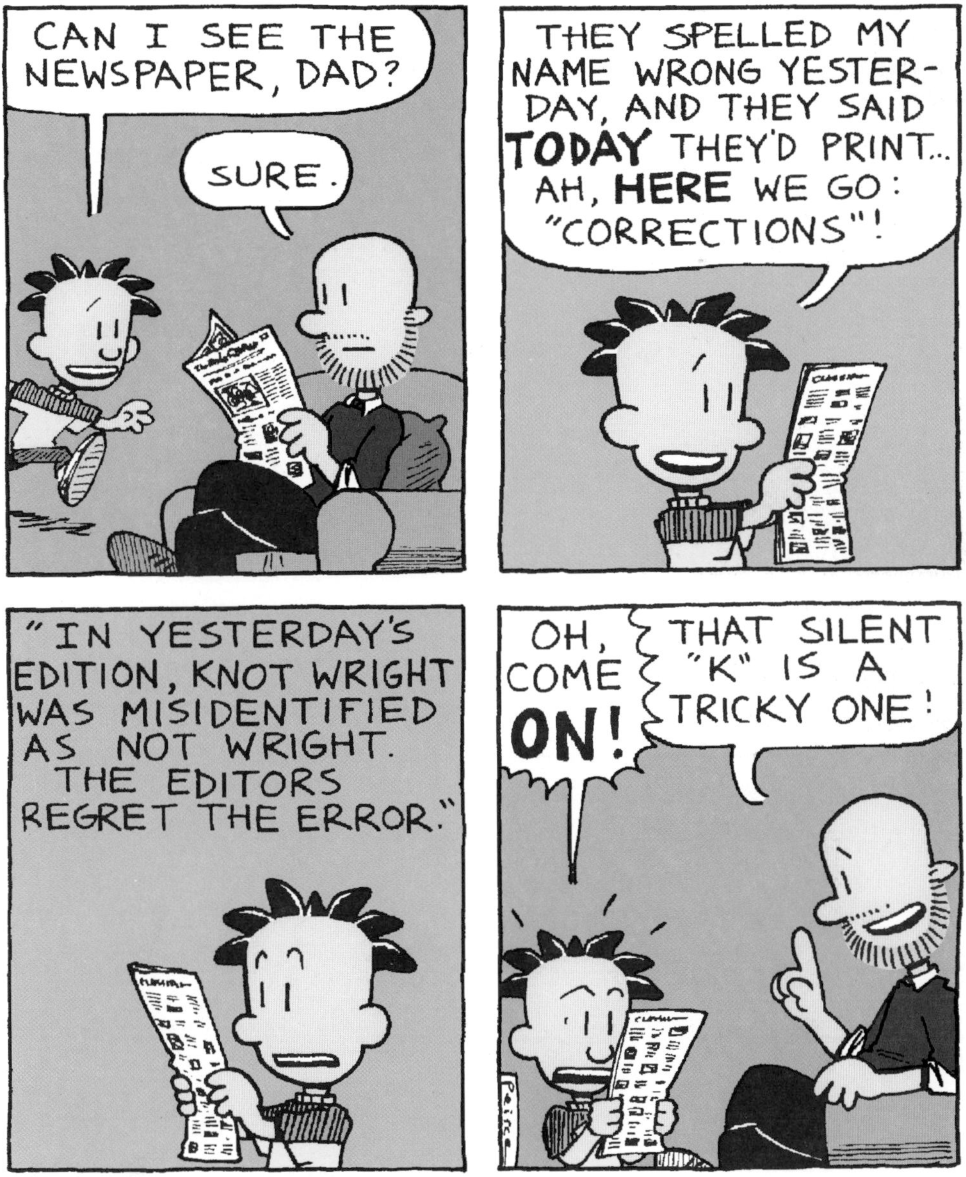
CAN I SEE THE NEWSPAPER, DAD?
SURE.
THEY SPELLED MY NAME WRONG YESTERDAY, AND THEY SAID **TODAY** THEY'D PRINT... AH, **HERE** WE GO: "CORRECTIONS"!
"IN YESTERDAY'S EDITION, KNOT WRIGHT WAS MISIDENTIFIED AS NOT WRIGHT. THE EDITORS REGRET THE ERROR."
OH, COME **ON!**
THAT SILENT "K" IS A TRICKY ONE!

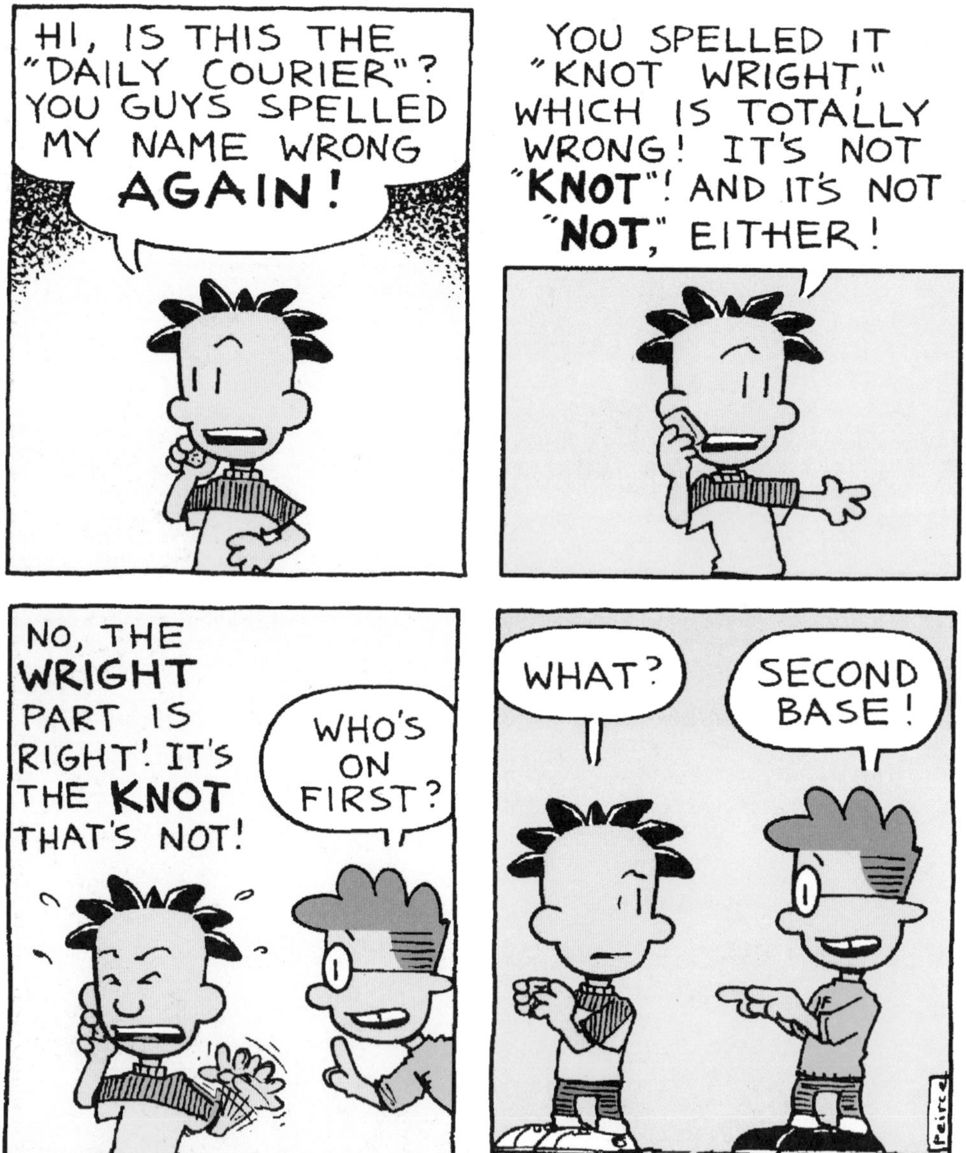
HI, IS THIS THE "DAILY COURIER"? YOU GUYS SPELLED MY NAME WRONG **AGAIN**!
YOU SPELLED IT "KNOT WRIGHT," WHICH IS TOTALLY WRONG! IT'S NOT "**KNOT**"! AND IT'S NOT "**NOT**," EITHER!
NO, THE **WRIGHT** PART IS RIGHT! IT'S THE **KNOT** THAT'S NOT!
WHO'S ON FIRST?
WHAT?
SECOND BASE!
Peirce

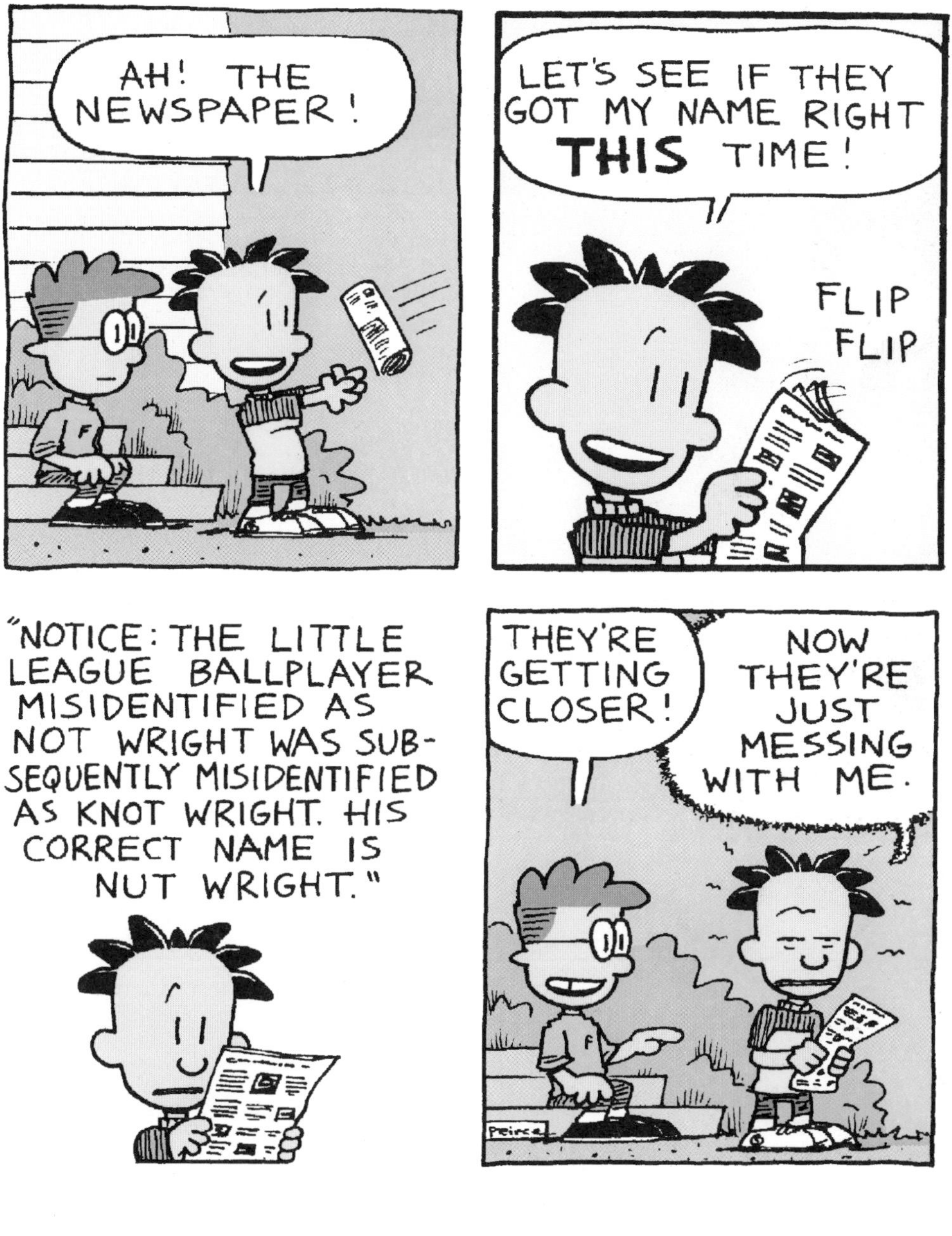
AH! THE NEWSPAPER!
LET'S SEE IF THEY GOT MY NAME RIGHT **THIS** TIME!
FLIP FLIP
"NOTICE: THE LITTLE LEAGUE BALLPLAYER MISIDENTIFIED AS NOT WRIGHT WAS SUBSEQUENTLY MISIDENTIFIED AS KNOT WRIGHT. HIS CORRECT NAME IS NUT WRIGHT."
THEY'RE GETTING CLOSER!
NOW THEY'RE JUST MESSING WITH ME.
Peirce

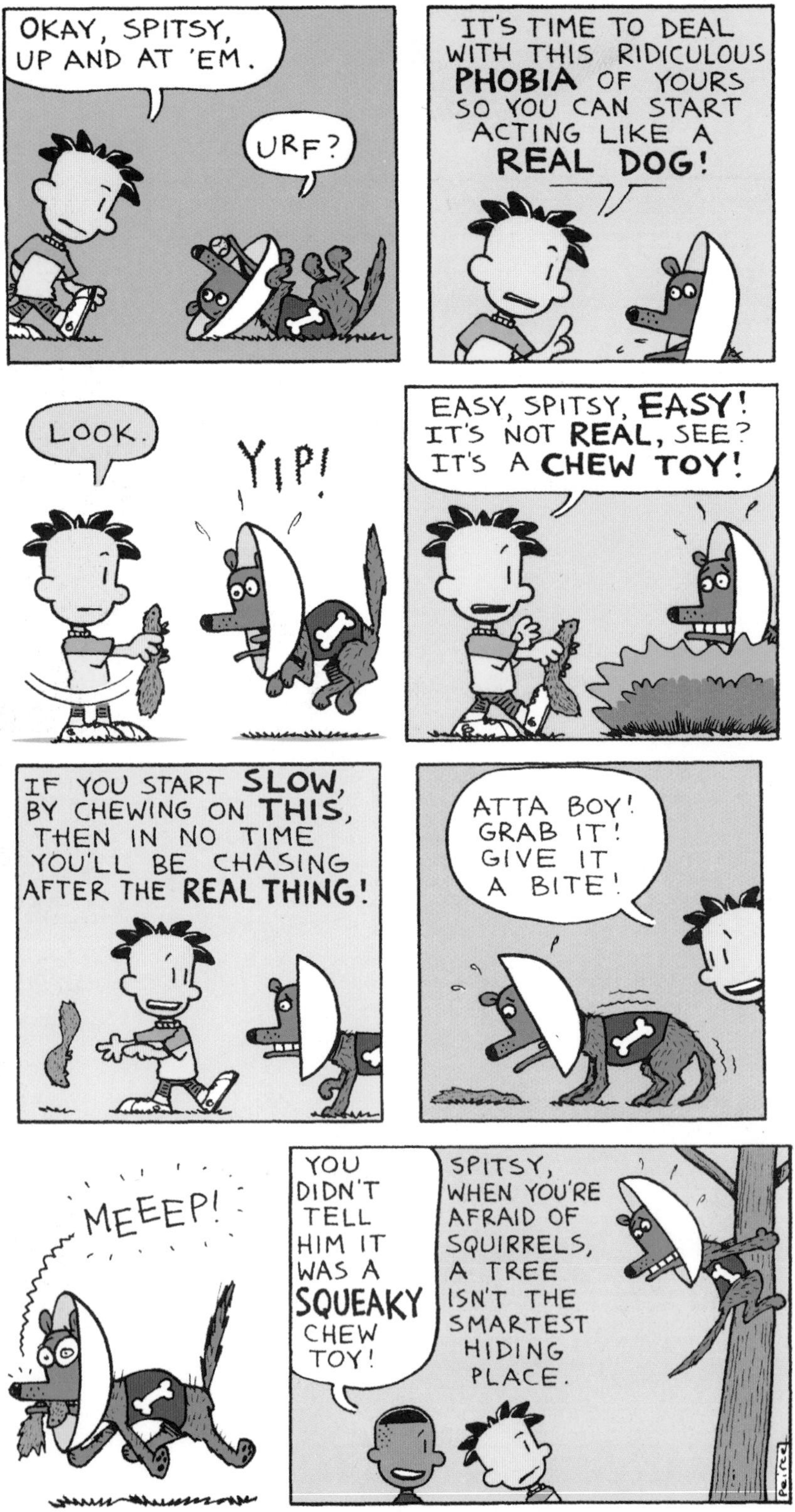
OKAY, SPITSY, UP AND AT 'EM.
URF?
IT'S TIME TO DEAL WITH THIS RIDICULOUS PHOBIA OF YOURS SO YOU CAN START ACTING LIKE A REAL DOG!
LOOK.
YIP!
EASY, SPITSY, EASY! IT'S NOT REAL, SEE? IT'S A CHEW TOY!
IF YOU START SLOW, BY CHEWING ON THIS, THEN IN NO TIME YOU'LL BE CHASING AFTER THE REAL THING!
ATTA BOY! GRAB IT! GIVE IT A BITE!
MEEEP!
YOU DIDN'T TELL HIM IT WAS A SQUEAKY CHEW TOY!
SPITSY, WHEN YOU'RE AFRAID OF SQUIRRELS, A TREE ISN'T THE SMARTEST HIDING PLACE.
Peirce

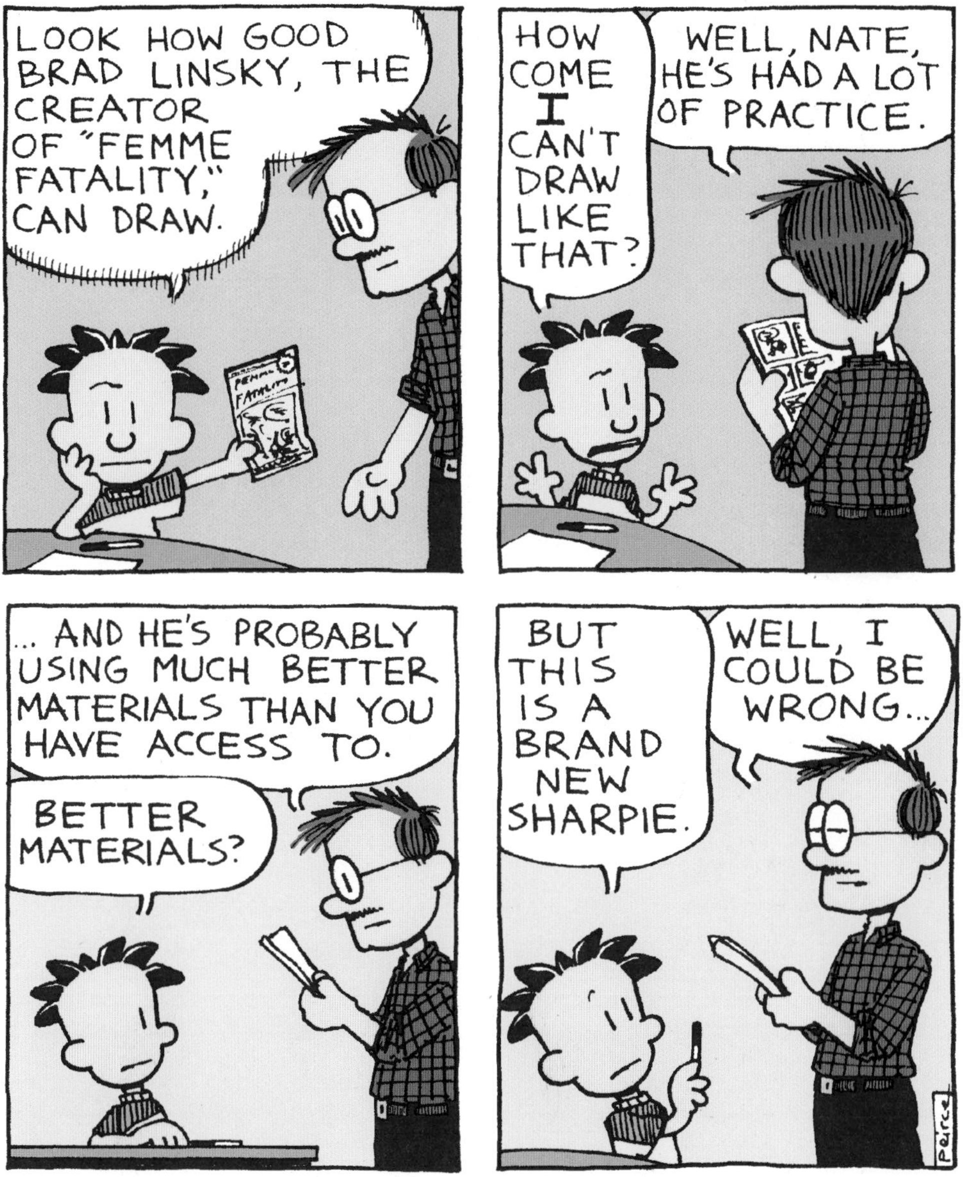
LOOK HOW GOOD BRAD LINSKY, THE CREATOR OF "FEMME FATALITY," CAN DRAW.
HOW COME I CAN'T DRAW LIKE THAT?
WELL, NATE, HE'S HAD A LOT OF PRACTICE.
... AND HE'S PROBABLY USING MUCH BETTER MATERIALS THAN YOU HAVE ACCESS TO.
BETTER MATERIALS?
BUT THIS IS A BRAND NEW SHARPIE.
WELL, I COULD BE WRONG...
peirce

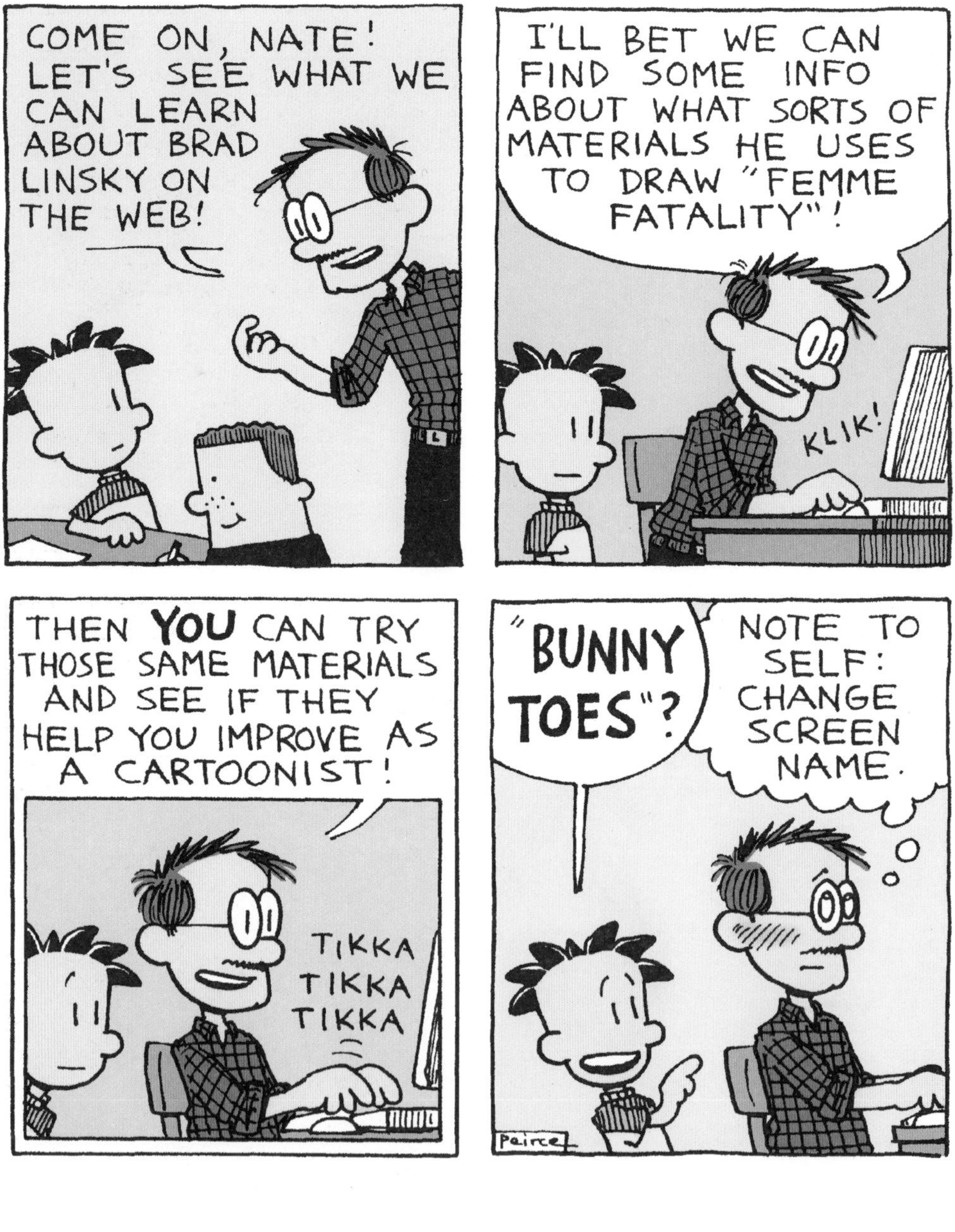
COME ON, NATE! LET'S SEE WHAT WE CAN LEARN ABOUT BRAD LINSKY ON THE WEB!
I'LL BET WE CAN FIND SOME INFO ABOUT WHAT SORTS OF MATERIALS HE USES TO DRAW "FEMME FATALITY"!
KLIK!
THEN **YOU** CAN TRY THOSE SAME MATERIALS AND SEE IF THEY HELP YOU IMPROVE AS A CARTOONIST!
TIKKA TIKKA TIKKA
"**BUNNY TOES**"?
NOTE TO SELF: CHANGE SCREEN NAME.
Peirce

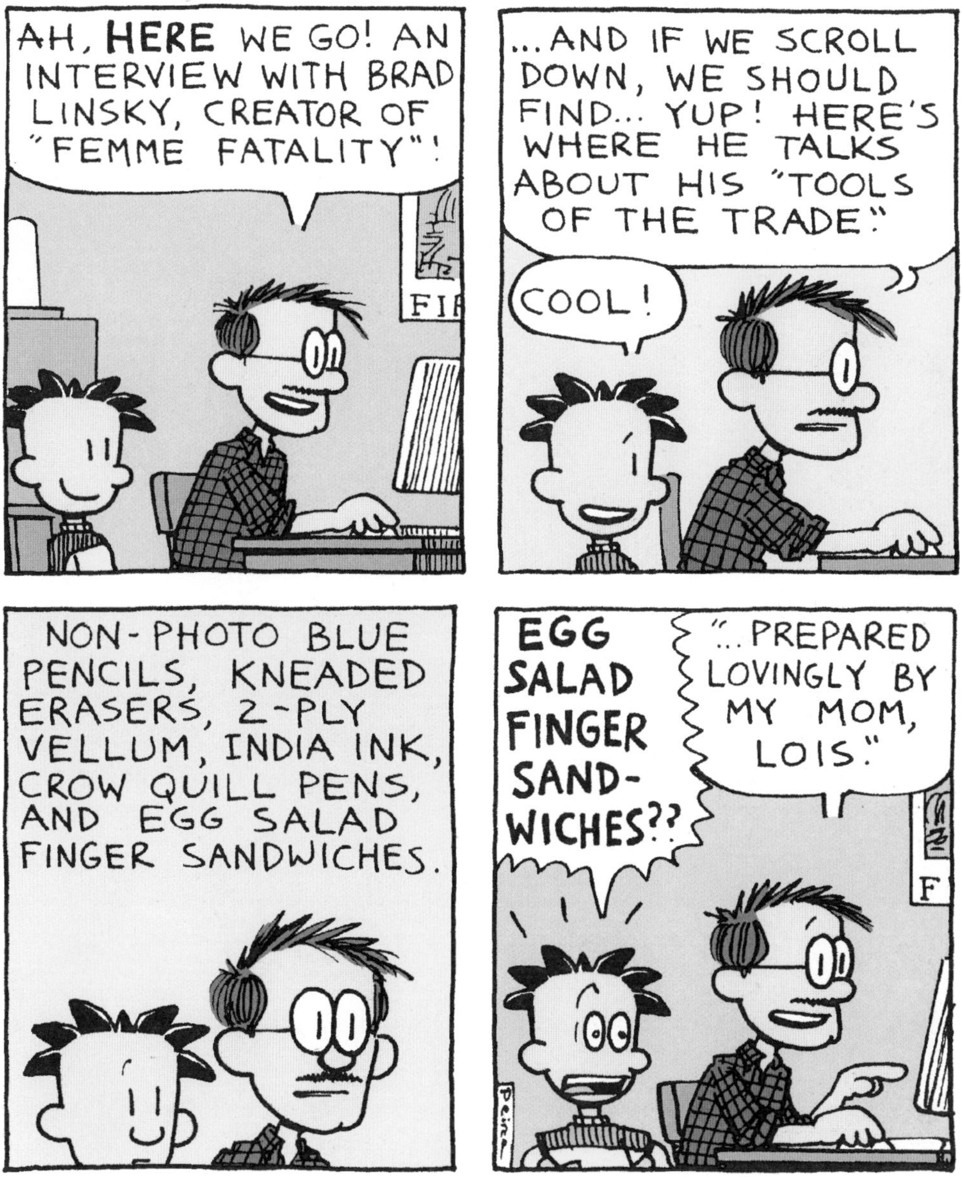
AH, HERE WE GO! AN INTERVIEW WITH BRAD LINSKY, CREATOR OF "FEMME FATALITY"!
...AND IF WE SCROLL DOWN, WE SHOULD FIND... YUP! HERE'S WHERE HE TALKS ABOUT HIS "TOOLS OF THE TRADE."
COOL!
NON-PHOTO BLUE PENCILS, KNEADED ERASERS, 2-PLY VELLUM, INDIA INK, CROW QUILL PENS, AND EGG SALAD FINGER SANDWICHES.
EGG SALAD FINGER SANDWICHES??
"...PREPARED LOVINGLY BY MY MOM, LOIS."

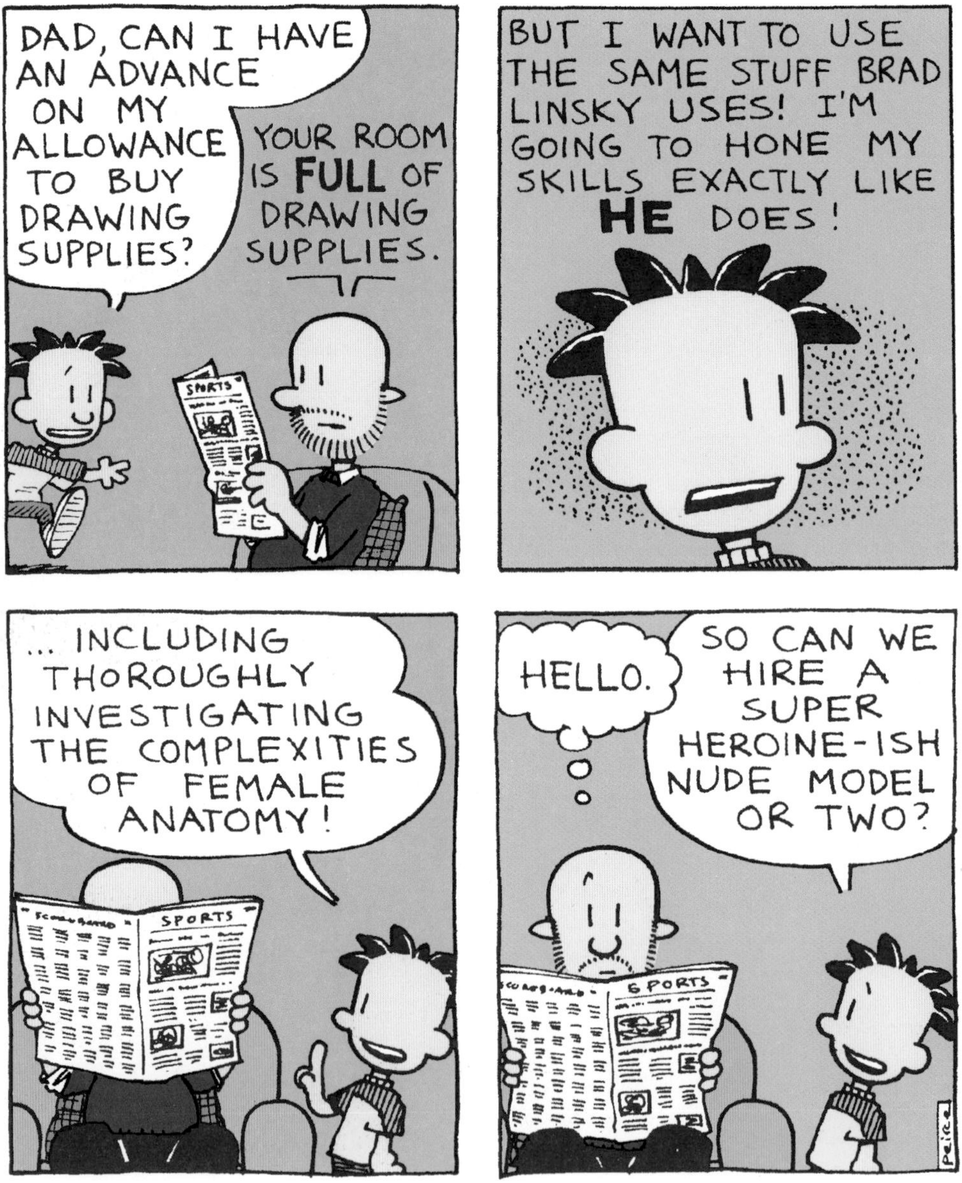
DAD, CAN I HAVE AN ADVANCE ON MY ALLOWANCE TO BUY DRAWING SUPPLIES?
YOUR ROOM IS FULL OF DRAWING SUPPLIES.
SPORTS
BUT I WANT TO USE THE SAME STUFF BRAD LINSKY USES! I'M GOING TO HONE MY SKILLS EXACTLY LIKE HE DOES!
... INCLUDING THOROUGHLY INVESTIGATING THE COMPLEXITIES OF FEMALE ANATOMY!
SPORTS
HELLO.
SO CAN WE HIRE A SUPER HEROINE-ISH NUDE MODEL OR TWO?
SPORTS
peirce

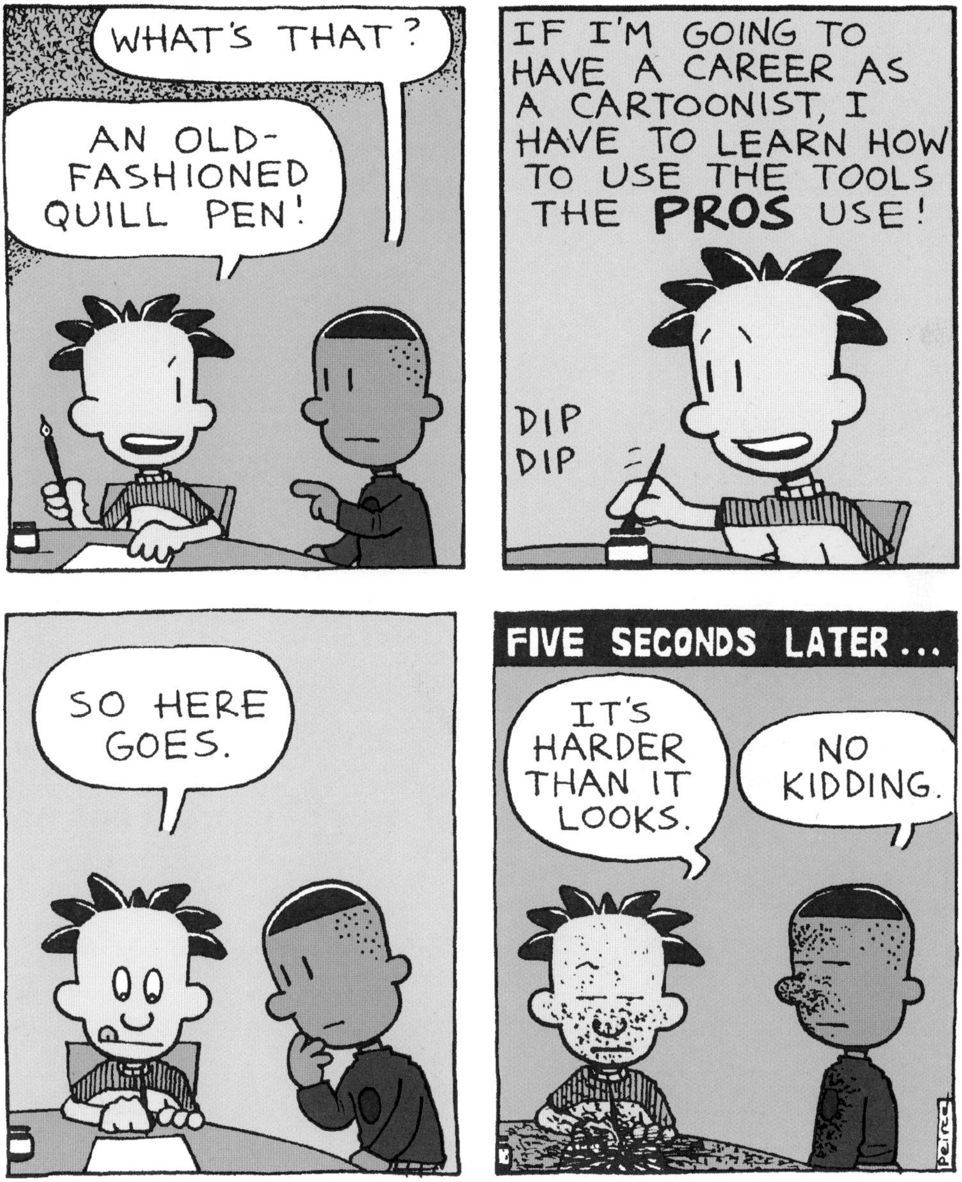
WHAT'S THAT?
AN OLD-FASHIONED QUILL PEN!
IF I'M GOING TO HAVE A CAREER AS A CARTOONIST, I HAVE TO LEARN HOW TO USE THE TOOLS THE **PROS** USE!
DIP DIP
SO HERE GOES.
FIVE SECONDS LATER...
IT'S HARDER THAN IT LOOKS.
NO KIDDING.
Peirce

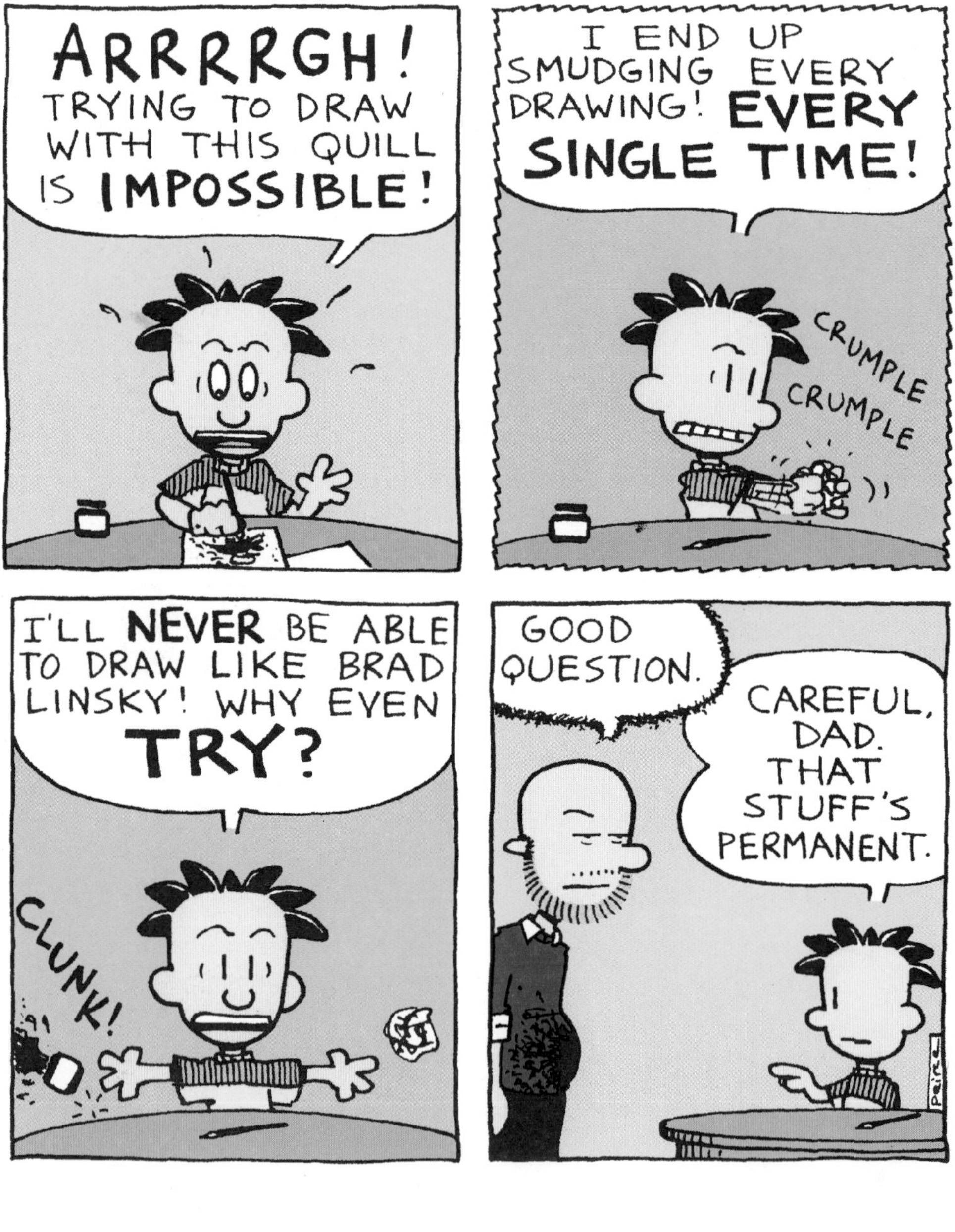
ARRRRGH! TRYING TO DRAW WITH THIS QUILL IS IMPOSSIBLE!
I END UP SMUDGING EVERY DRAWING! EVERY SINGLE TIME!
CRUMPLE
CRUMPLE
I'LL NEVER BE ABLE TO DRAW LIKE BRAD LINSKY! WHY EVEN TRY?
CLUNK!
GOOD QUESTION.
CAREFUL, DAD. THAT STUFF'S PERMANENT.

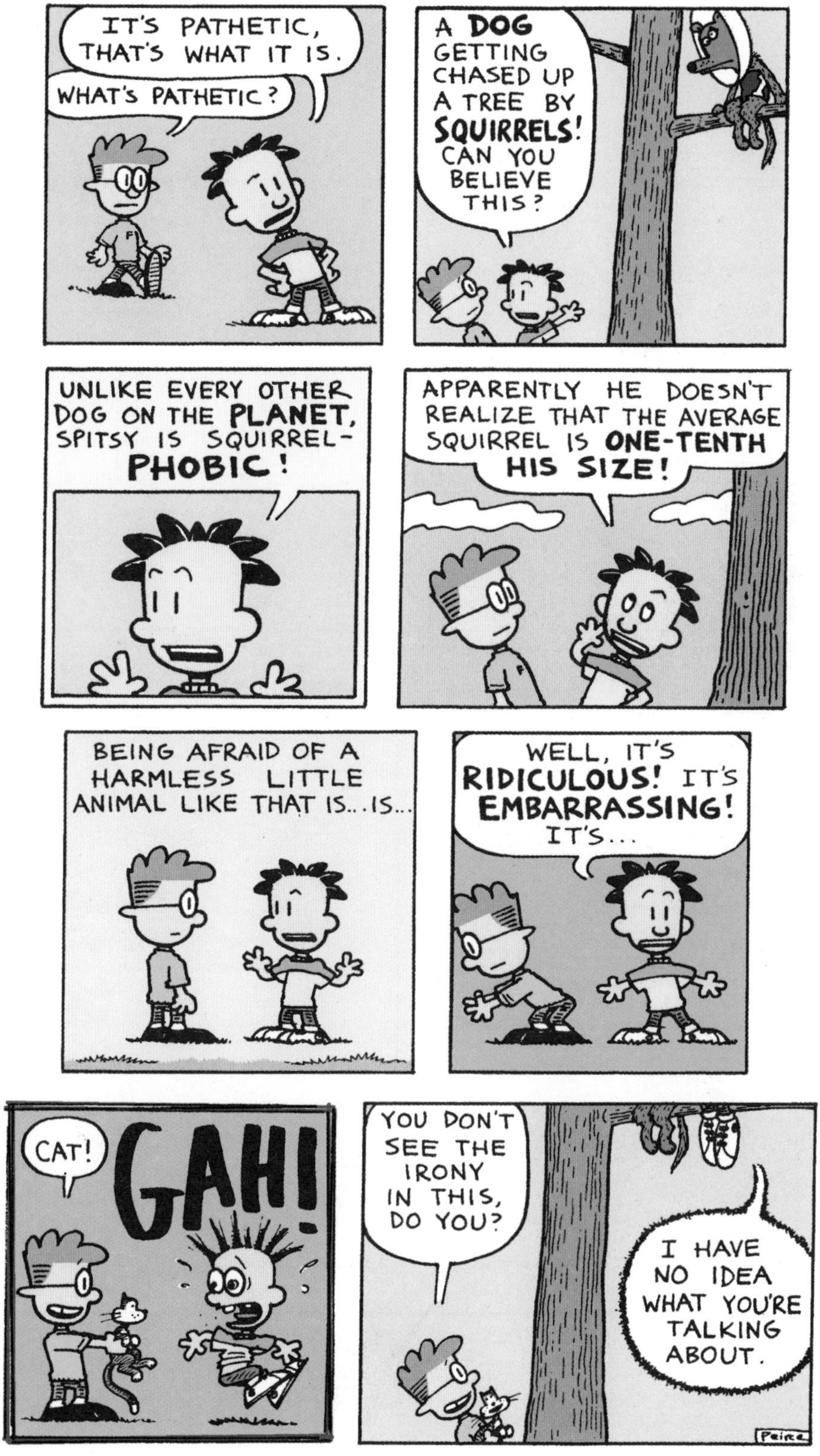
IT'S PATHETIC, THAT'S WHAT IT IS.
WHAT'S PATHETIC?
A DOG GETTING CHASED UP A TREE BY SQUIRRELS! CAN YOU BELIEVE THIS?
UNLIKE EVERY OTHER DOG ON THE PLANET, SPITSY IS SQUIRREL-PHOBIC!
APPARENTLY HE DOESN'T REALIZE THAT THE AVERAGE SQUIRREL IS ONE-TENTH HIS SIZE!
BEING AFRAID OF A HARMLESS LITTLE ANIMAL LIKE THAT IS...IS...
WELL, IT'S RIDICULOUS! IT'S EMBARRASSING! IT'S...
CAT!
GAH!
YOU DON'T SEE THE IRONY IN THIS, DO YOU?
I HAVE NO IDEA WHAT YOU'RE TALKING ABOUT.
Peirce

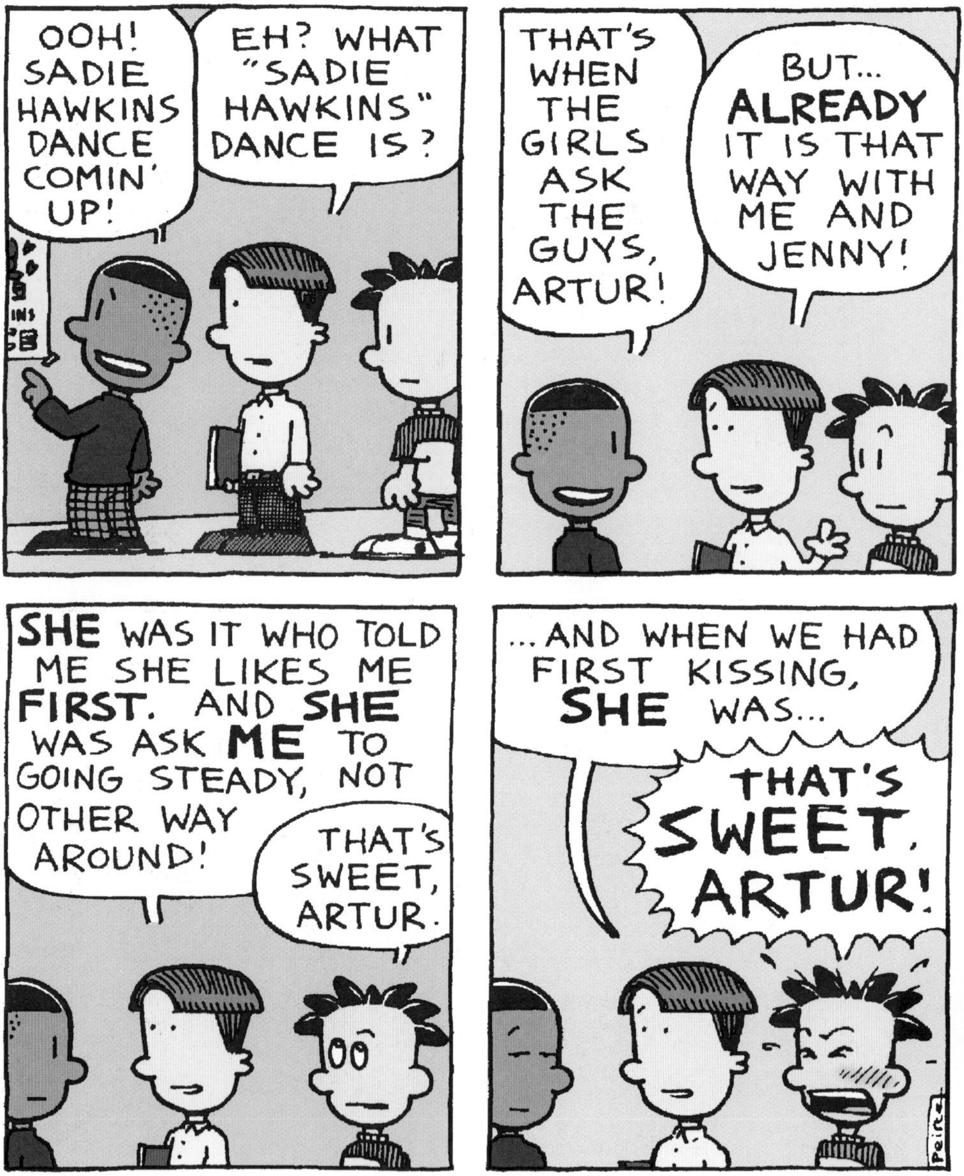
OOH! SADIE HAWKINS DANCE COMIN' UP!
EH? WHAT "SADIE HAWKINS" DANCE IS?
THAT'S WHEN THE GIRLS ASK THE GUYS, ARTUR!
BUT... ALREADY IT IS THAT WAY WITH ME AND JENNY!
SHE WAS IT WHO TOLD ME SHE LIKES ME FIRST. AND SHE WAS ASK ME TO GOING STEADY, NOT OTHER WAY AROUND!
THAT'S SWEET, ARTUR.
...AND WHEN WE HAD FIRST KISSING, SHE WAS...
THAT'S SWEET, ARTUR!
Peirce

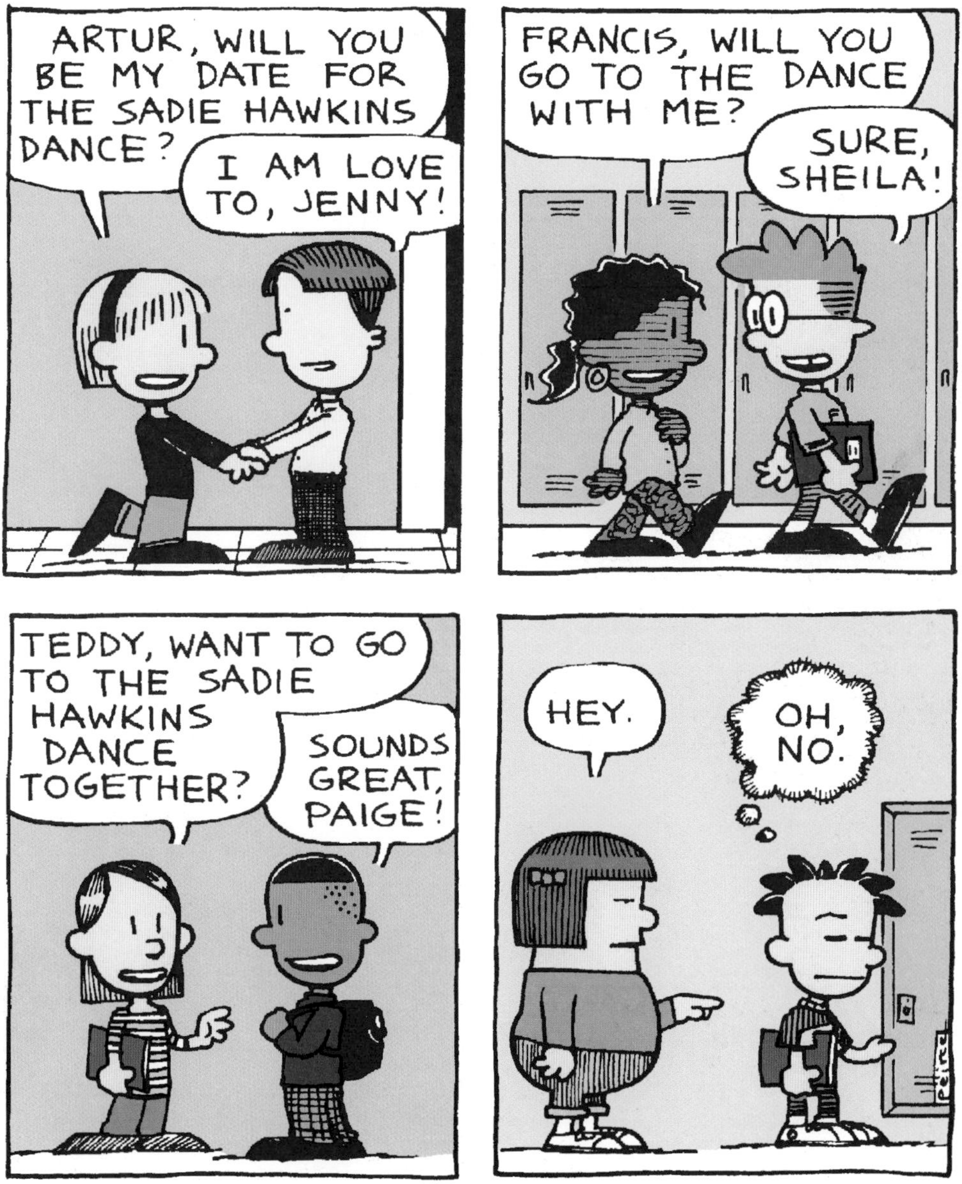
ARTUR, WILL YOU BE MY DATE FOR THE SADIE HAWKINS DANCE?
I AM LOVE TO, JENNY!
FRANCIS, WILL YOU GO TO THE DANCE WITH ME?
SURE, SHEILA!
TEDDY, WANT TO GO TO THE SADIE HAWKINS DANCE TOGETHER?
SOUNDS GREAT, PAIGE!
HEY.
OH, NO.
peirce

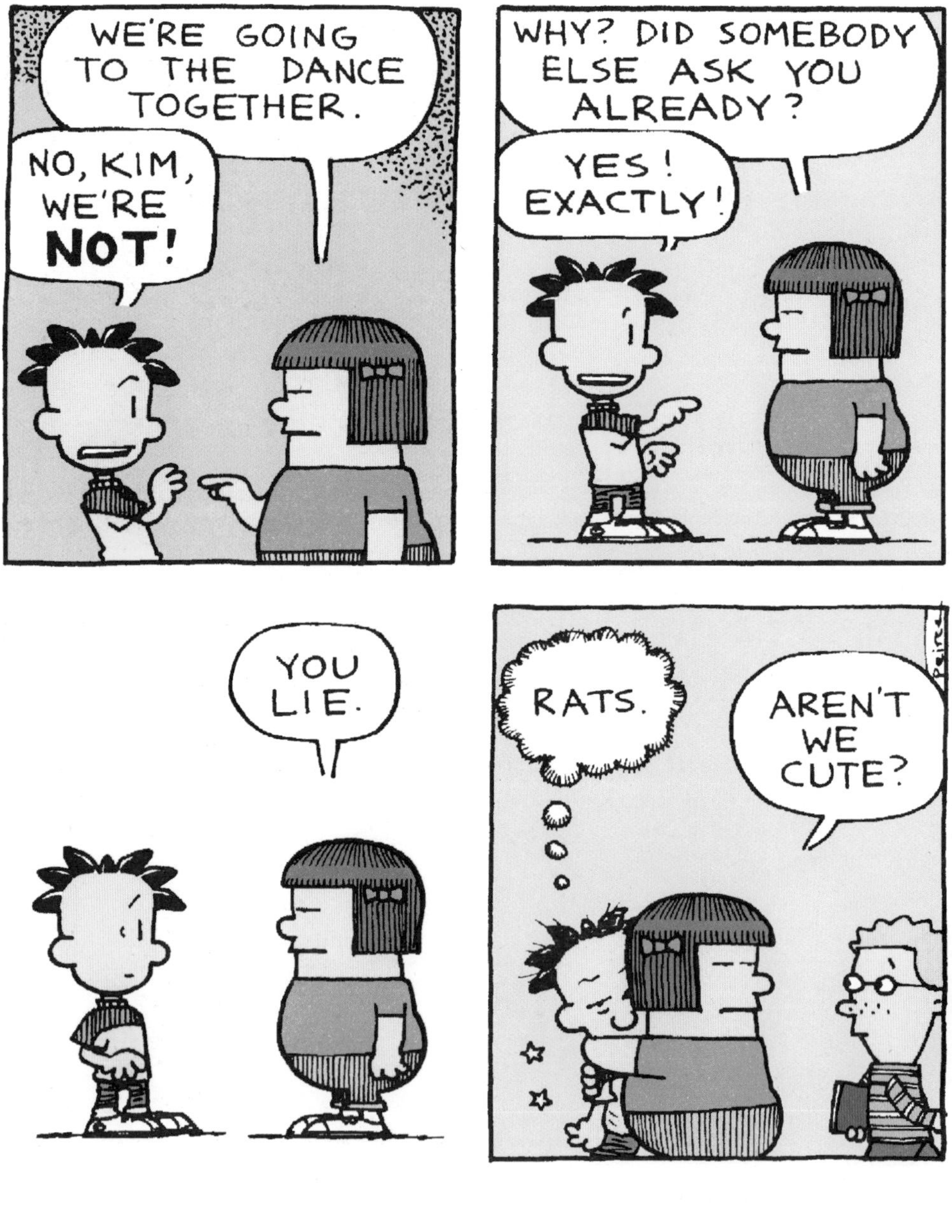
WE'RE GOING TO THE DANCE TOGETHER.
NO, KIM, WE'RE **NOT**!
WHY? DID SOMEBODY ELSE ASK YOU ALREADY?
YES! EXACTLY!
YOU LIE.
RATS.
AREN'T WE CUTE?

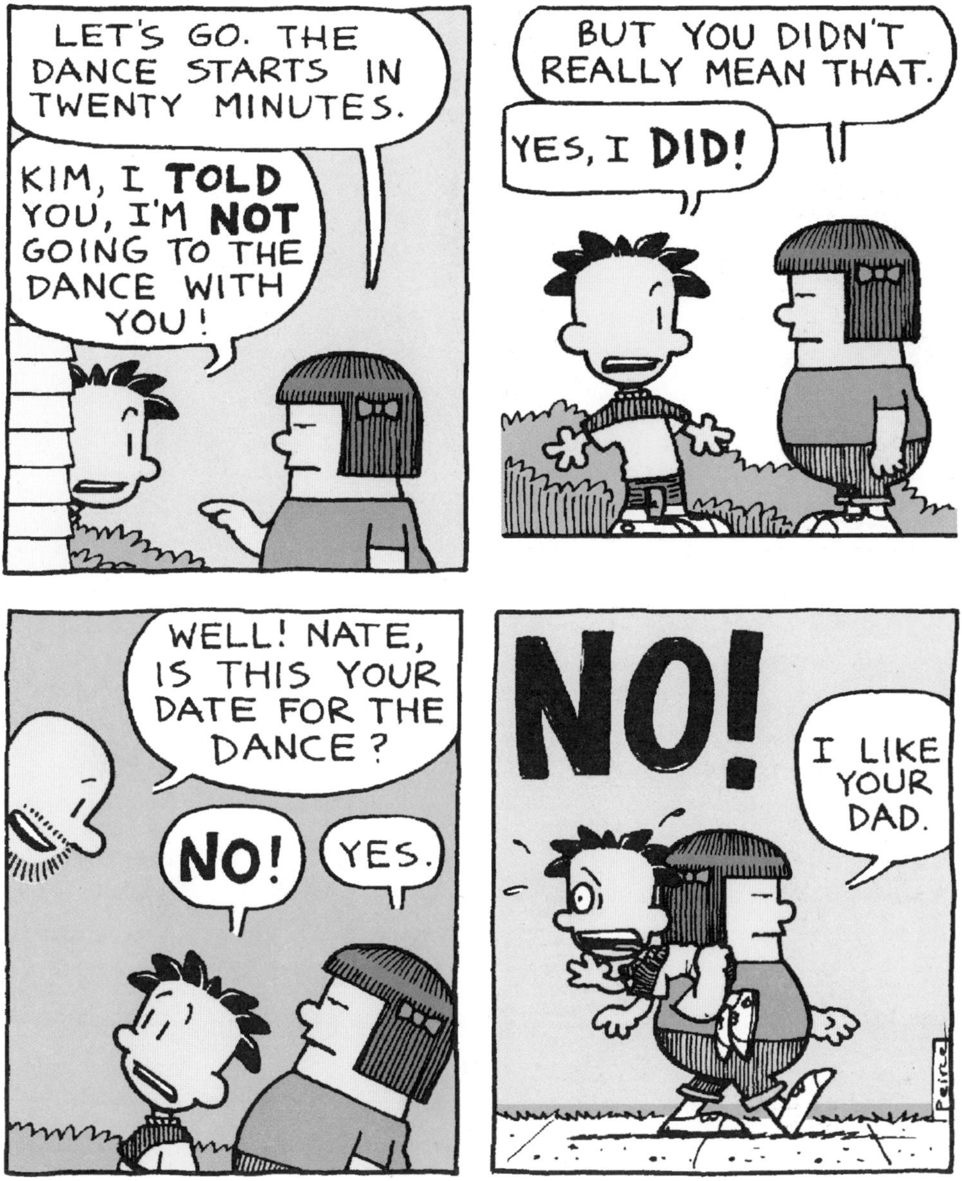
LET'S GO. THE DANCE STARTS IN TWENTY MINUTES.
KIM, I **TOLD** YOU, I'M **NOT** GOING TO THE DANCE WITH YOU!
BUT YOU DIDN'T REALLY MEAN THAT.
YES, I **DID!**
WELL! NATE, IS THIS YOUR DATE FOR THE DANCE?
NO!
YES.
NO!
I LIKE YOUR DAD.
Peirce

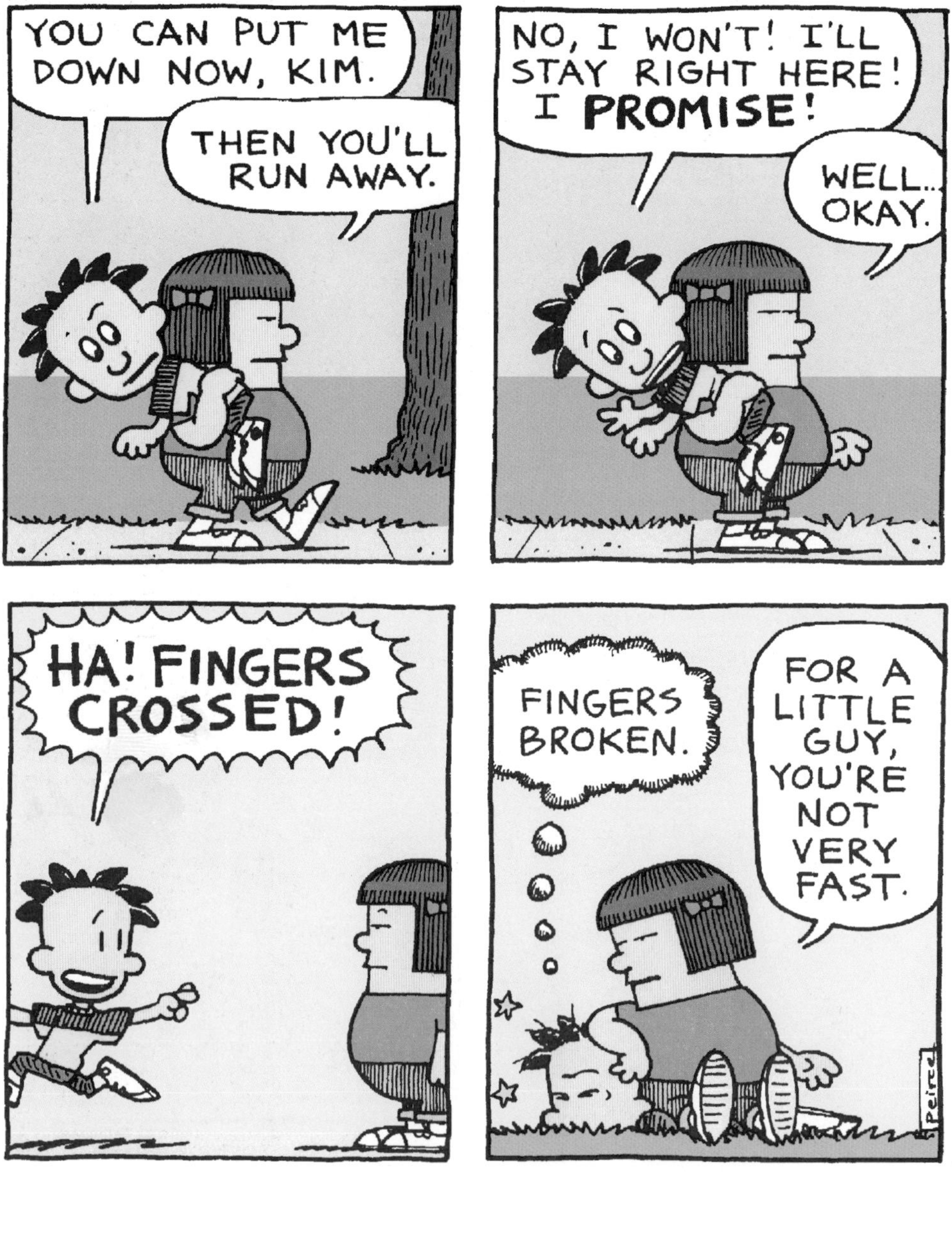
YOU CAN PUT ME DOWN NOW, KIM.
THEN YOU'LL RUN AWAY.
NO, I WON'T! I'LL STAY RIGHT HERE! I **PROMISE**!
WELL... OKAY.
HA! FINGERS CROSSED!
FINGERS BROKEN.
FOR A LITTLE GUY, YOU'RE NOT VERY FAST.
Peirce

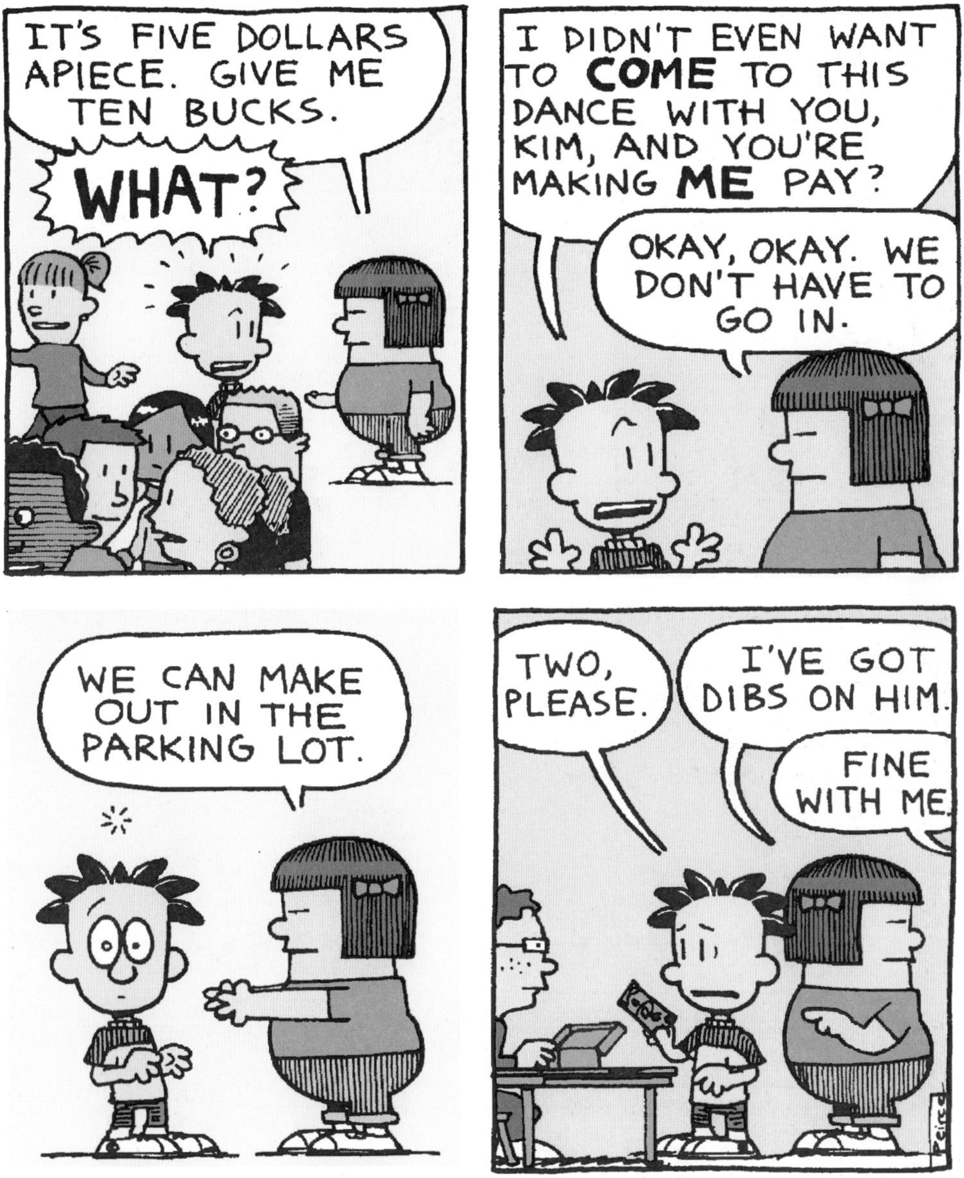
IT'S FIVE DOLLARS APIECE. GIVE ME TEN BUCKS.
WHAT?
I DIDN'T EVEN WANT TO **COME** TO THIS DANCE WITH YOU, KIM, AND YOU'RE MAKING **ME** PAY?
OKAY, OKAY. WE DON'T HAVE TO GO IN.
WE CAN MAKE OUT IN THE PARKING LOT.
TWO, PLEASE.
I'VE GOT DIBS ON HIM.
FINE WITH ME.

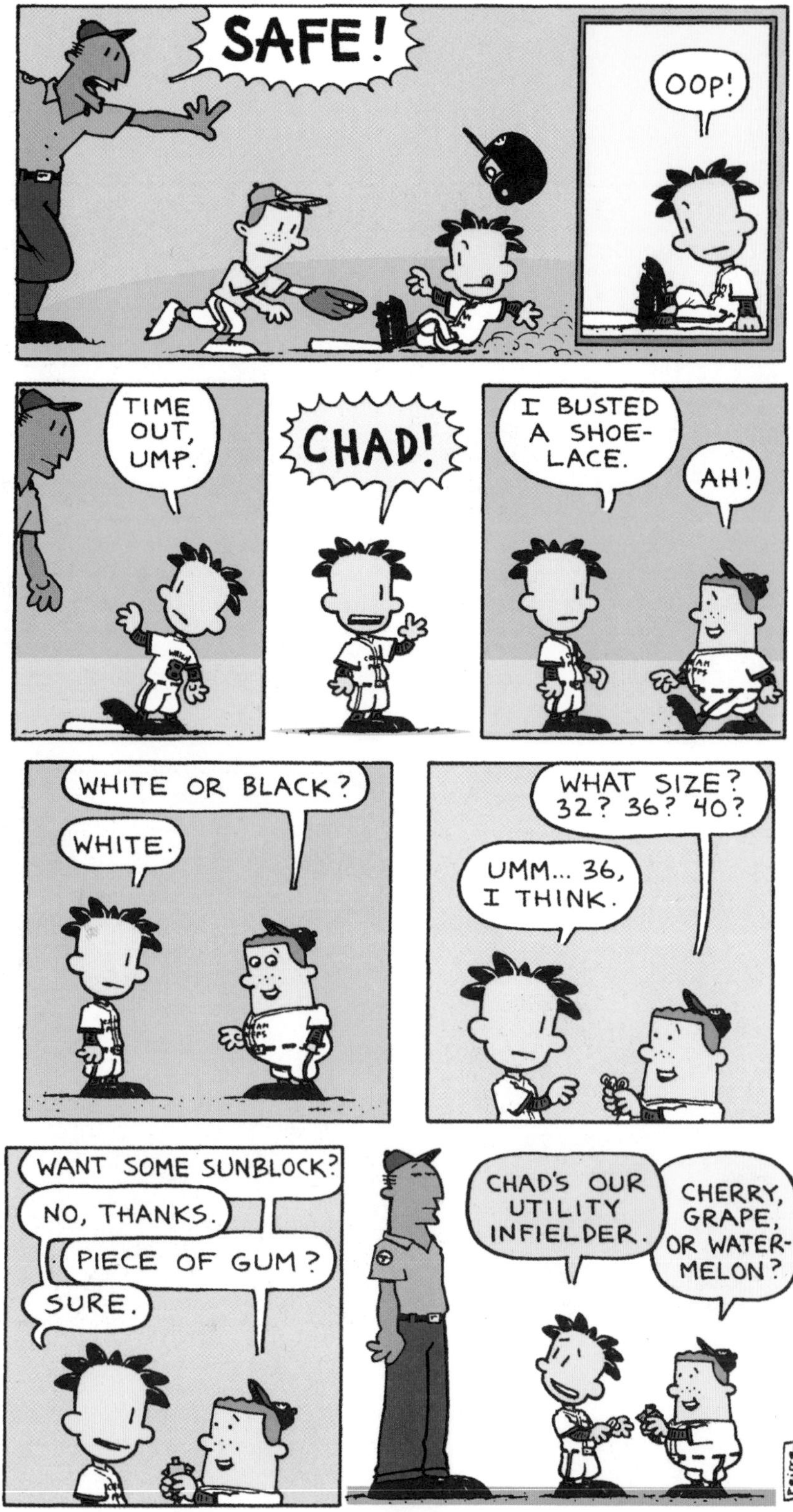
SAFE!
OOP!
TIME OUT, UMP.
CHAD!
I BUSTED A SHOE-LACE.
AH!
WHITE OR BLACK?
WHITE.
WHAT SIZE? 32? 36? 40?
UMM... 36, I THINK.
WANT SOME SUNBLOCK?
NO, THANKS.
PIECE OF GUM?
SURE.
CHAD'S OUR UTILITY INFIELDER.
CHERRY, GRAPE, OR WATER-MELON?

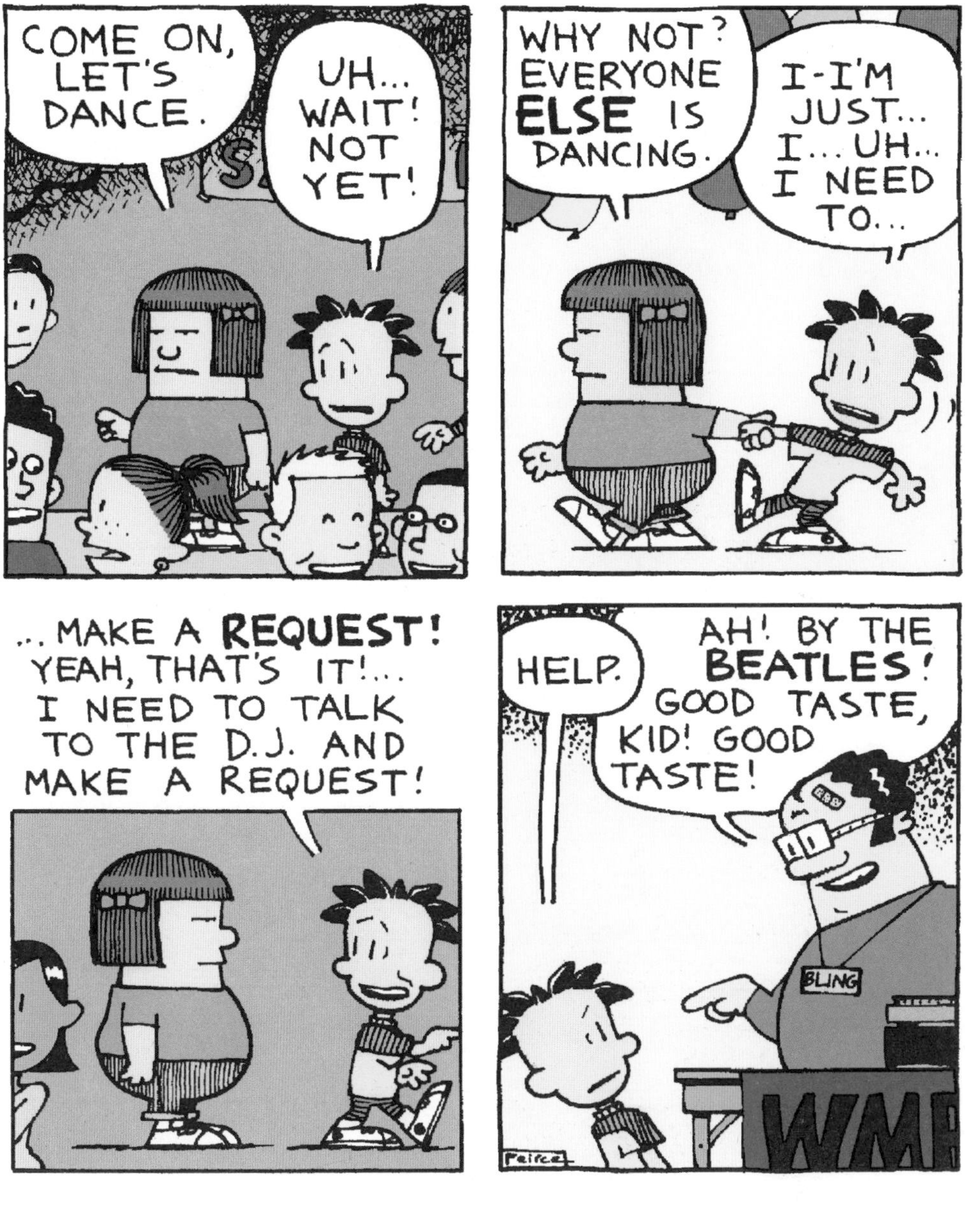
COME ON, LET'S DANCE.
UH... WAIT! NOT YET!
WHY NOT? EVERYONE **ELSE** IS DANCING.
I-I'M JUST... I... UH... I NEED TO...
... MAKE A **REQUEST!** YEAH, THAT'S IT!... I NEED TO TALK TO THE D.J. AND MAKE A REQUEST!
HELP.
AH! BY THE **BEATLES!** GOOD TASTE, KID! GOOD TASTE!
BLING
Peirce

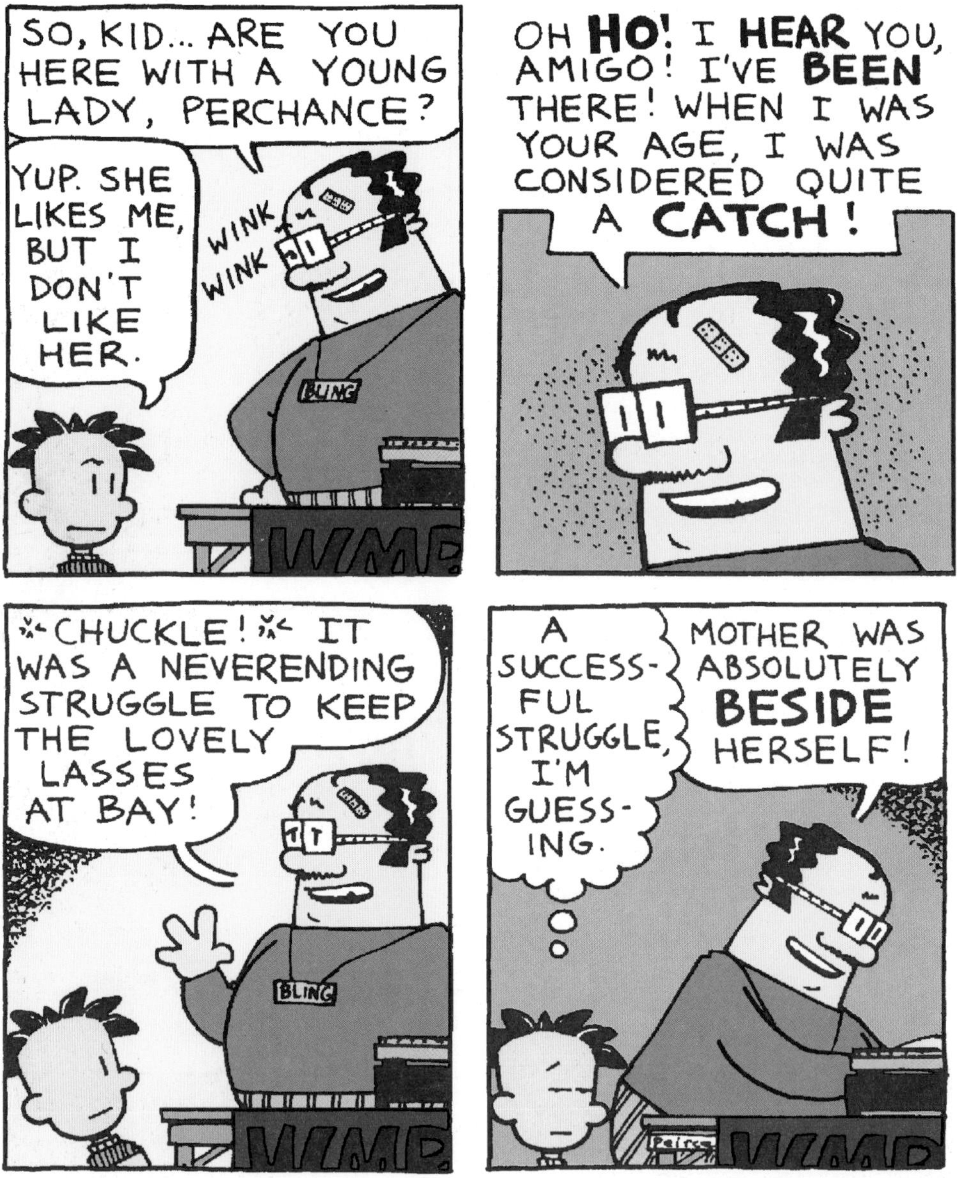
SO, KID... ARE YOU HERE WITH A YOUNG LADY, PERCHANCE?
WINK WINK
YUP. SHE LIKES ME, BUT I DON'T LIKE HER.
BLING
WIMP
OH HO! I HEAR YOU, AMIGO! I'VE BEEN THERE! WHEN I WAS YOUR AGE, I WAS CONSIDERED QUITE A CATCH!
CHUCKLE! IT WAS A NEVERENDING STRUGGLE TO KEEP THE LOVELY LASSES AT BAY!
BLING
WIMP
A SUCCESSFUL STRUGGLE, I'M GUESSING.
MOTHER WAS ABSOLUTELY BESIDE HERSELF!
Peirce
WIMP

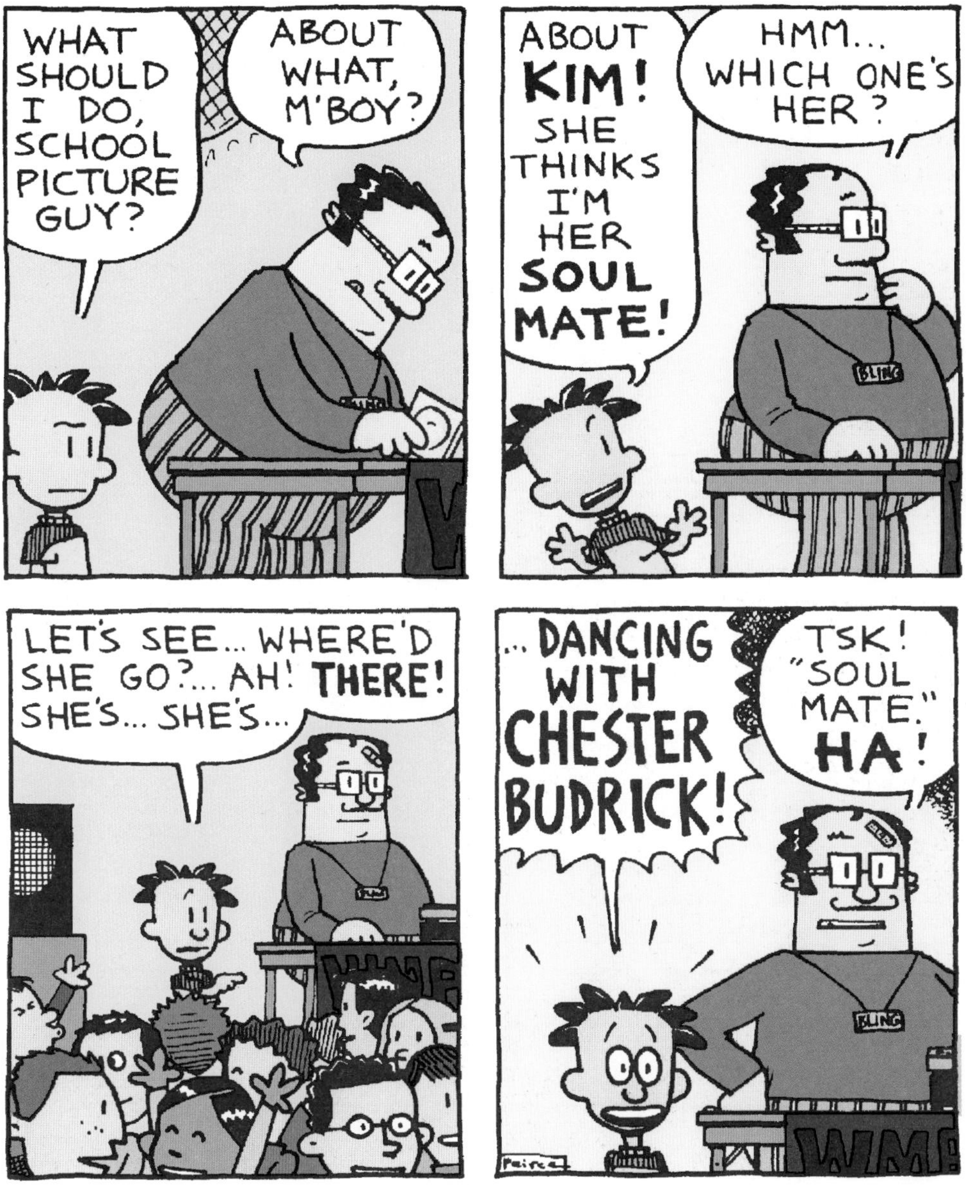
WHAT SHOULD I DO, SCHOOL PICTURE GUY?
ABOUT WHAT, M'BOY?
ABOUT KIM! SHE THINKS I'M HER SOUL MATE!
HMM... WHICH ONE'S HER?
LET'S SEE... WHERE'D SHE GO?... AH! THERE! SHE'S... SHE'S...
...DANCING WITH CHESTER BUDRICK!
TSK! "SOUL MATE." HA!

60

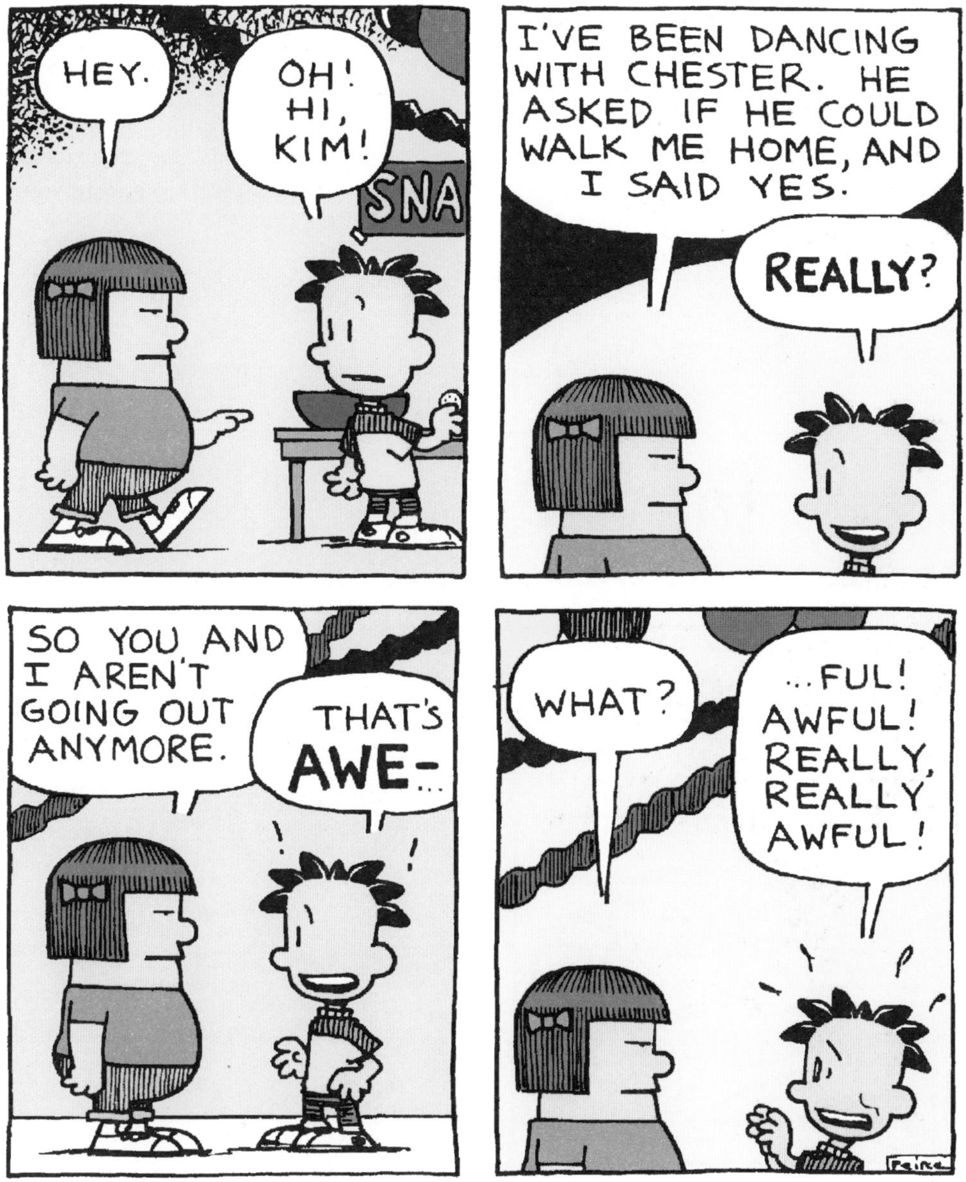
HEY.
OH! HI, KIM!
SNA
I'VE BEEN DANCING WITH CHESTER. HE ASKED IF HE COULD WALK ME HOME, AND I SAID YES.
REALLY?
SO YOU AND I AREN'T GOING OUT ANYMORE.
THAT'S AWE-...
WHAT?
...FUL! AWFUL! REALLY, REALLY AWFUL!

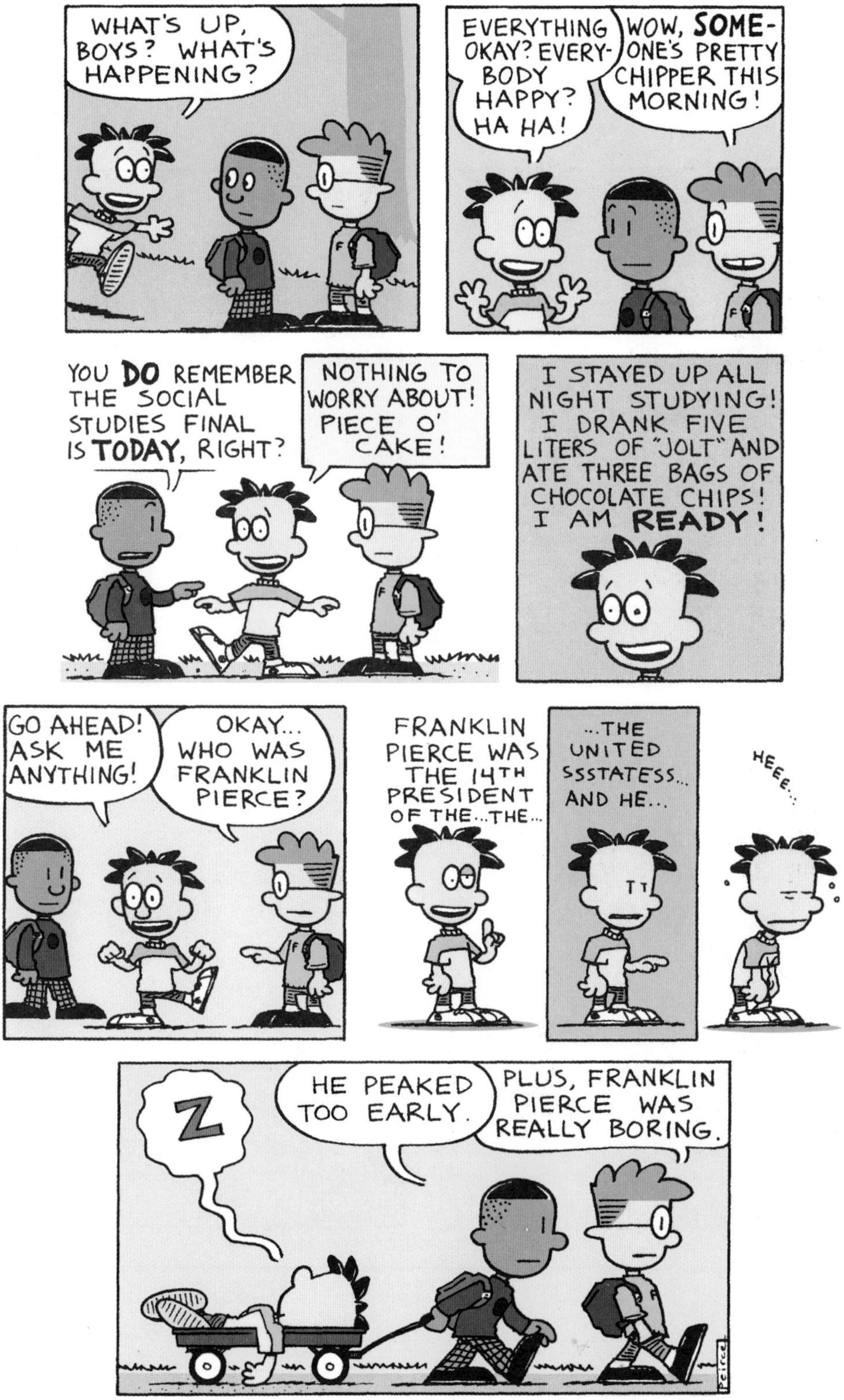

WHAT'S UP, BOYS? WHAT'S HAPPENING?
EVERYTHING OKAY? EVERY-BODY HAPPY? HA HA!
WOW, SOME-ONE'S PRETTY CHIPPER THIS MORNING!
YOU DO REMEMBER THE SOCIAL STUDIES FINAL IS TODAY, RIGHT?
NOTHING TO WORRY ABOUT! PIECE O' CAKE!
I STAYED UP ALL NIGHT STUDYING! I DRANK FIVE LITERS OF "JOLT" AND ATE THREE BAGS OF CHOCOLATE CHIPS! I AM READY!
GO AHEAD! ASK ME ANYTHING!
OKAY... WHO WAS FRANKLIN PIERCE?
FRANKLIN PIERCE WAS THE 14TH PRESIDENT OF THE...THE...
...THE UNITED SSSTATESS... AND HE...
HEEE...
Z
HE PEAKED TOO EARLY.
PLUS, FRANKLIN PIERCE WAS REALLY BORING.

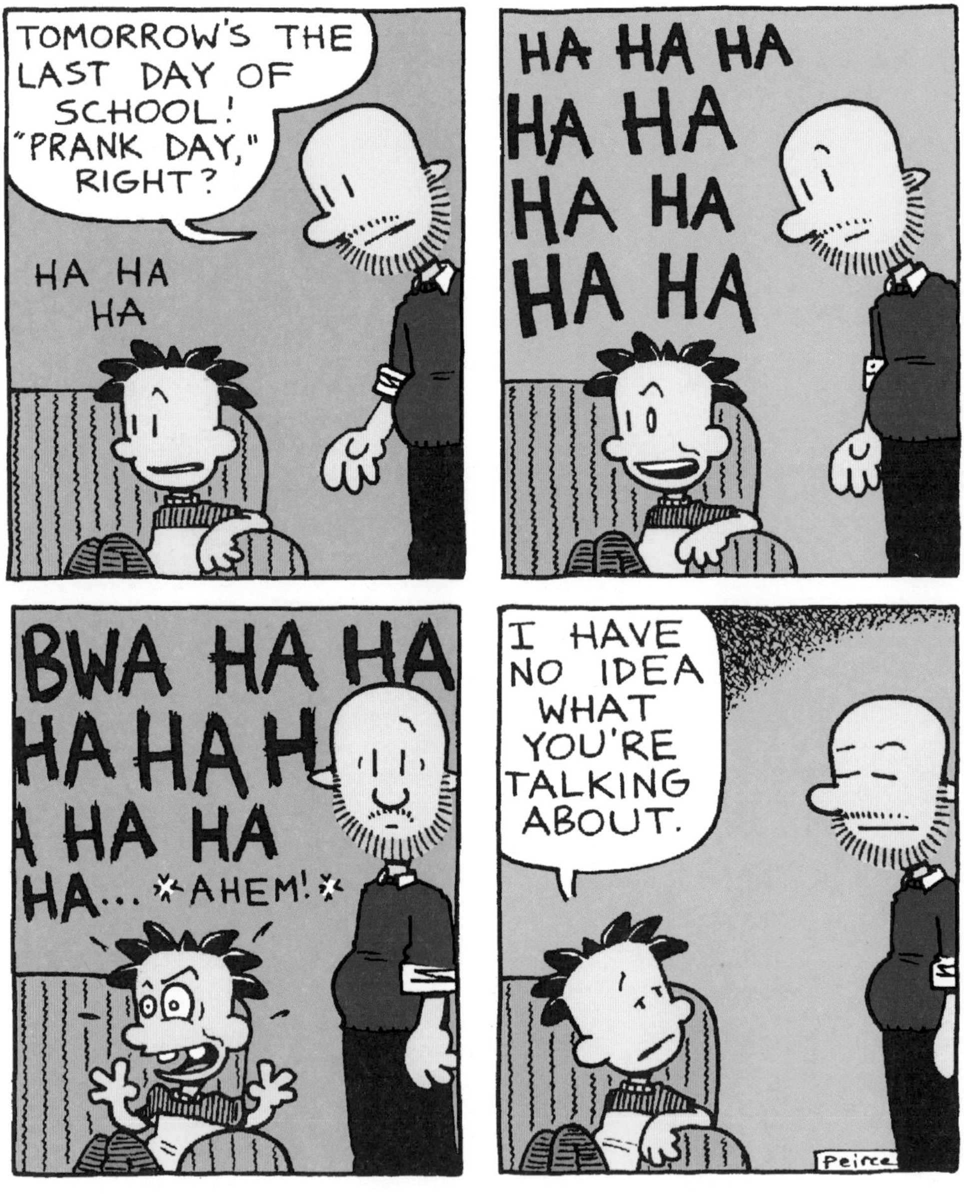
TOMORROW'S THE LAST DAY OF SCHOOL! "PRANK DAY," RIGHT?
HA HA HA
HA HA HA HA HA HA HA HA HA
BWA HA HA HA HA H
A HA HA HA...
AHEM!
I HAVE NO IDEA WHAT YOU'RE TALKING ABOUT.
Peirce

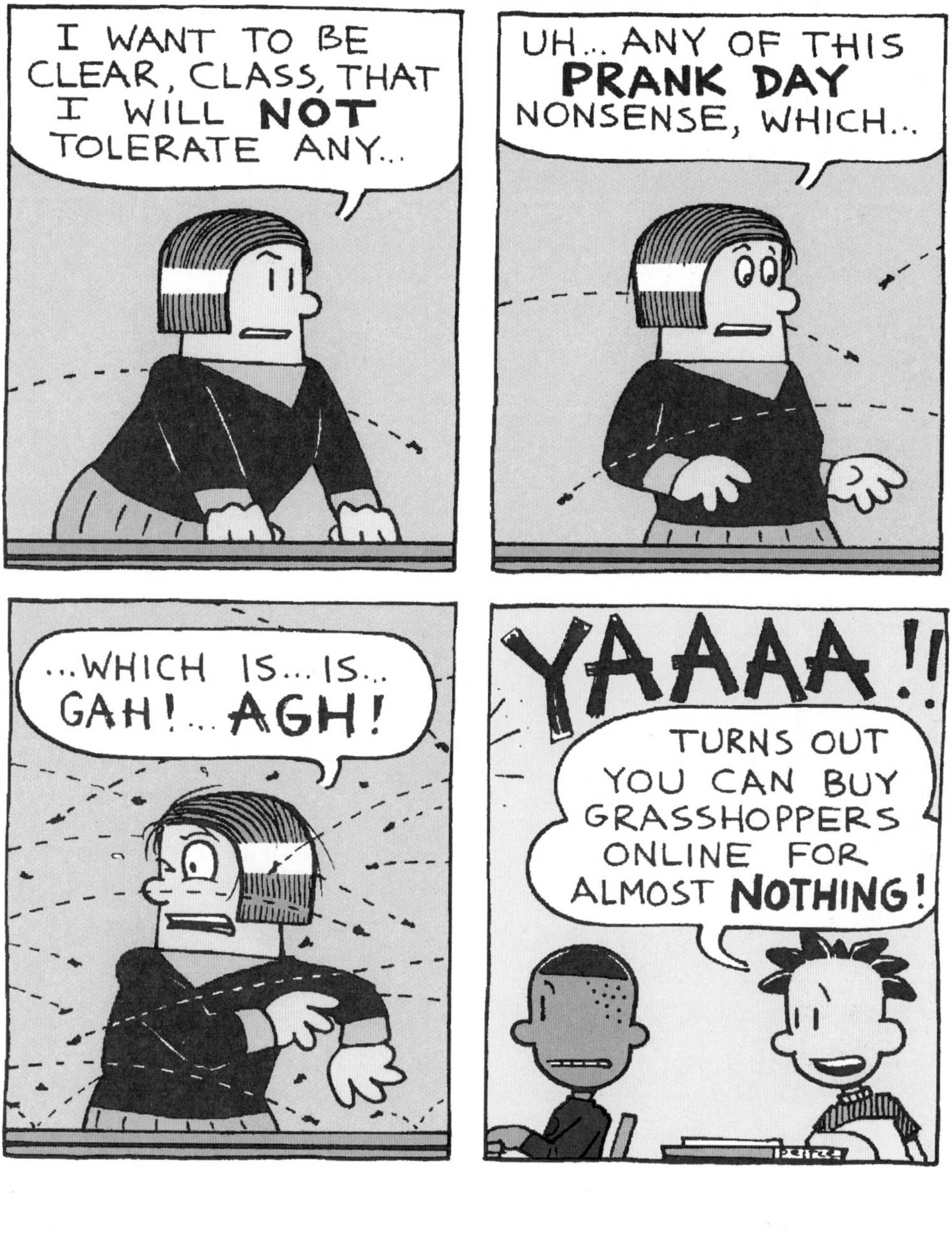
I WANT TO BE CLEAR, CLASS, THAT I WILL **NOT** TOLERATE ANY...
UH... ANY OF THIS **PRANK DAY** NONSENSE, WHICH...
...WHICH IS... IS... GAH!... **AGH!**
YAAAA!!
TURNS OUT YOU CAN BUY GRASSHOPPERS ONLINE FOR ALMOST **NOTHING**!

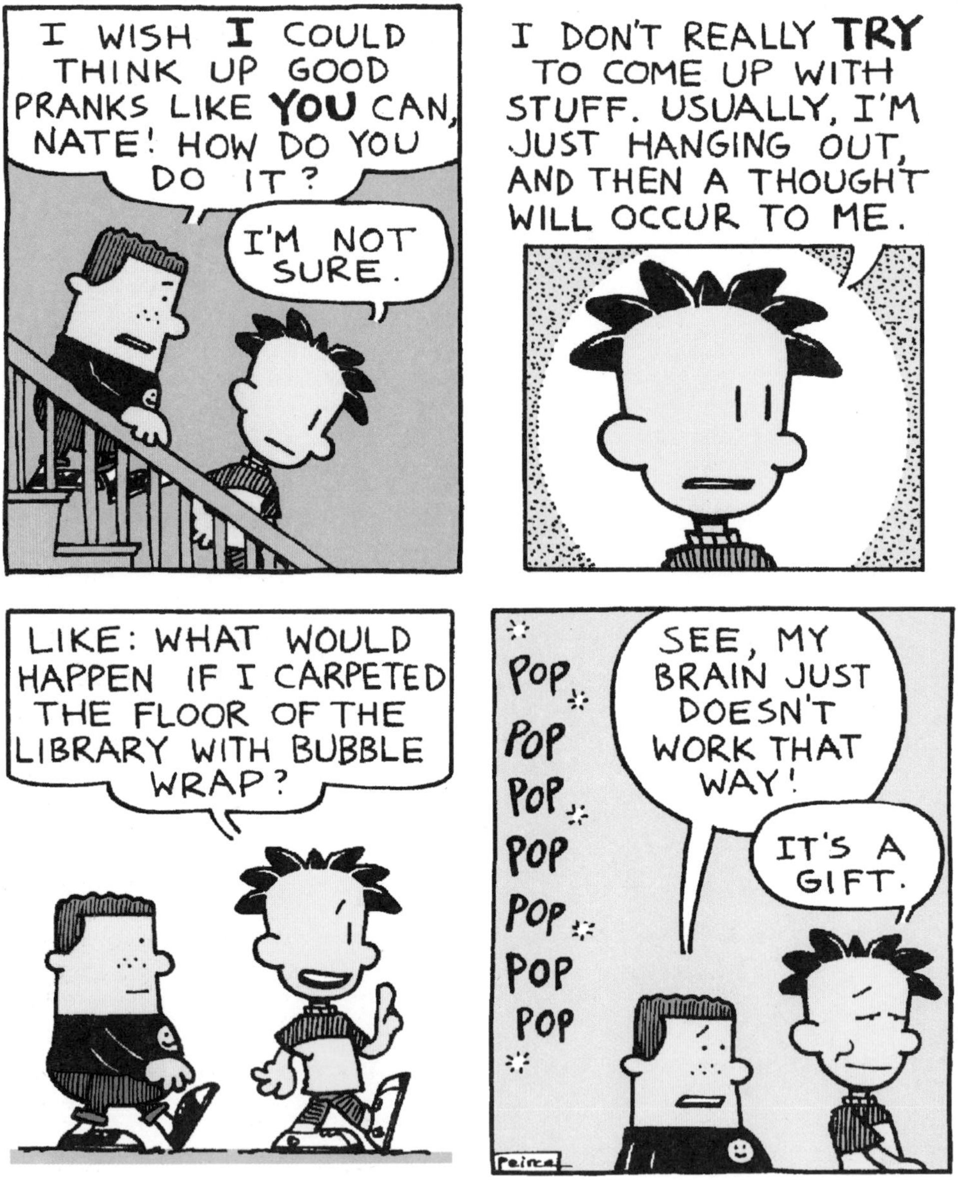
I WISH **I** COULD THINK UP GOOD PRANKS LIKE **YOU** CAN, NATE! HOW DO YOU DO IT?
I'M NOT SURE.
I DON'T REALLY **TRY** TO COME UP WITH STUFF. USUALLY, I'M JUST HANGING OUT, AND THEN A THOUGHT WILL OCCUR TO ME.
LIKE: WHAT WOULD HAPPEN IF I CARPETED THE FLOOR OF THE LIBRARY WITH BUBBLE WRAP?
POP POP POP POP POP POP POP
SEE, MY BRAIN JUST DOESN'T WORK THAT WAY!
IT'S A GIFT.
Peirce

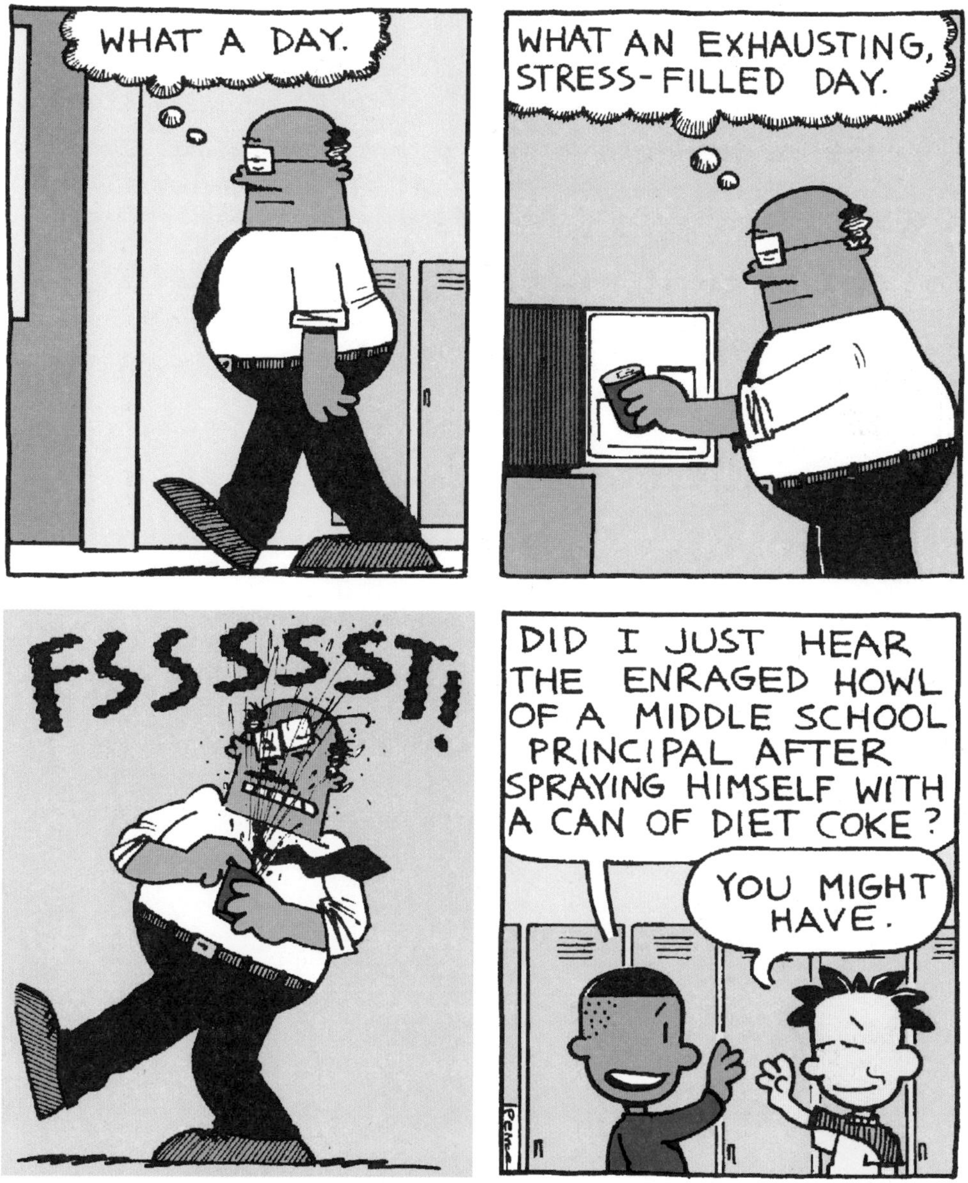
WHAT A DAY.
WHAT AN EXHAUSTING, STRESS-FILLED DAY.
FSSSSST!
DID I JUST HEAR THE ENRAGED HOWL OF A MIDDLE SCHOOL PRINCIPAL AFTER SPRAYING HIMSELF WITH A CAN OF DIET COKE?
YOU MIGHT HAVE.

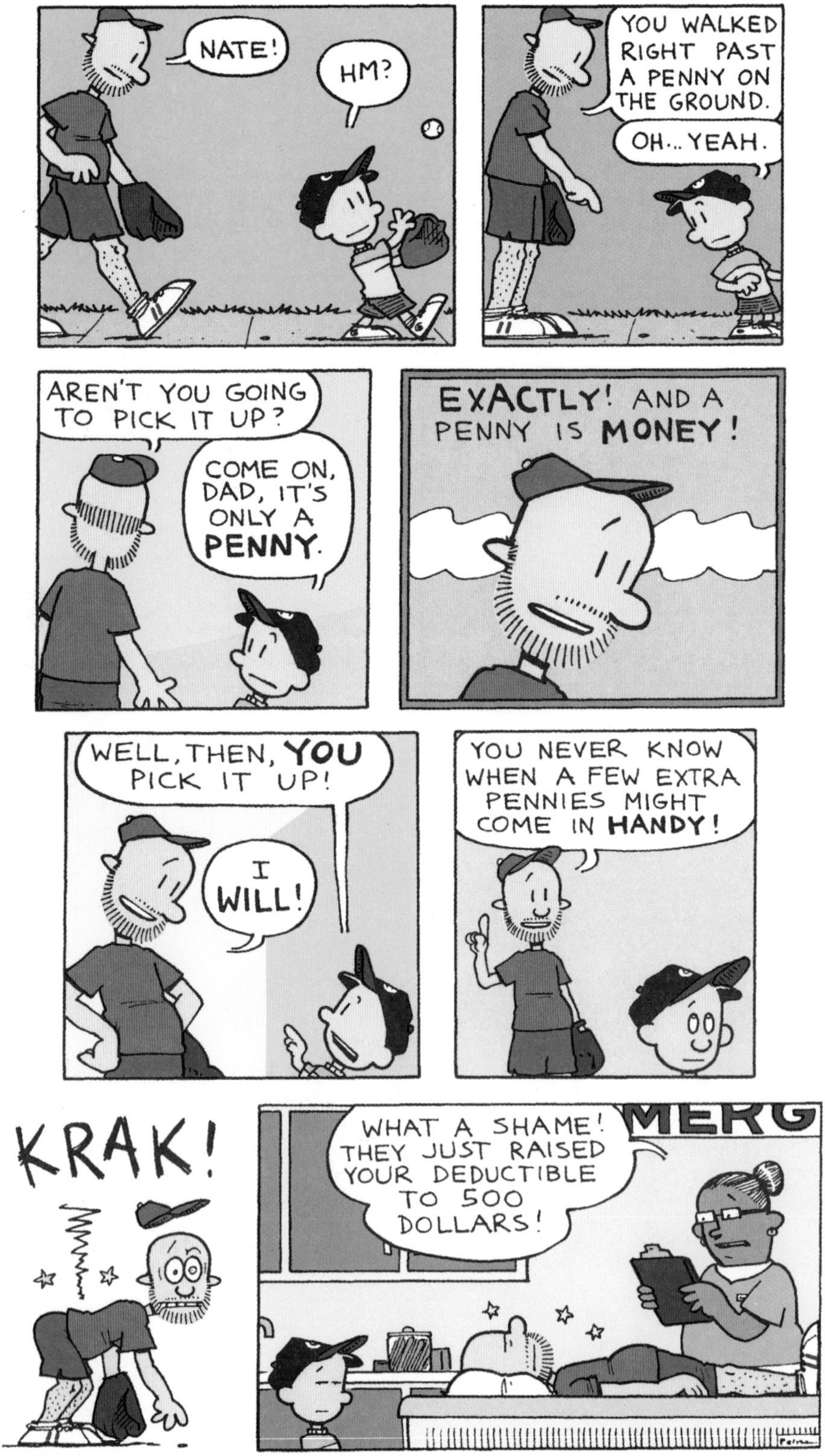
NATE!
HM?
YOU WALKED RIGHT PAST A PENNY ON THE GROUND.
OH... YEAH.
AREN'T YOU GOING TO PICK IT UP?
COME ON, DAD, IT'S ONLY A PENNY.
EXACTLY! AND A PENNY IS MONEY!
WELL, THEN, YOU PICK IT UP!
I WILL!
YOU NEVER KNOW WHEN A FEW EXTRA PENNIES MIGHT COME IN HANDY!
KRAK!
WHAT A SHAME! THEY JUST RAISED YOUR DEDUCTIBLE TO 500 DOLLARS!
MERG

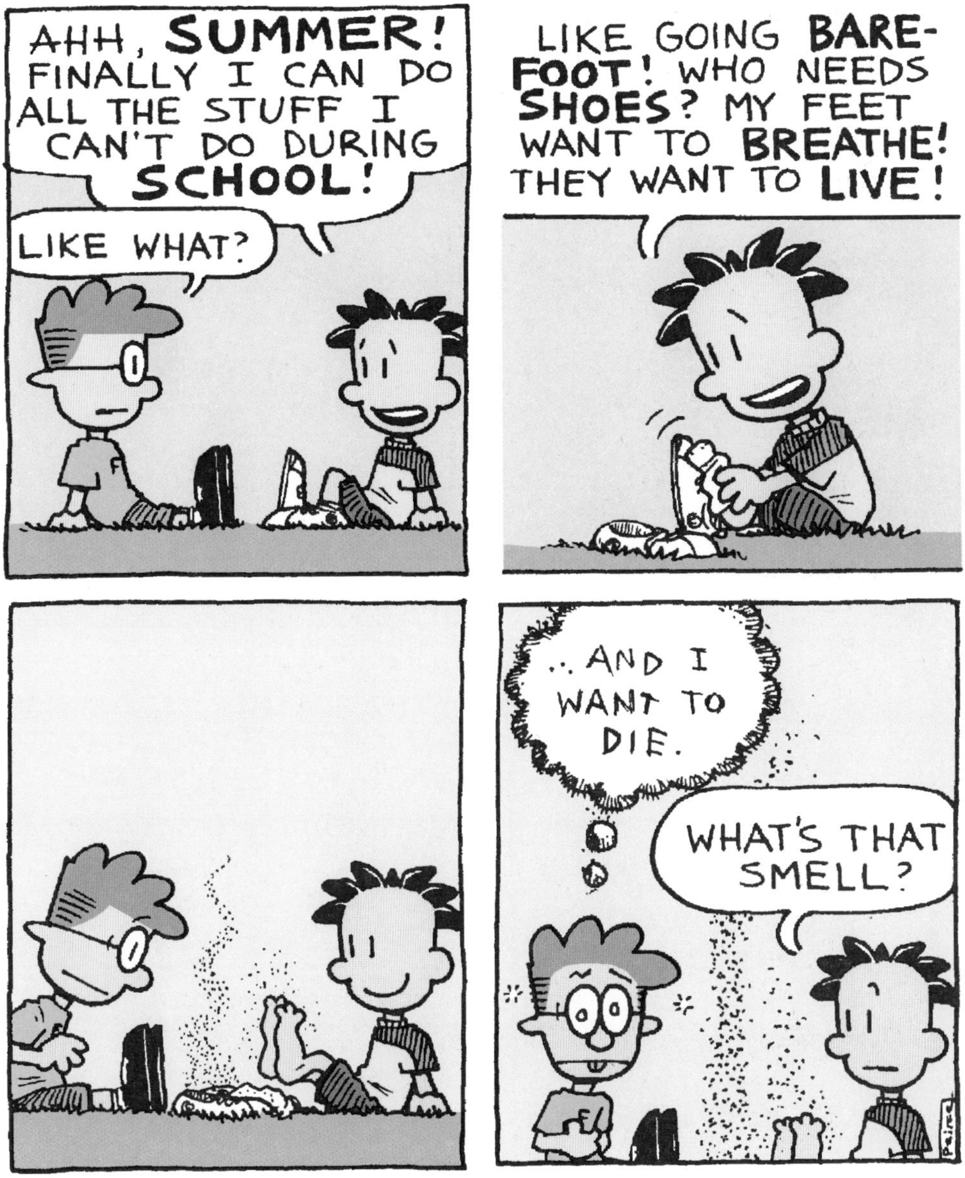
AHH, SUMMER! FINALLY I CAN DO ALL THE STUFF I CAN'T DO DURING SCHOOL!
LIKE WHAT?
LIKE GOING BARE-FOOT! WHO NEEDS SHOES? MY FEET WANT TO BREATHE! THEY WANT TO LIVE!
...AND I WANT TO DIE.
WHAT'S THAT SMELL?

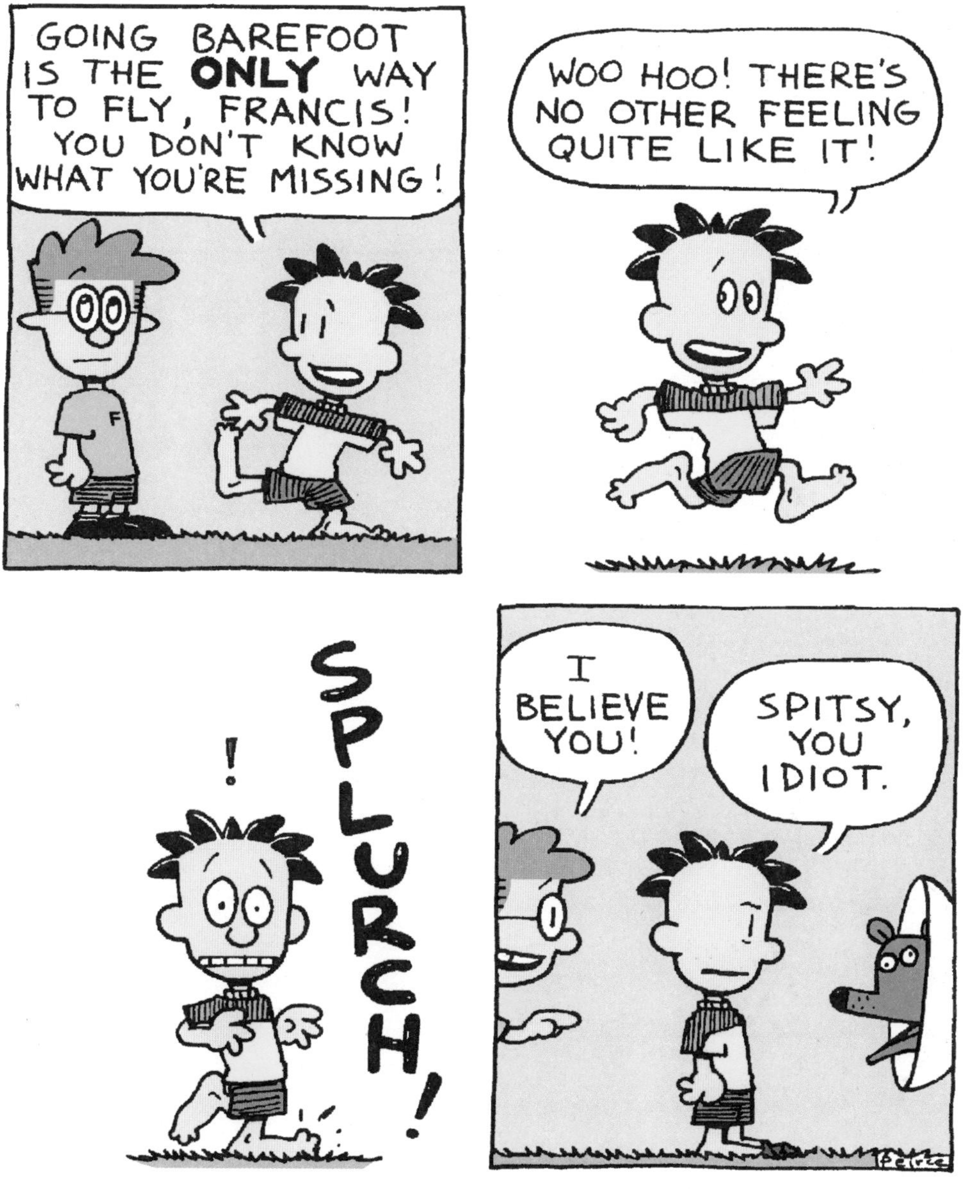

GOING BAREFOOT IS THE **ONLY** WAY TO FLY, FRANCIS! YOU DON'T KNOW WHAT YOU'RE MISSING!
F
WOO HOO! THERE'S NO OTHER FEELING QUITE LIKE IT!
!
SPLURCH!
I BELIEVE YOU!
SPITSY, YOU IDIOT.

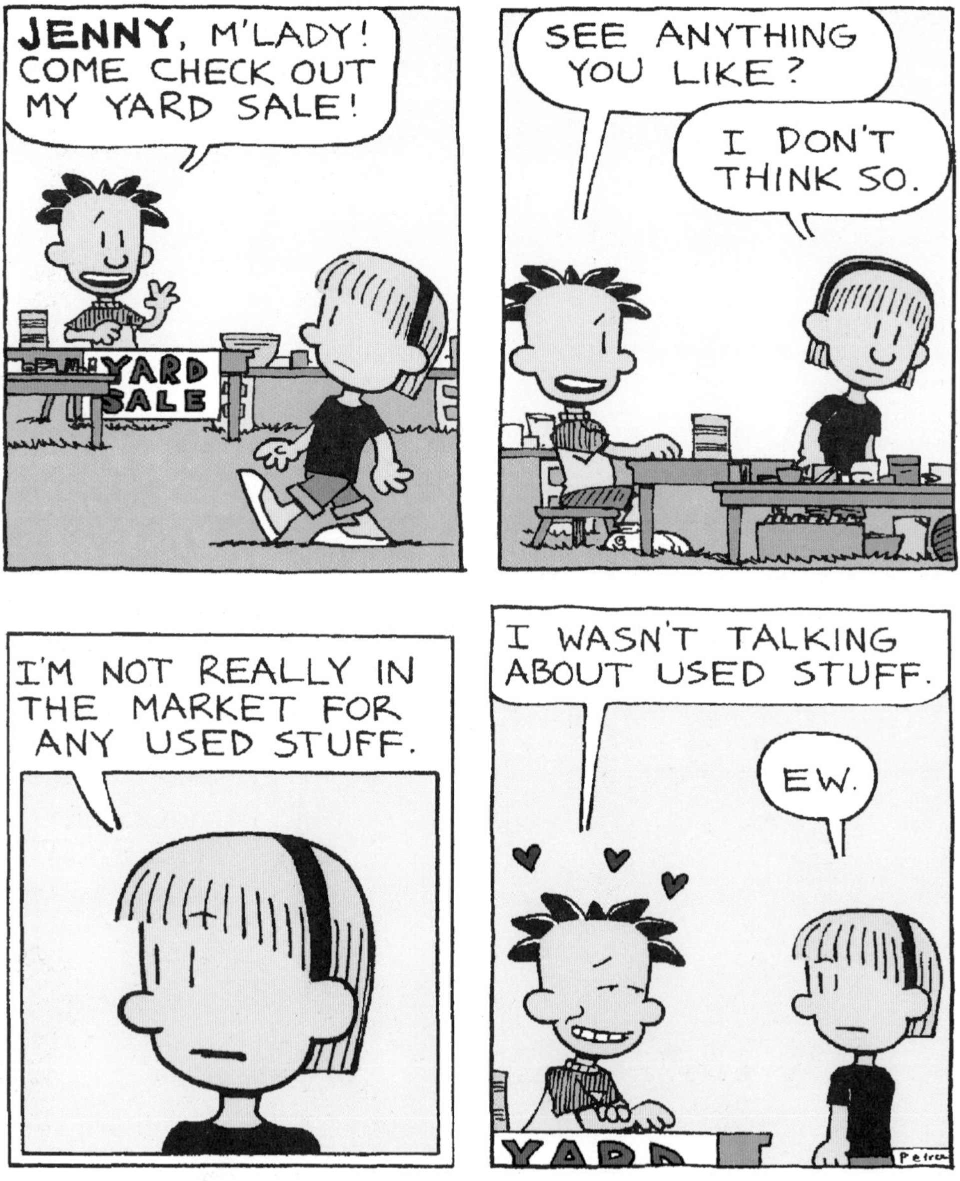
JENNY, M'LADY! COME CHECK OUT MY YARD SALE!
YARD SALE
SEE ANYTHING YOU LIKE?
I DON'T THINK SO.
I'M NOT REALLY IN THE MARKET FOR ANY USED STUFF.
I WASN'T TALKING ABOUT USED STUFF.
EW.
Peirce

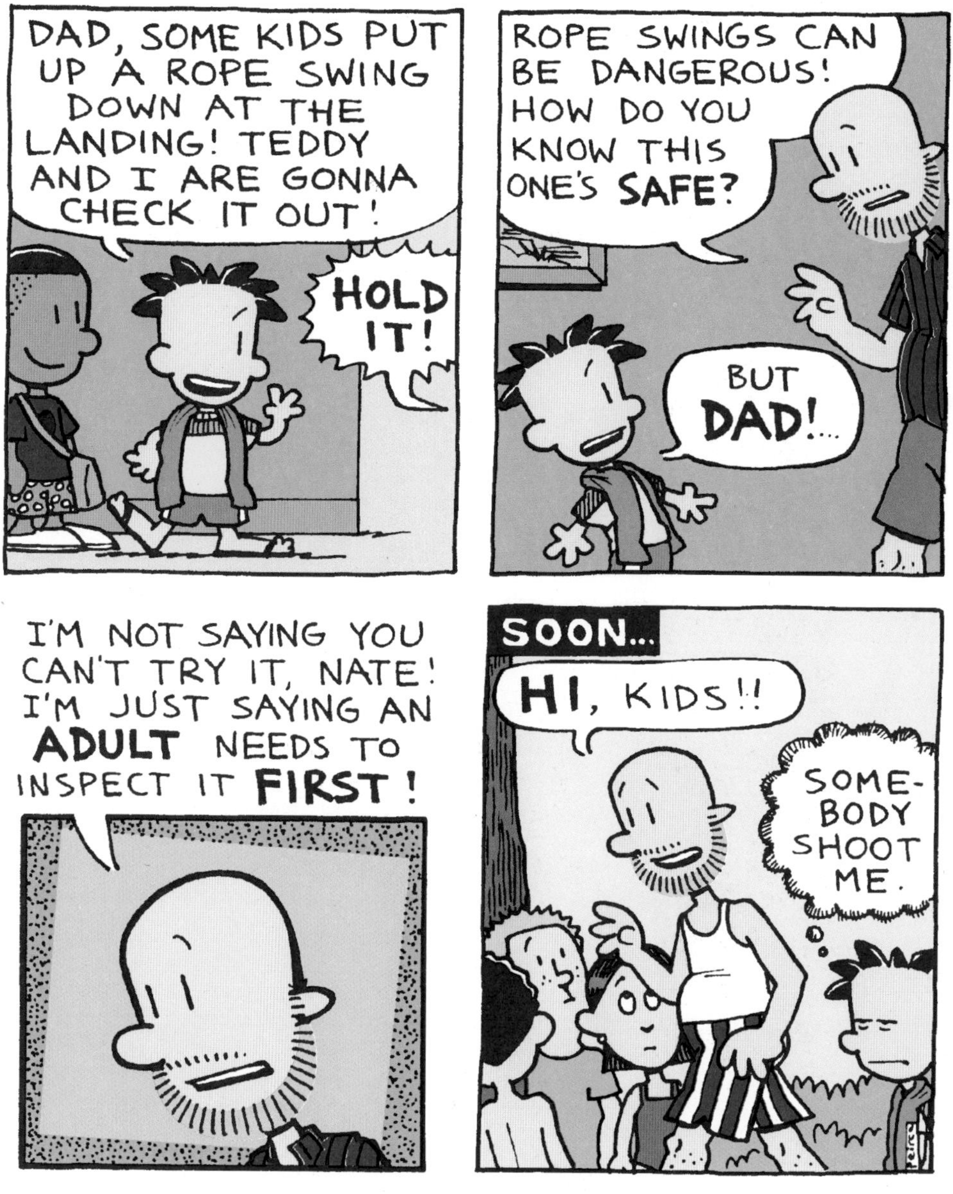
DAD, SOME KIDS PUT UP A ROPE SWING DOWN AT THE LANDING! TEDDY AND I ARE GONNA CHECK IT OUT!
HOLD IT!
ROPE SWINGS CAN BE DANGEROUS! HOW DO YOU KNOW THIS ONE'S SAFE?
BUT DAD!...
I'M NOT SAYING YOU CAN'T TRY IT, NATE! I'M JUST SAYING AN ADULT NEEDS TO INSPECT IT FIRST!
SOON...
HI, KIDS!!
SOME-BODY SHOOT ME.

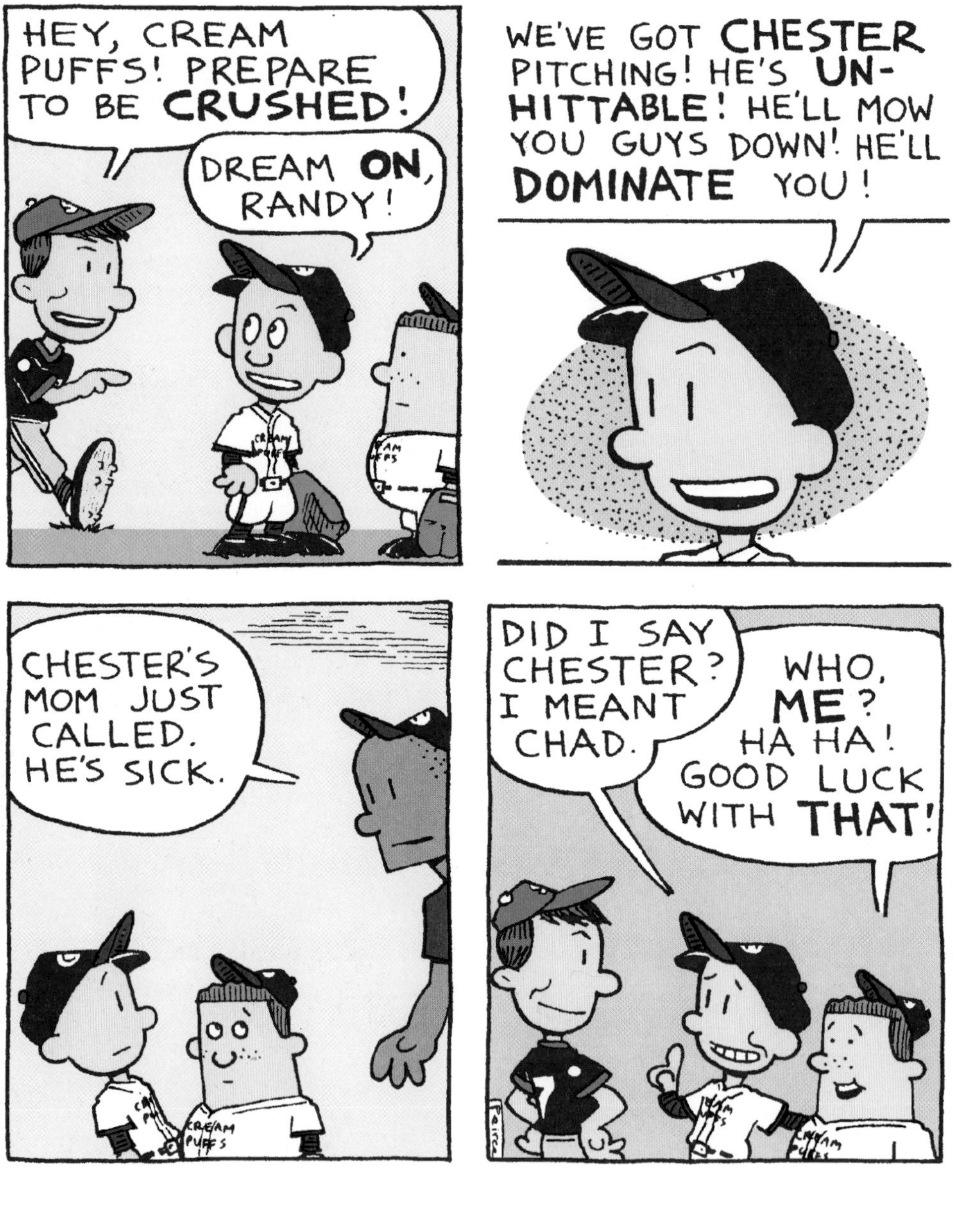
HEY, CREAM PUFFS! PREPARE TO BE **CRUSHED**!
DREAM **ON**, RANDY!
WE'VE GOT **CHESTER** PITCHING! HE'S **UN-HITTABLE**! HE'LL MOW YOU GUYS DOWN! HE'LL **DOMINATE** YOU!
CHESTER'S MOM JUST CALLED. HE'S SICK.
DID I SAY CHESTER? I MEANT CHAD.
WHO, **ME**? HA HA! GOOD LUCK WITH **THAT**!

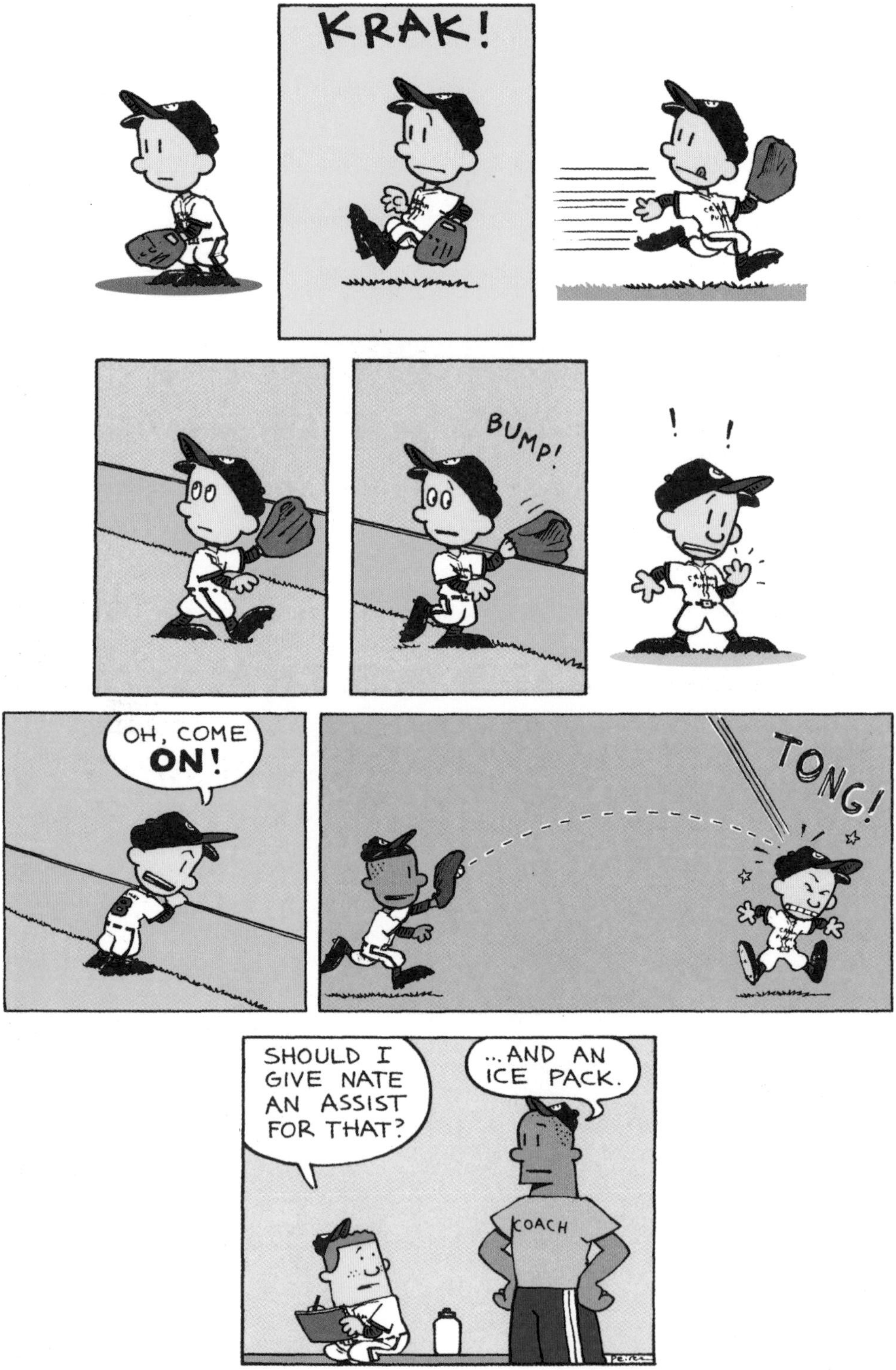
KRAK!
BUMP!
! !
OH, COME ON!
TONG!
SHOULD I GIVE NATE AN ASSIST FOR THAT?
...AND AN ICE PACK.
COACH

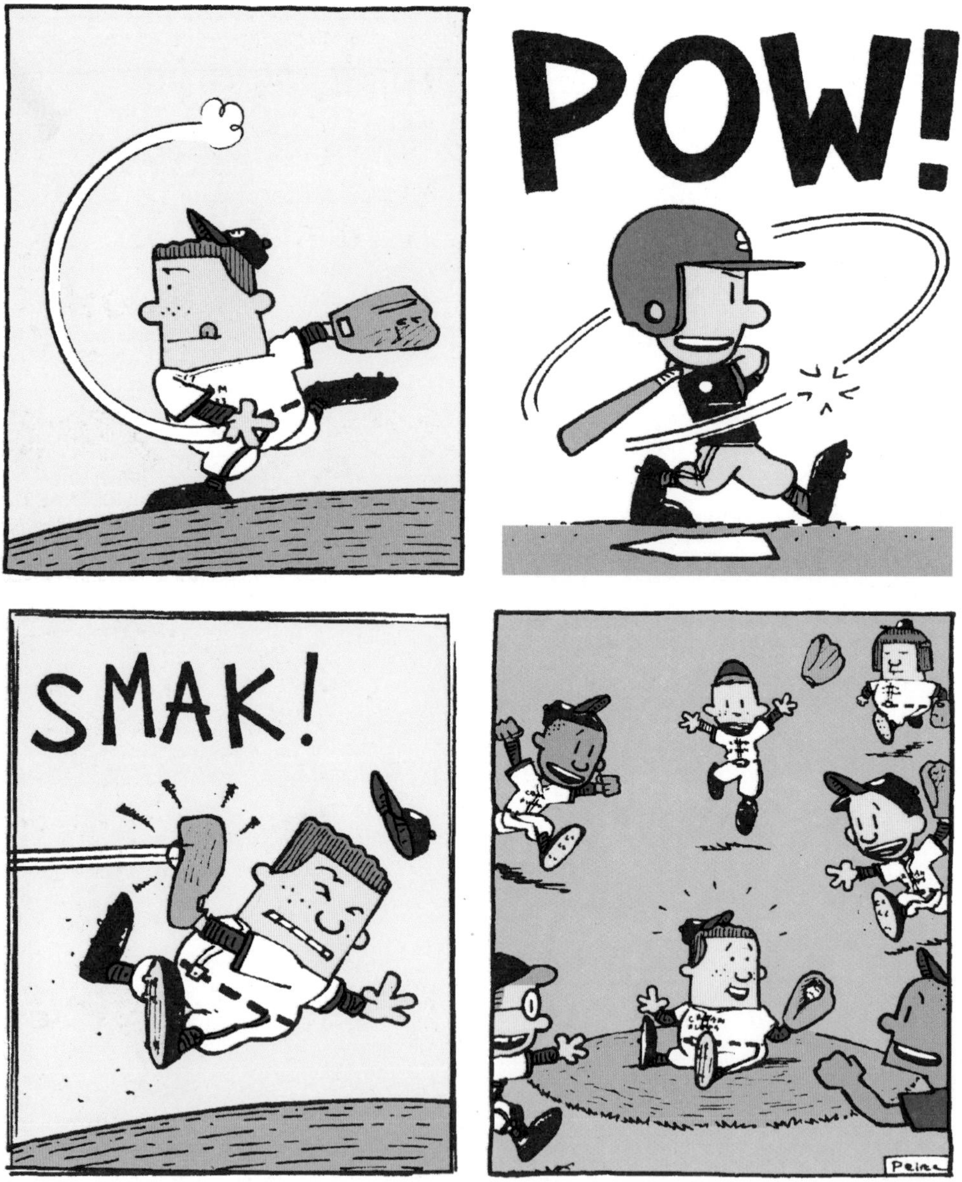
POW!
SMAK!

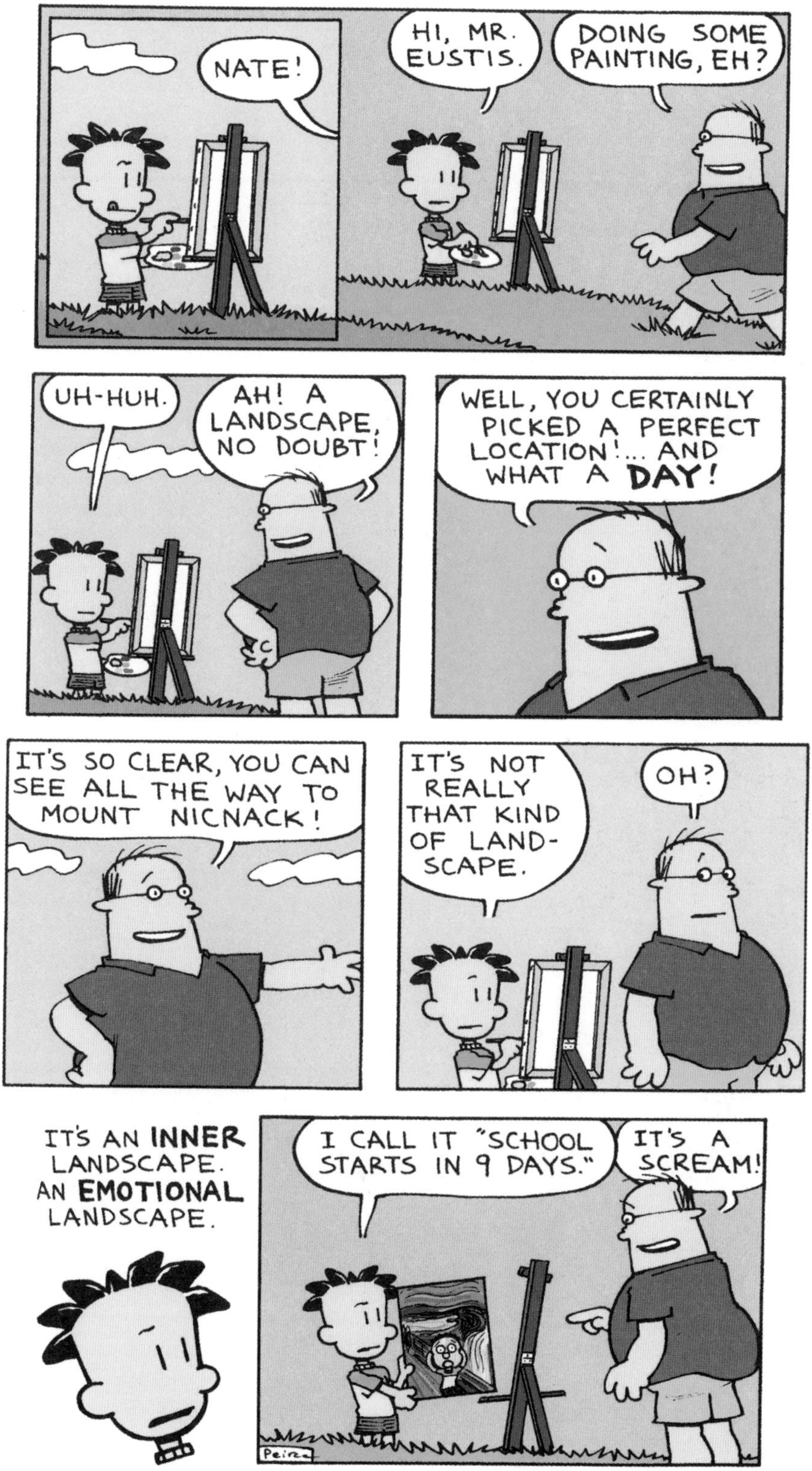
NATE!
HI, MR. EUSTIS.
DOING SOME PAINTING, EH?
UH-HUH.
AH! A LANDSCAPE, NO DOUBT!
WELL, YOU CERTAINLY PICKED A PERFECT LOCATION!... AND WHAT A DAY!
IT'S SO CLEAR, YOU CAN SEE ALL THE WAY TO MOUNT NICNACK!
IT'S NOT REALLY THAT KIND OF LAND-SCAPE.
OH?
IT'S AN INNER LANDSCAPE. AN EMOTIONAL LANDSCAPE.
I CALL IT "SCHOOL STARTS IN 9 DAYS."
IT'S A SCREAM!
Peirce

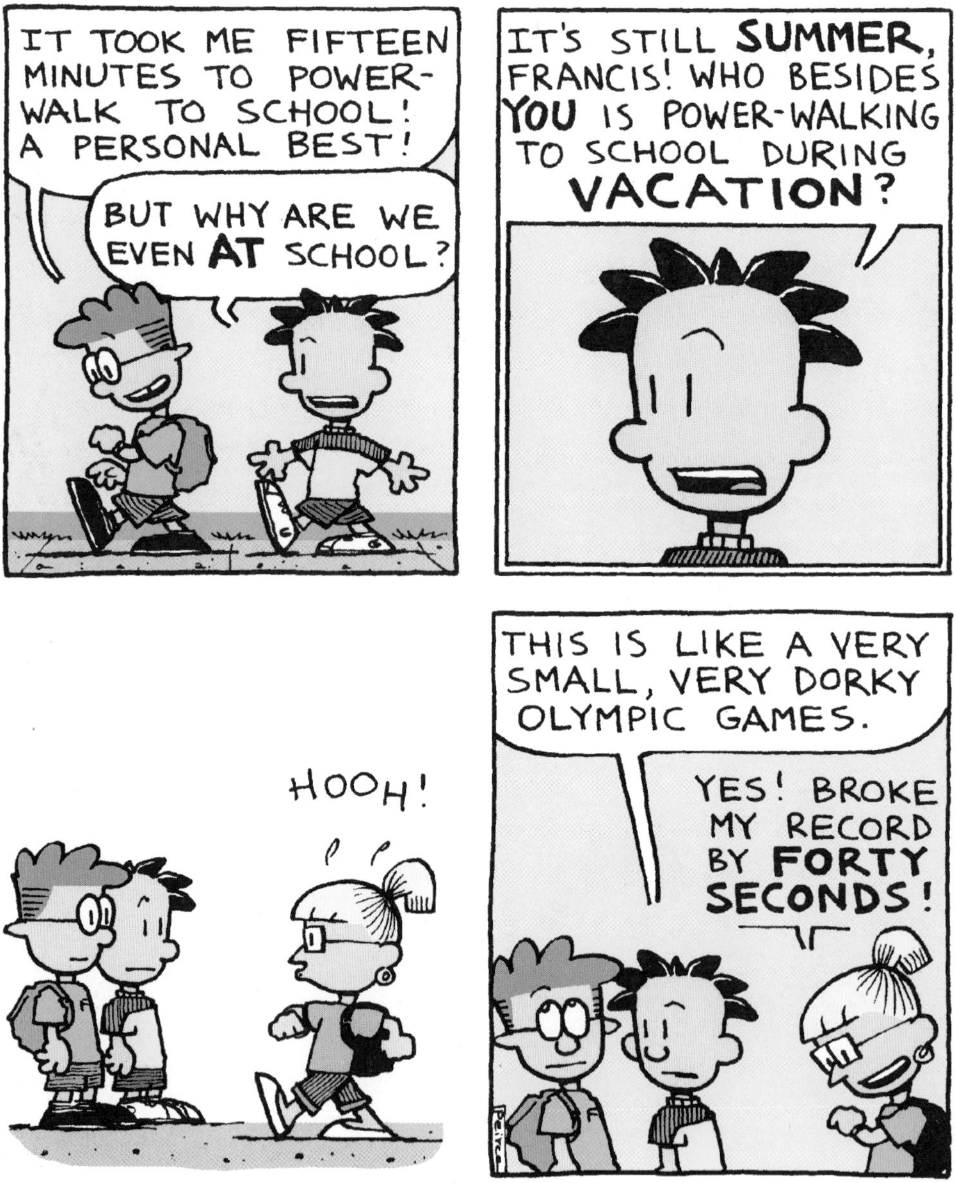
IT TOOK ME FIFTEEN MINUTES TO POWER-WALK TO SCHOOL! A PERSONAL BEST!
BUT WHY ARE WE EVEN AT SCHOOL?
IT'S STILL SUMMER, FRANCIS! WHO BESIDES YOU IS POWER-WALKING TO SCHOOL DURING VACATION?
HOOH!
THIS IS LIKE A VERY SMALL, VERY DORKY OLYMPIC GAMES.
YES! BROKE MY RECORD BY FORTY SECONDS!
Peirce

LOOK, FRANCIS, **GINA'S** HERE! YOU'RE NOT THE **ONLY** ONE GETTING READY FOR SCHOOL A WEEK EARLY!

WELL, WHAT'S WRONG WITH BEING PREPARED?

IT'S **WEIRD**, THAT'S WHAT!

IT OBVIOUSLY **WORKS**! BOTH OF US GET BETTER GRADES THAN **YOU** DO!

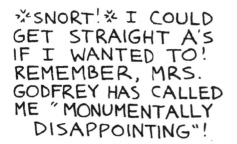

✳SNORT!✳ I COULD GET STRAIGHT A'S IF I WANTED TO! REMEMBER, MRS. GODFREY HAS CALLED ME "MONUMENTALLY DISAPPOINTING"!

SHE ONLY DOES THAT FOR HER VERY **BEST** C-PLUS STUDENTS.

RIGHT! I'VE SQUANDERED MORE POTENTIAL THAN MOST PEOPLE CAN SHAKE A STICK AT!

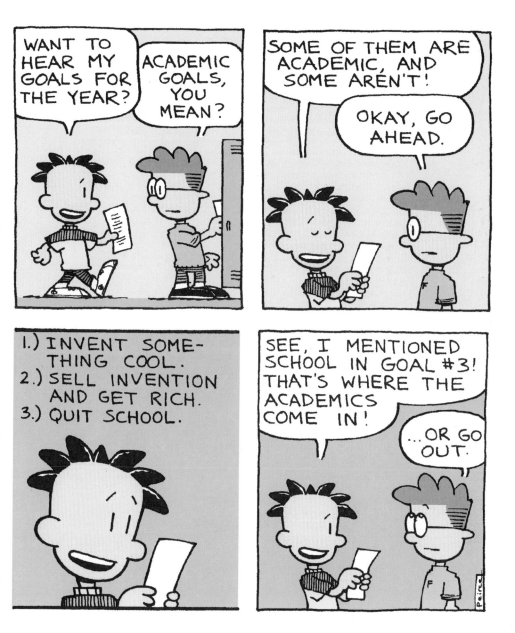

GEORGE WASHINGTON, FATHER OF OUR COUNTRY
By Nate Wright

People sometimes call George Washington the father of our country. I think those people are right, because indeed, George Washington truly WAS the father of our country, which as we all know is called the United States of America. But HOW did a shy young man from the humble little town of Wakefield, Virginia, grow up to become our first president? Well, allow me to give you some of the startling facts that will PROVE my point, which is that George Washington is the real father of our country. When young George was born, on February 22nd, 1732, he was just a baby. But soon, as so often happens, he grew up. Then George got smallpox, which was a disease back in the old days. As a result, George had bad skin.

Then his dad died. Oh, by the way, George's dad was named Augustine and his mother had the very simple name of Mary. Heartbroken, George chopped down a cherry tree and became a surveyor. After that he joined the army, which was in the middle of a war with France. George fought against the French in Ohio, which is kind of weird, and got them to surrender some forts. For example: one of those forts was called Fort Duquesne. George got out of the army and decided it was time to get married. He found a widow named Martha Custis who agreed to marry him even though he had wooden teeth. So they got married and went to live at George's mansion, which is called Mount Vernon. It is open 365 days a year and contains a museum, orientation center, and gift shop. Everything was going great until England came along and started raising taxes. George got so mad, he declared WAR ON ENGLAND!!

George was made commander of the Continental Army, and then he crossed the Delaware to fight the British at Valley Forge. There were many fierce battles, but thanks to George and his very, very good leadership, the British eventually gave up and went back to England. George wanted to retire to Mount Vernon, but the rest of the country was like: we don't THINK so. So they elected George as the first president.

George was inaugurated on April 30th, 1789, in New York City. Why New York City? Because George had not invented the city of Washington, DC yet. Pretty soon he did, though, and he made it the capital of the whole country. That was the first of many impressive accomplishments he accomplished as president. Most of them he did while he was alive, but some he achieved when he was dead, like getting his face carved into Mount Rushmore. On December 14th, 1799, tragedy struck. George went horseback riding in the snow, came down with acute laryngitis, and died. But what a very amazing life he led. As the first president and father of our country, George Washington definitely made history.

THE END

FIVE HUNDRED WORDS **EXACTLY!**

SOME MAKE HISTORY, AND SOME MAKE **UP** HISTORY.

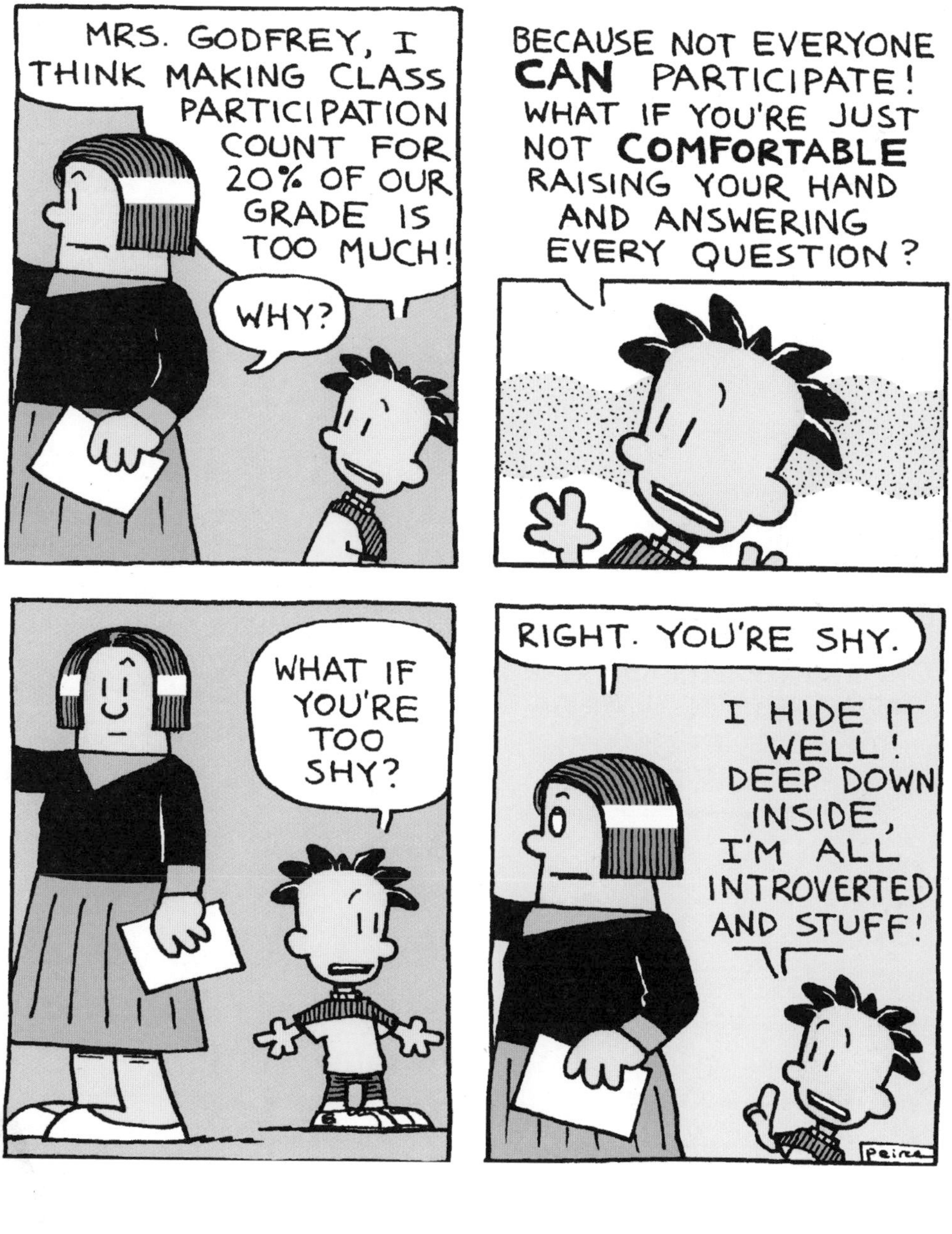
MRS. GODFREY, I THINK MAKING CLASS PARTICIPATION COUNT FOR 20% OF OUR GRADE IS TOO MUCH!
WHY?
BECAUSE NOT EVERYONE **CAN** PARTICIPATE! WHAT IF YOU'RE JUST NOT **COMFORTABLE** RAISING YOUR HAND AND ANSWERING EVERY QUESTION?
WHAT IF YOU'RE TOO SHY?
RIGHT. YOU'RE SHY.
I HIDE IT WELL! DEEP DOWN INSIDE, I'M ALL INTROVERTED AND STUFF!
peirce

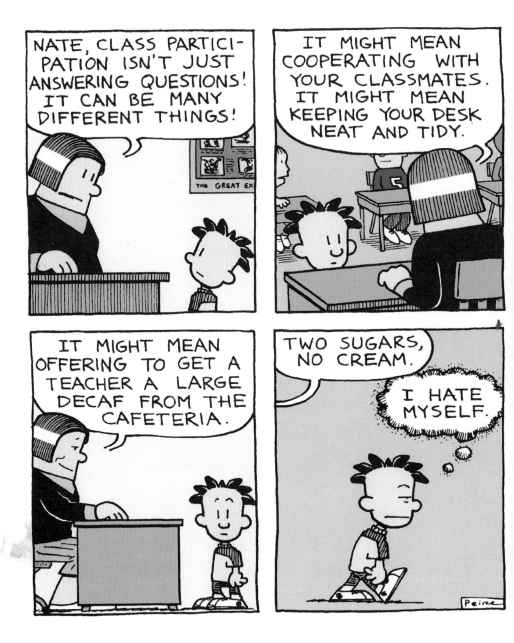

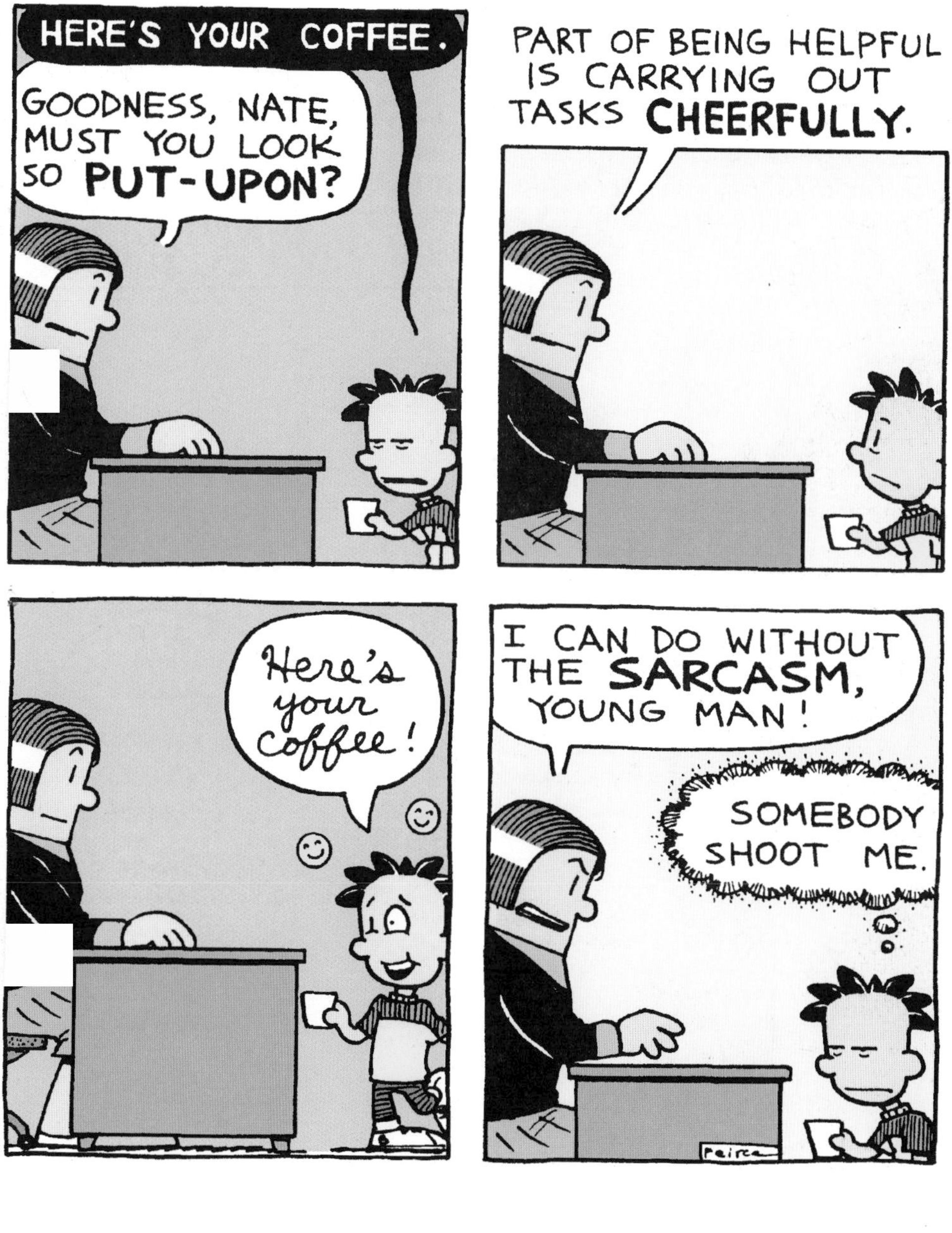
HERE'S YOUR COFFEE.
GOODNESS, NATE, MUST YOU LOOK SO PUT-UPON?
PART OF BEING HELPFUL IS CARRYING OUT TASKS CHEERFULLY.
Here's your coffee!
I CAN DO WITHOUT THE SARCASM, YOUNG MAN!
SOMEBODY SHOOT ME.
Peirce

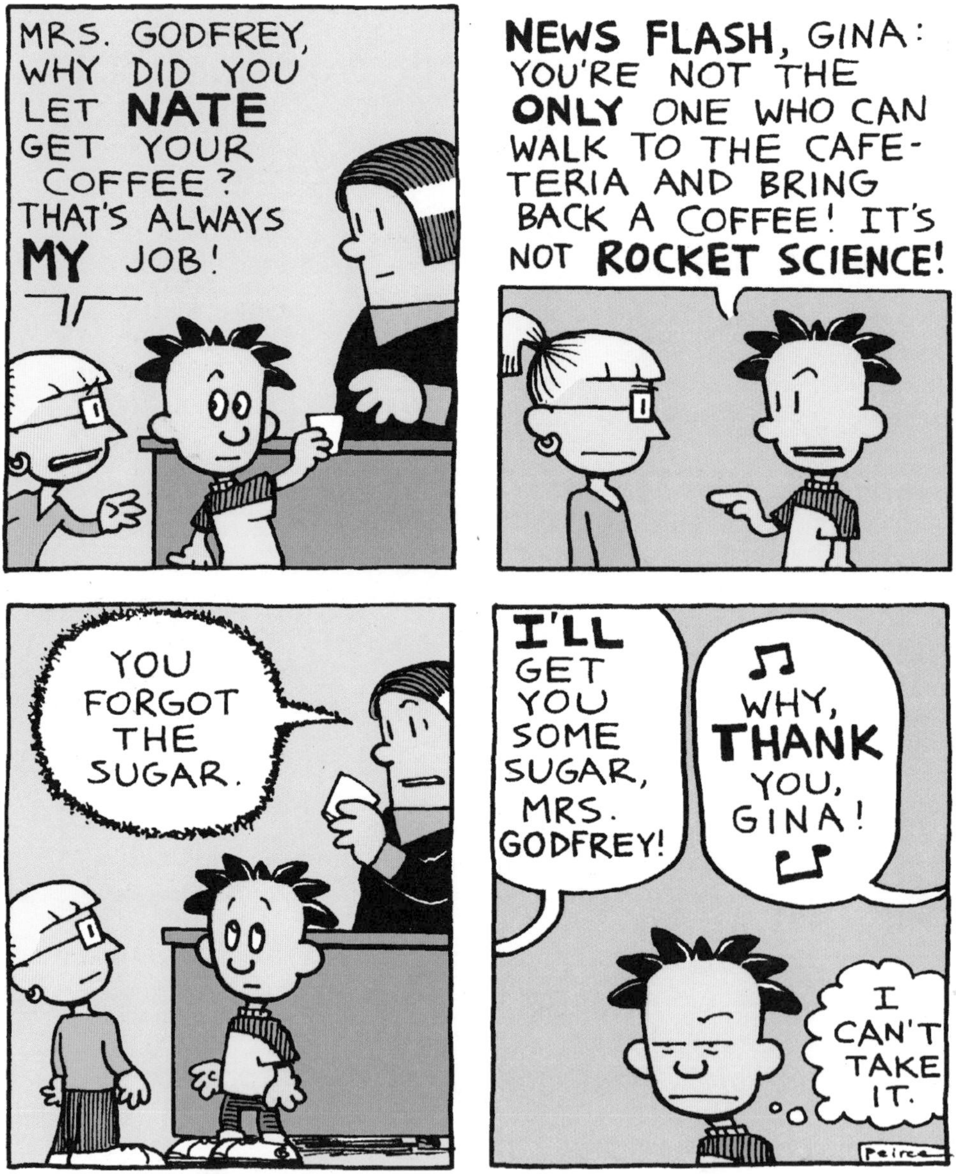
MRS. GODFREY, WHY DID YOU LET **NATE** GET YOUR COFFEE? THAT'S ALWAYS **MY** JOB!
NEWS FLASH, GINA: YOU'RE NOT THE **ONLY** ONE WHO CAN WALK TO THE CAFETERIA AND BRING BACK A COFFEE! IT'S NOT **ROCKET SCIENCE**!
YOU FORGOT THE SUGAR.
I'LL GET YOU SOME SUGAR, MRS. GODFREY!
WHY, **THANK** YOU, GINA!
I CAN'T TAKE IT.
Peirce

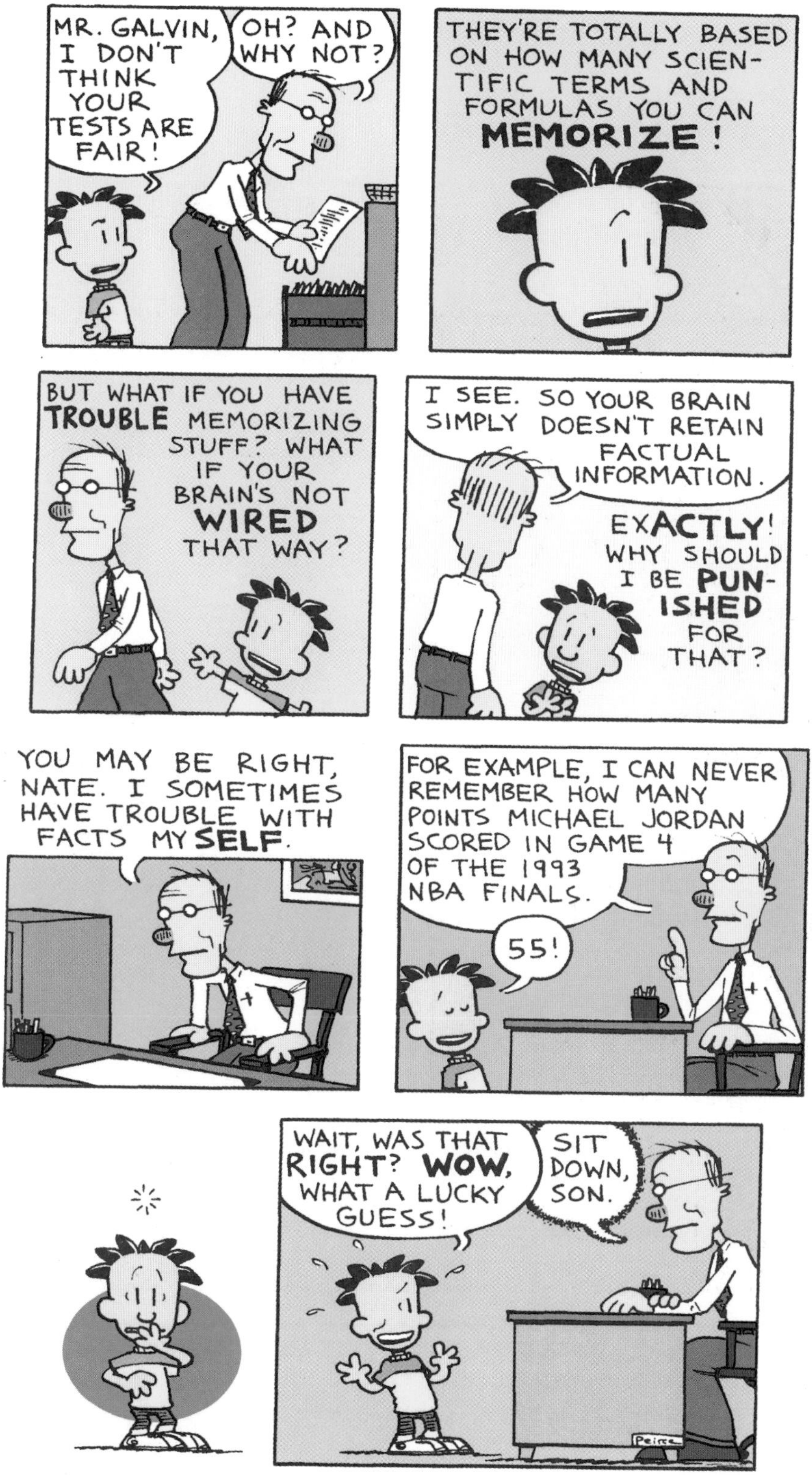
MR. GALVIN, I DON'T THINK YOUR TESTS ARE FAIR!
OH? AND WHY NOT?
THEY'RE TOTALLY BASED ON HOW MANY SCIENTIFIC TERMS AND FORMULAS YOU CAN **MEMORIZE**!
BUT WHAT IF YOU HAVE **TROUBLE** MEMORIZING STUFF? WHAT IF YOUR BRAIN'S NOT **WIRED** THAT WAY?
I SEE. SO YOUR BRAIN SIMPLY DOESN'T RETAIN FACTUAL INFORMATION.
EX**ACTLY**! WHY SHOULD I BE **PUNISHED** FOR THAT?
YOU MAY BE RIGHT, NATE. I SOMETIMES HAVE TROUBLE WITH FACTS MY**SELF**.
FOR EXAMPLE, I CAN NEVER REMEMBER HOW MANY POINTS MICHAEL JORDAN SCORED IN GAME 4 OF THE 1993 NBA FINALS.
55!
WAIT, WAS THAT **RIGHT**? **WOW**, WHAT A LUCKY GUESS!
SIT DOWN, SON.

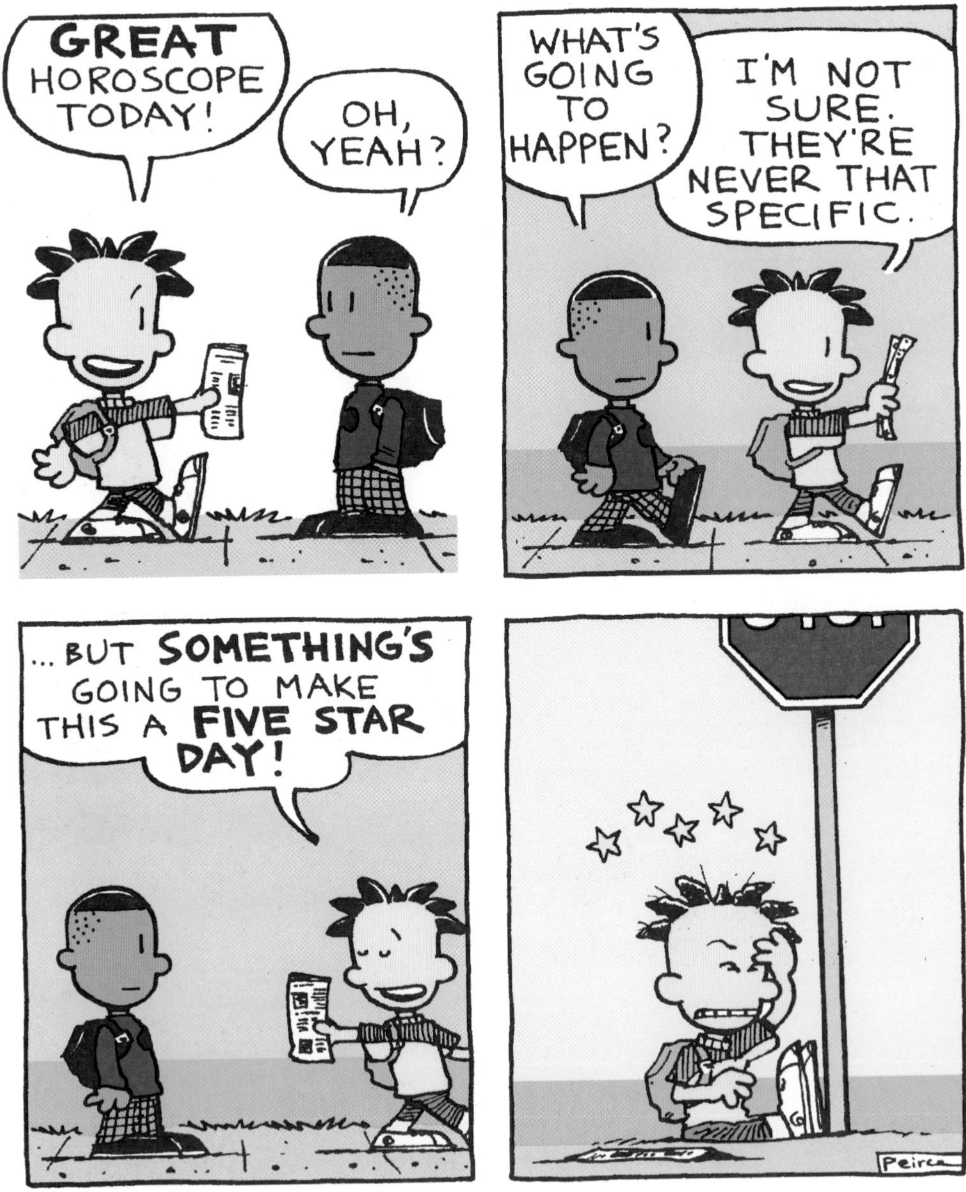

GREAT HOROSCOPE TODAY!
OH, YEAH?
WHAT'S GOING TO HAPPEN?
I'M NOT SURE. THEY'RE NEVER THAT SPECIFIC.
...BUT SOMETHING'S GOING TO MAKE THIS A FIVE STAR DAY!
Peirce

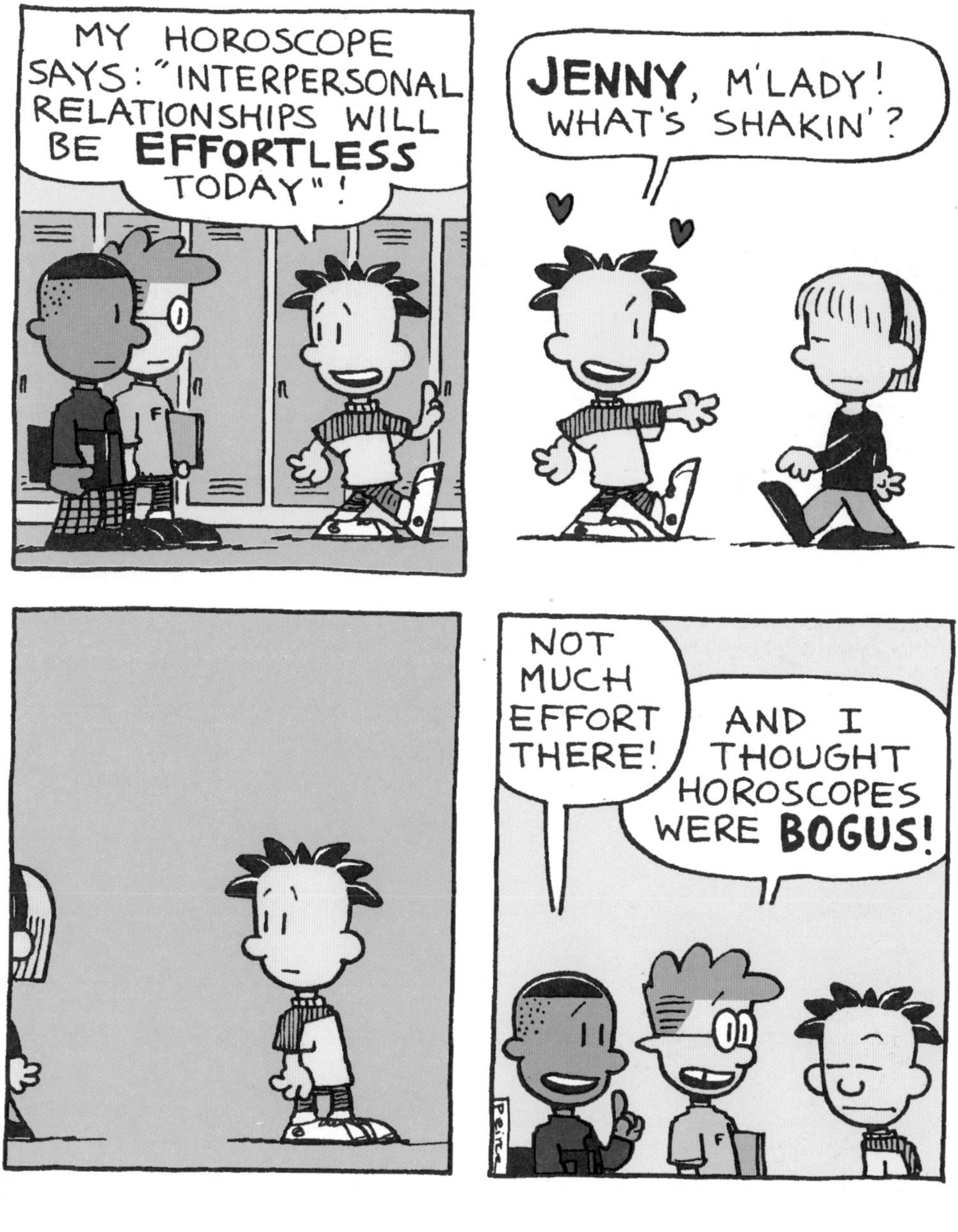

MY HOROSCOPE SAYS: "INTERPERSONAL RELATIONSHIPS WILL BE EFFORTLESS TODAY"!
JENNY, M'LADY! WHAT'S SHAKIN'?
NOT MUCH EFFORT THERE!
AND I THOUGHT HOROSCOPES WERE BOGUS!

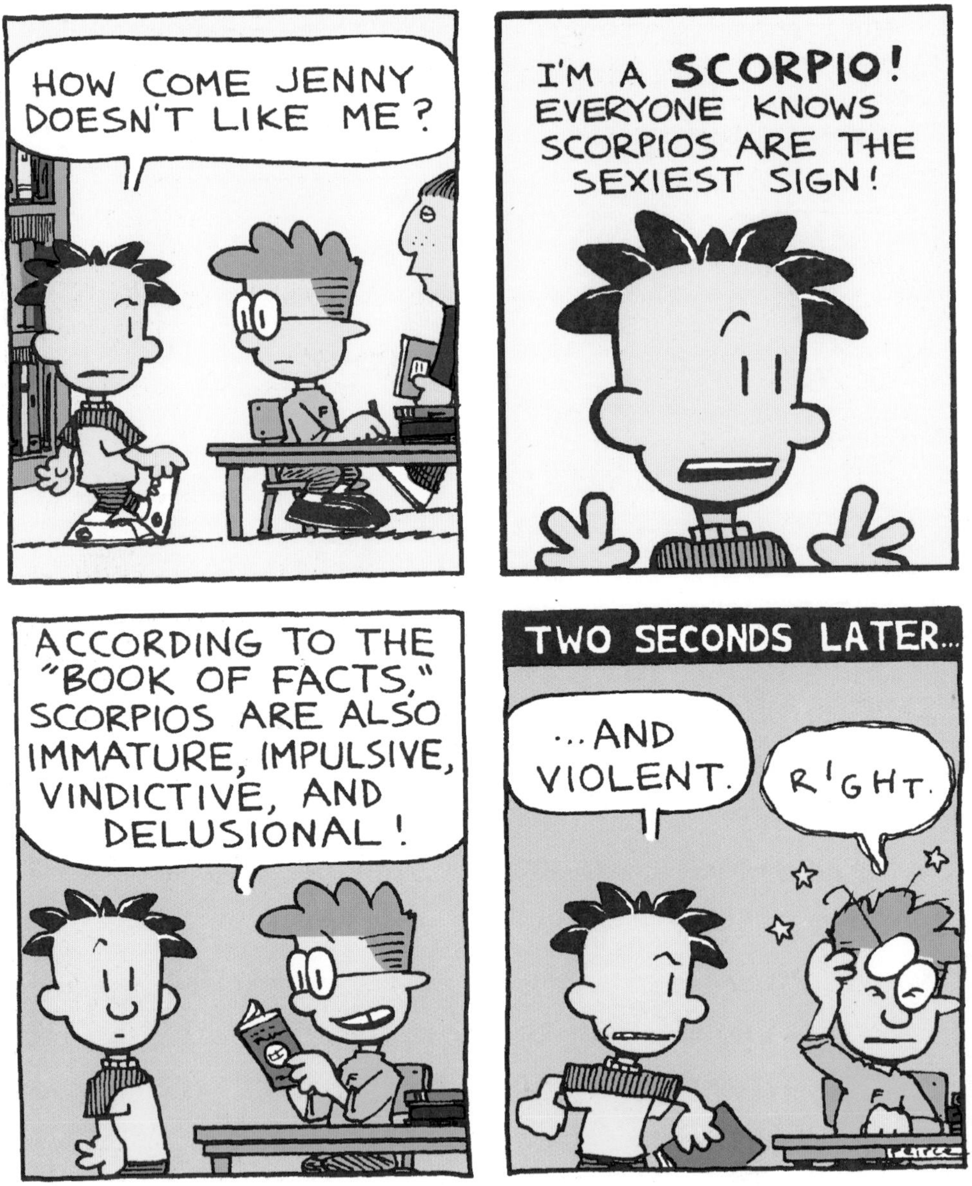
HOW COME JENNY DOESN'T LIKE ME?
I'M A SCORPIO! EVERYONE KNOWS SCORPIOS ARE THE SEXIEST SIGN!
ACCORDING TO THE "BOOK OF FACTS," SCORPIOS ARE ALSO IMMATURE, IMPULSIVE, VINDICTIVE, AND DELUSIONAL!
TWO SECONDS LATER...
...AND VIOLENT.
RIGHT.

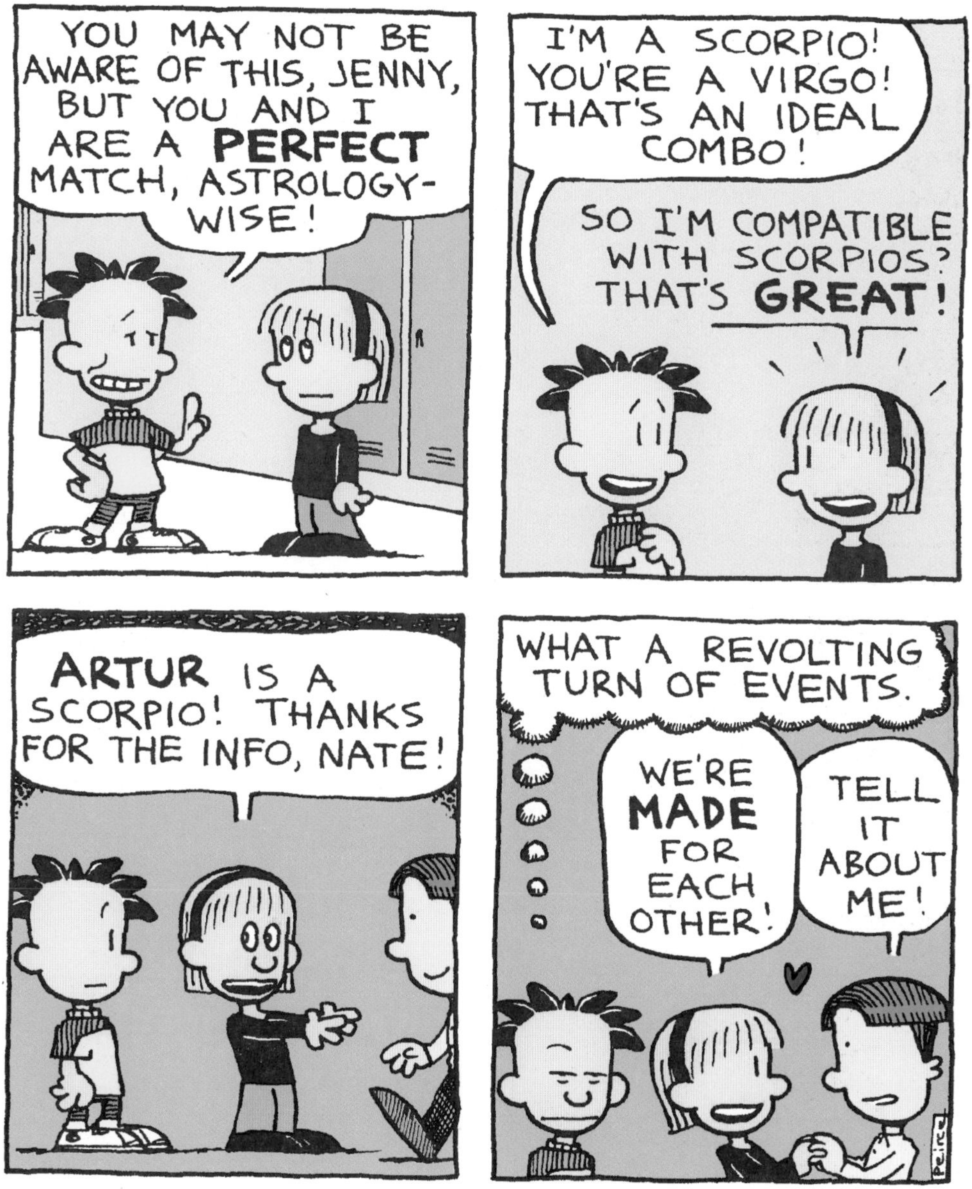
YOU MAY NOT BE AWARE OF THIS, JENNY, BUT YOU AND I ARE A **PERFECT** MATCH, ASTROLOGY-WISE!
I'M A SCORPIO! YOU'RE A VIRGO! THAT'S AN IDEAL COMBO!
SO I'M COMPATIBLE WITH SCORPIOS? THAT'S **GREAT**!
ARTUR IS A SCORPIO! THANKS FOR THE INFO, NATE!
WHAT A REVOLTING TURN OF EVENTS.
WE'RE **MADE** FOR EACH OTHER!
TELL IT ABOUT ME!
Peirce

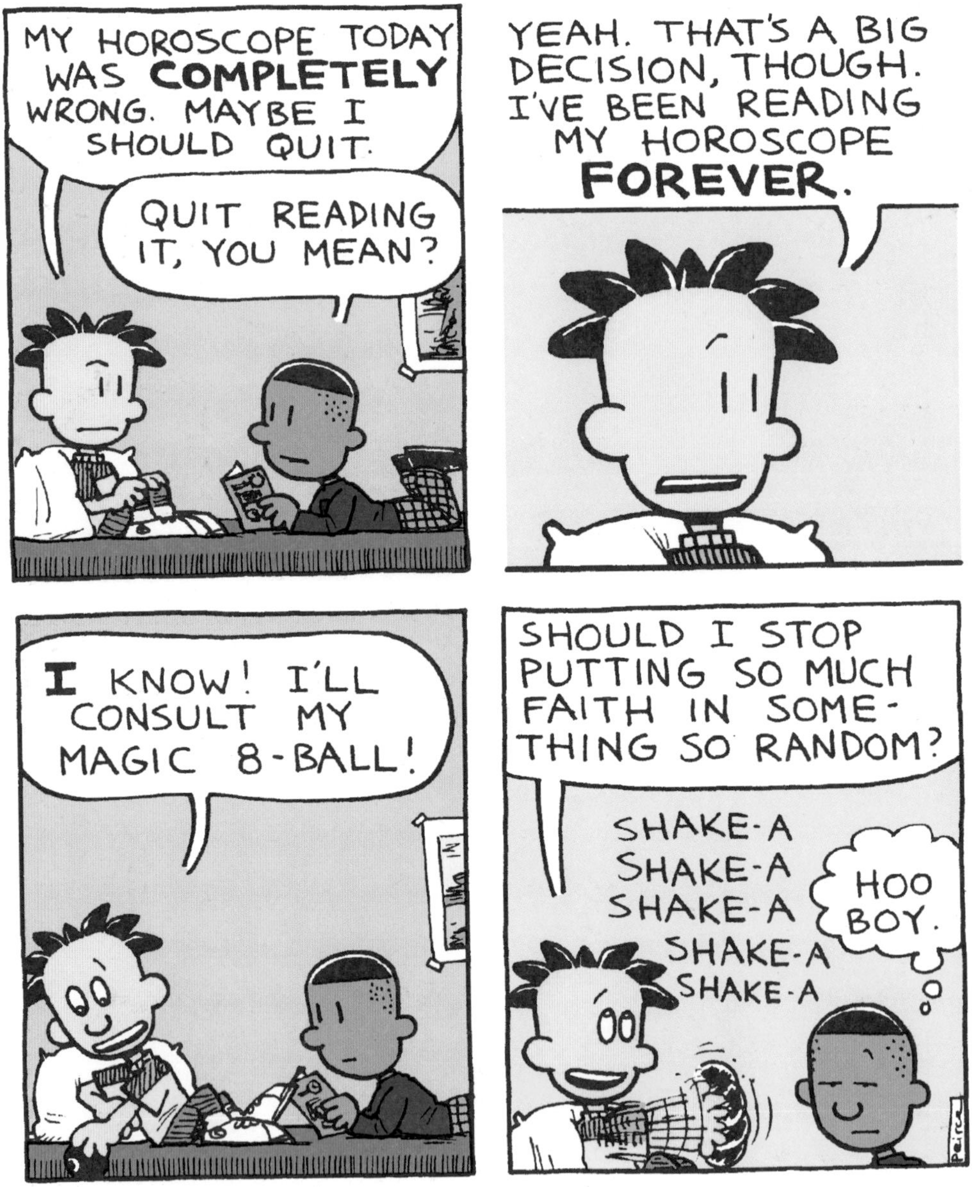
MY HOROSCOPE TODAY WAS **COMPLETELY** WRONG. MAYBE I SHOULD QUIT.
QUIT READING IT, YOU MEAN?
YEAH. THAT'S A BIG DECISION, THOUGH. I'VE BEEN READING MY HOROSCOPE **FOREVER**.
I KNOW! I'LL CONSULT MY MAGIC 8-BALL!
SHOULD I STOP PUTTING SO MUCH FAITH IN SOMETHING SO RANDOM?
SHAKE-A SHAKE-A SHAKE-A SHAKE-A SHAKE-A
HOO BOY.
Peirce

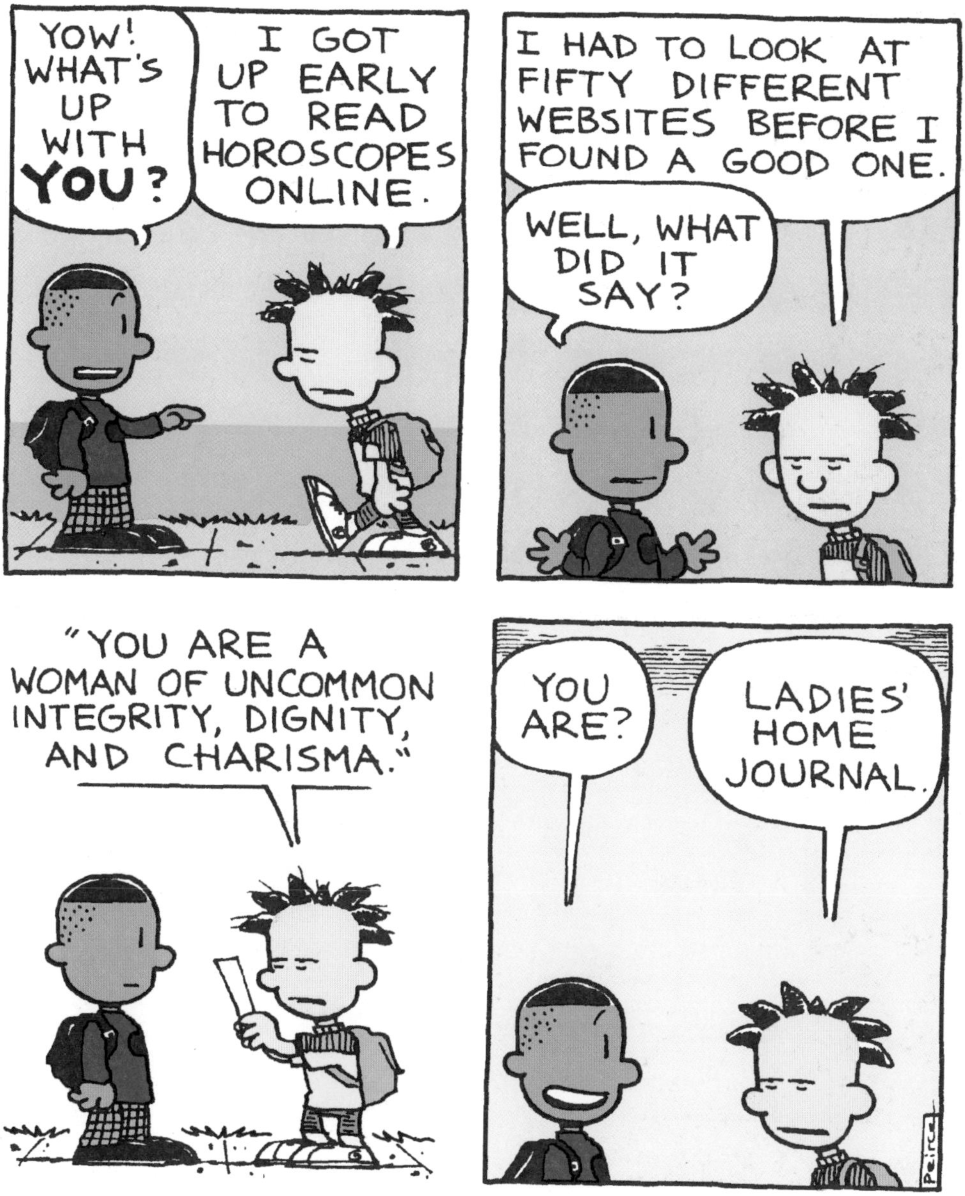
YOW! WHAT'S UP WITH YOU?
I GOT UP EARLY TO READ HOROSCOPES ONLINE.
I HAD TO LOOK AT FIFTY DIFFERENT WEBSITES BEFORE I FOUND A GOOD ONE.
WELL, WHAT DID IT SAY?
"YOU ARE A WOMAN OF UNCOMMON INTEGRITY, DIGNITY, AND CHARISMA."
YOU ARE?
LADIES' HOME JOURNAL.
Peirce

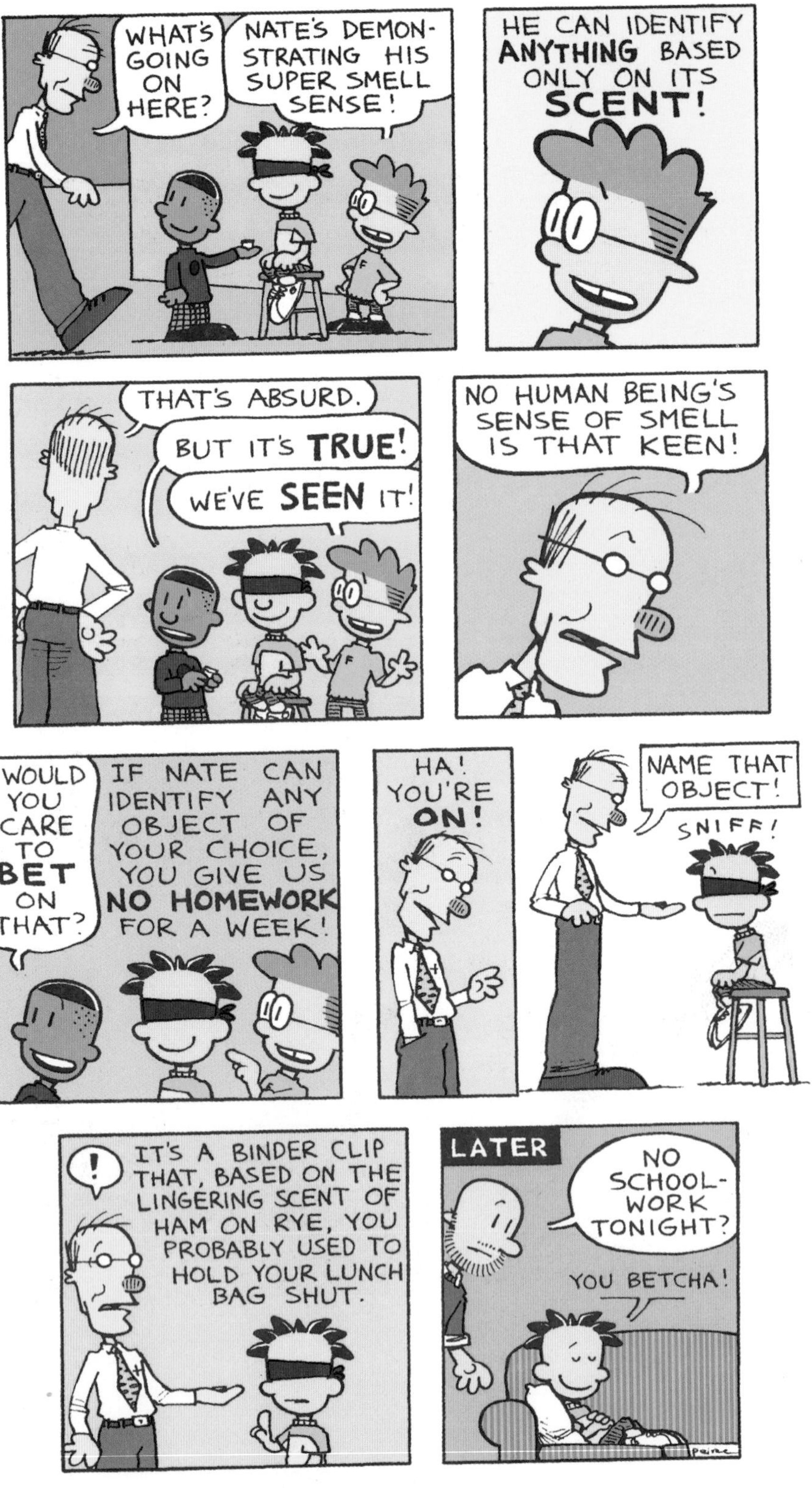
WHAT'S GOING ON HERE?
NATE'S DEMON-STRATING HIS SUPER SMELL SENSE!
HE CAN IDENTIFY **ANYTHING** BASED ONLY ON ITS **SCENT!**
THAT'S ABSURD.
BUT IT'S **TRUE!**
WE'VE **SEEN** IT!
NO HUMAN BEING'S SENSE OF SMELL IS THAT KEEN!
WOULD YOU CARE TO **BET** ON THAT?
IF NATE CAN IDENTIFY ANY OBJECT OF YOUR CHOICE, YOU GIVE US **NO HOMEWORK** FOR A WEEK!
HA! YOU'RE **ON!**
NAME THAT OBJECT!
SNIFF!
!
IT'S A BINDER CLIP THAT, BASED ON THE LINGERING SCENT OF HAM ON RYE, YOU PROBABLY USED TO HOLD YOUR LUNCH BAG SHUT.
LATER
NO SCHOOL-WORK TONIGHT?
YOU BETCHA!

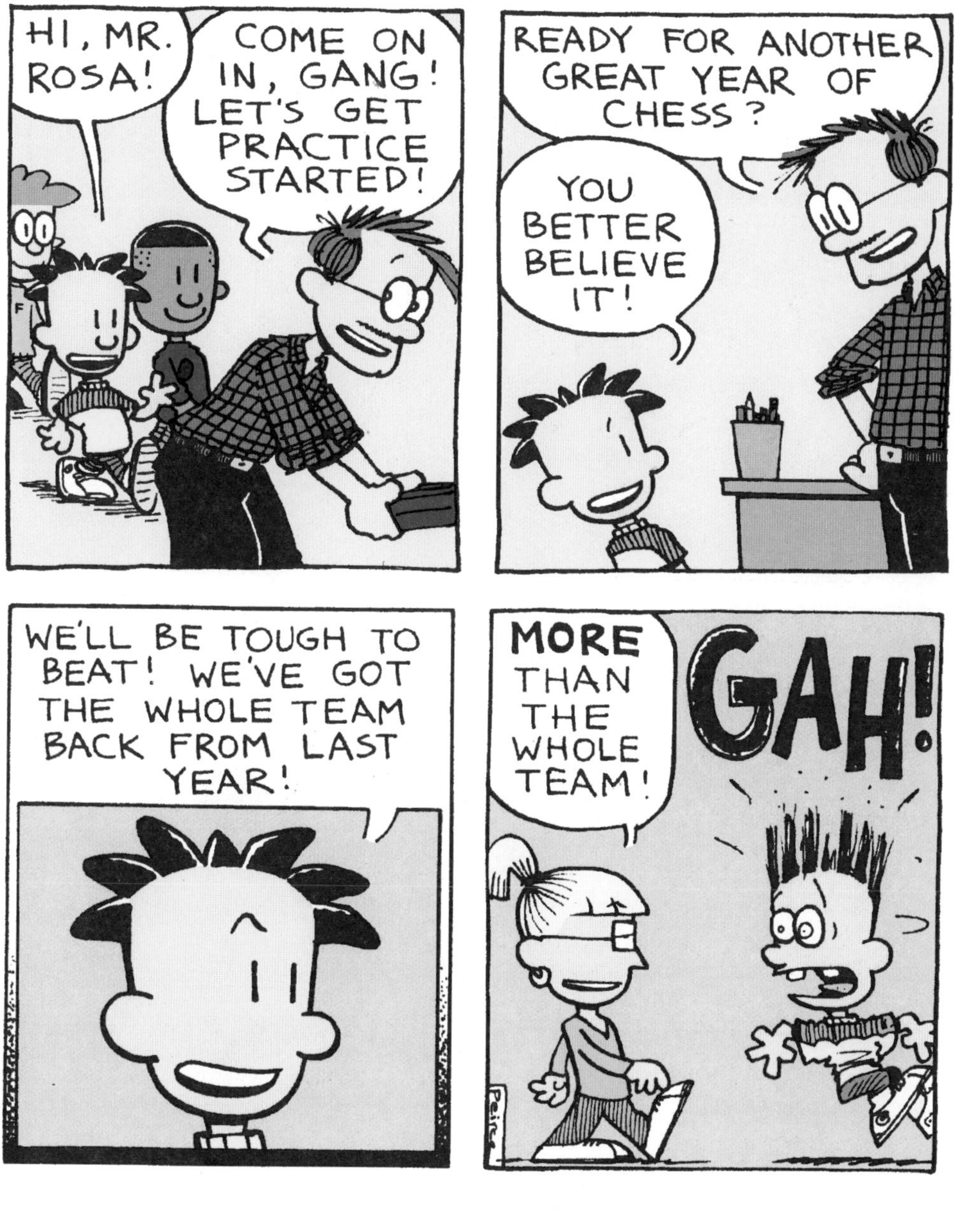
HI, MR. ROSA!
COME ON IN, GANG! LET'S GET PRACTICE STARTED!
READY FOR ANOTHER GREAT YEAR OF CHESS?
YOU BETTER BELIEVE IT!
WE'LL BE TOUGH TO BEAT! WE'VE GOT THE WHOLE TEAM BACK FROM LAST YEAR!
MORE THAN THE WHOLE TEAM!
GAH!
Peirce

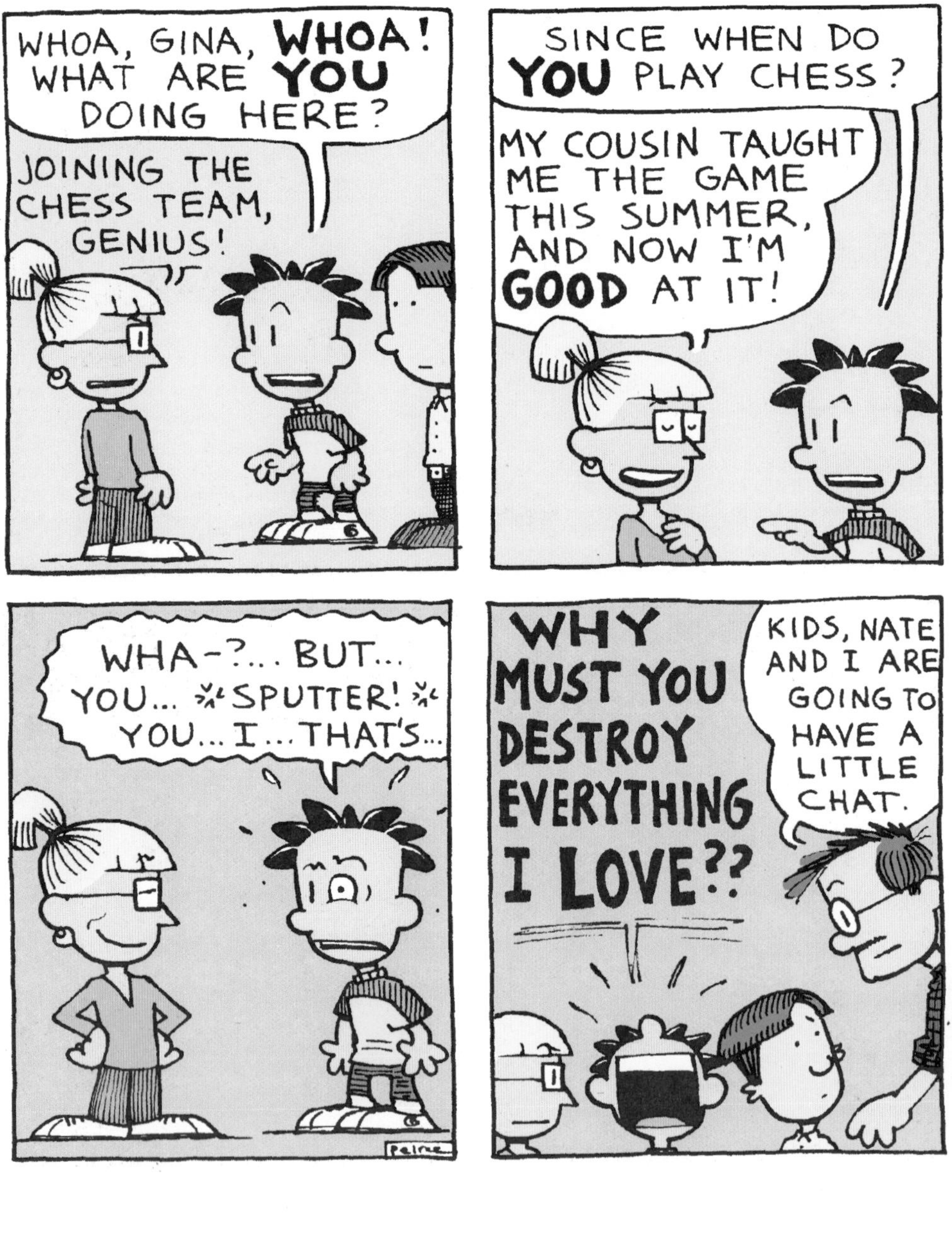
WHOA, GINA, WHOA! WHAT ARE YOU DOING HERE?
JOINING THE CHESS TEAM, GENIUS!
SINCE WHEN DO YOU PLAY CHESS?
MY COUSIN TAUGHT ME THE GAME THIS SUMMER, AND NOW I'M GOOD AT IT!
WHA-?... BUT... YOU... SPUTTER! YOU... I... THAT'S...
WHY MUST YOU DESTROY EVERYTHING I LOVE??
KIDS, NATE AND I ARE GOING TO HAVE A LITTLE CHAT.

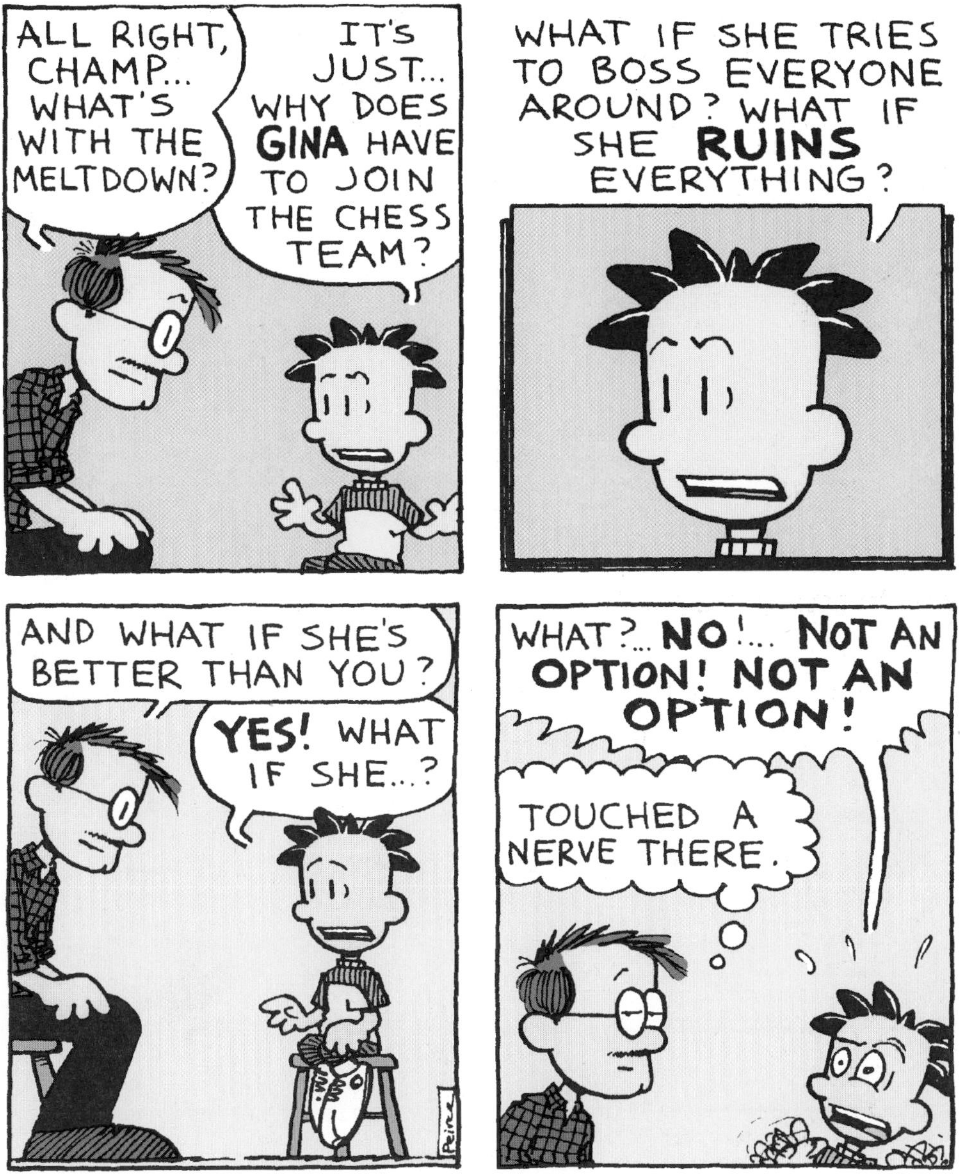
ALL RIGHT, CHAMP... WHAT'S WITH THE MELTDOWN?
IT'S JUST... WHY DOES GINA HAVE TO JOIN THE CHESS TEAM?
WHAT IF SHE TRIES TO BOSS EVERYONE AROUND? WHAT IF SHE RUINS EVERYTHING?
AND WHAT IF SHE'S BETTER THAN YOU?
YES! WHAT IF SHE...?
WHAT?... NO!... NOT AN OPTION! NOT AN OPTION!
TOUCHED A NERVE THERE.

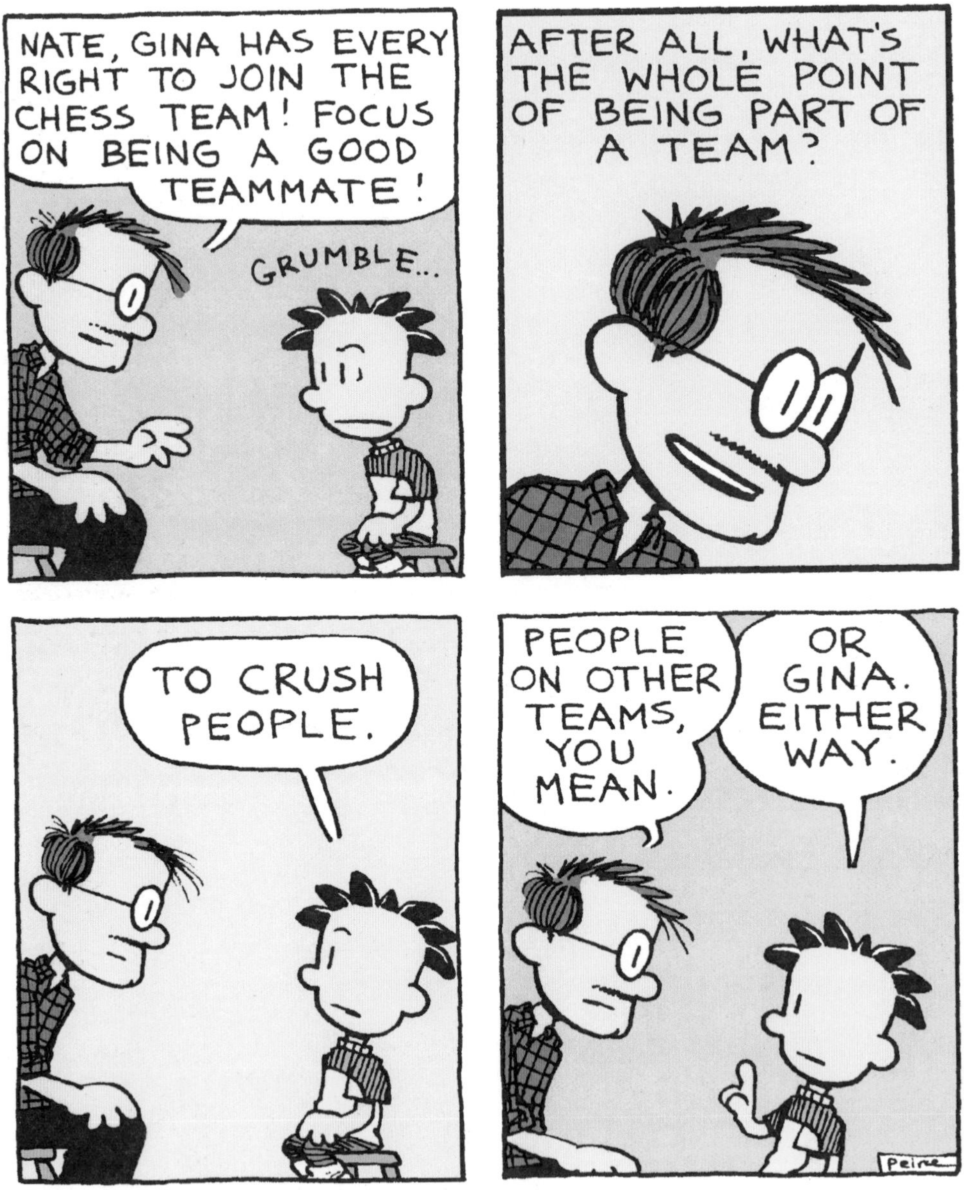
NATE, GINA HAS EVERY RIGHT TO JOIN THE CHESS TEAM! FOCUS ON BEING A GOOD TEAMMATE!
GRUMBLE...
AFTER ALL, WHAT'S THE WHOLE POINT OF BEING PART OF A TEAM?
TO CRUSH PEOPLE.
PEOPLE ON OTHER TEAMS, YOU MEAN.
OR GINA. EITHER WAY.
Peirce

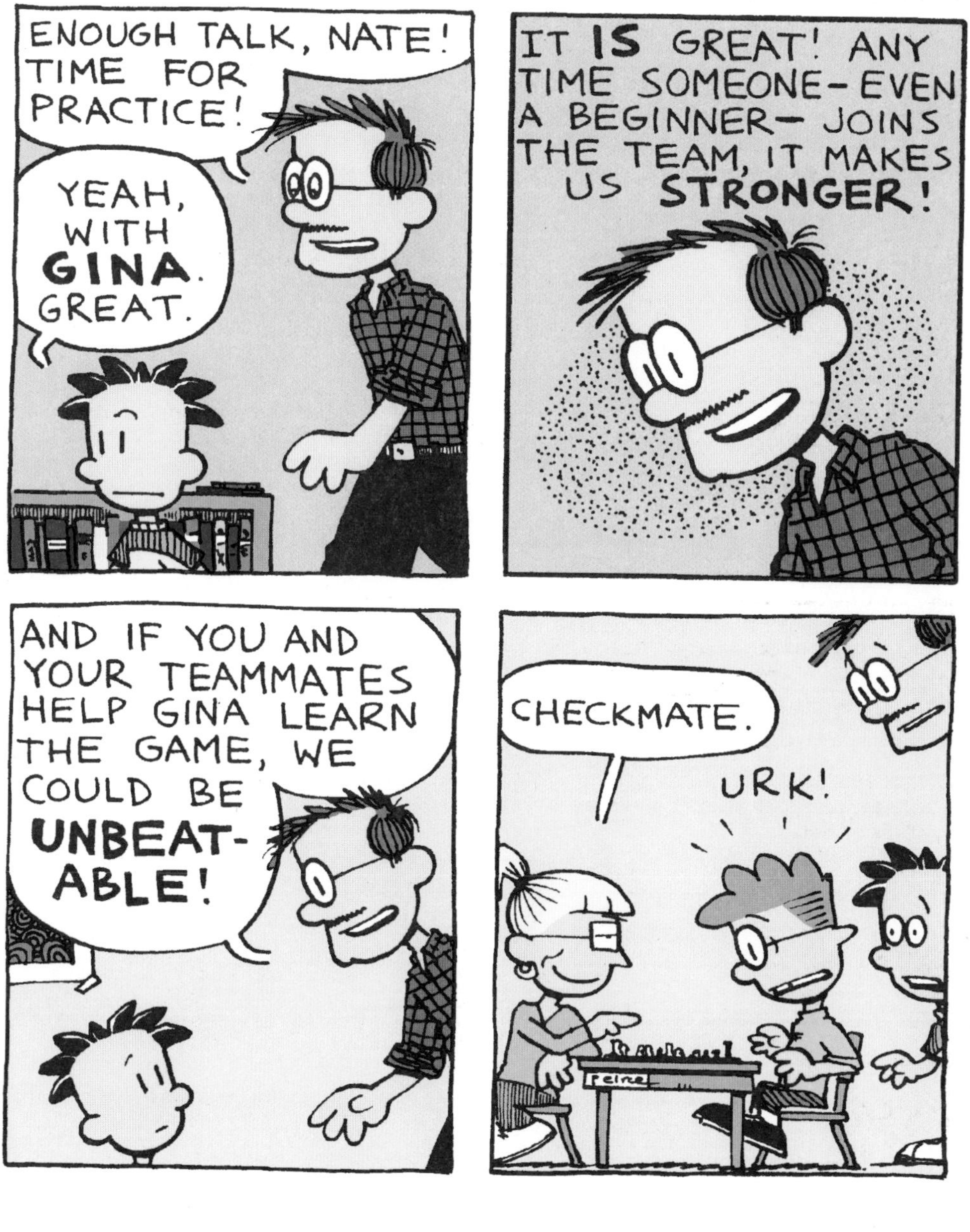
ENOUGH TALK, NATE! TIME FOR PRACTICE!
YEAH, WITH GINA. GREAT.
IT IS GREAT! ANY TIME SOMEONE—EVEN A BEGINNER—JOINS THE TEAM, IT MAKES US STRONGER!
AND IF YOU AND YOUR TEAMMATES HELP GINA LEARN THE GAME, WE COULD BE UNBEAT-ABLE!
CHECKMATE.
URK!

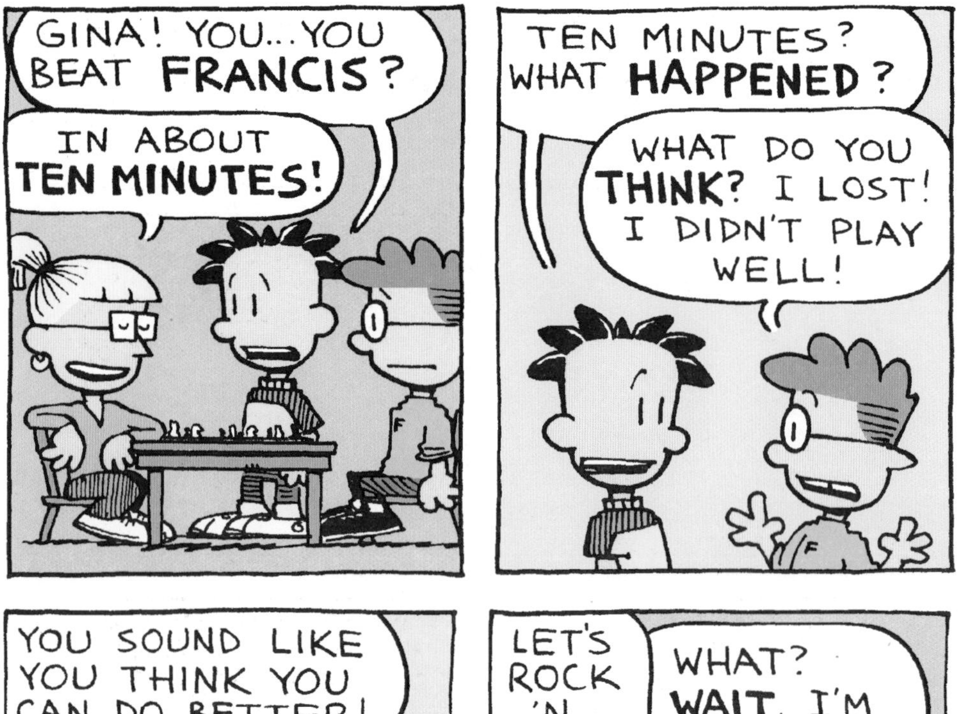
GINA! YOU...YOU BEAT FRANCIS?
IN ABOUT TEN MINUTES!
TEN MINUTES? WHAT HAPPENED?
WHAT DO YOU THINK? I LOST! I DIDN'T PLAY WELL!
YOU SOUND LIKE YOU THINK YOU CAN DO BETTER!
ME? NO, I DIDN'T SAY...
LET'S ROCK 'N ROLL!
WHAT? WAIT, I'M NOT READY!!
GRUDGE MATCH!
Peirce

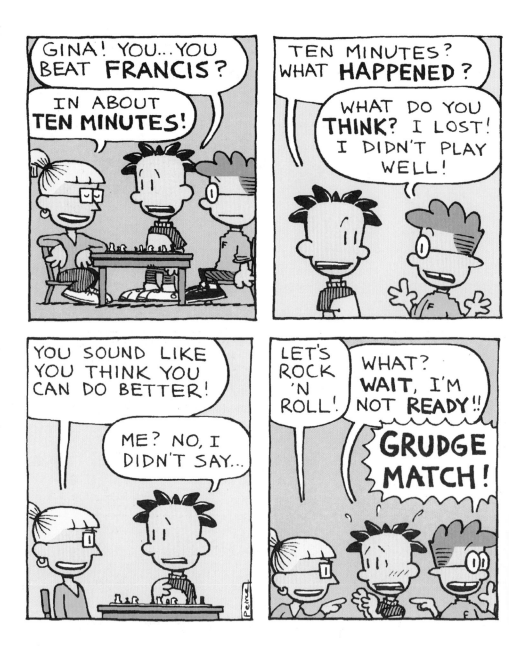

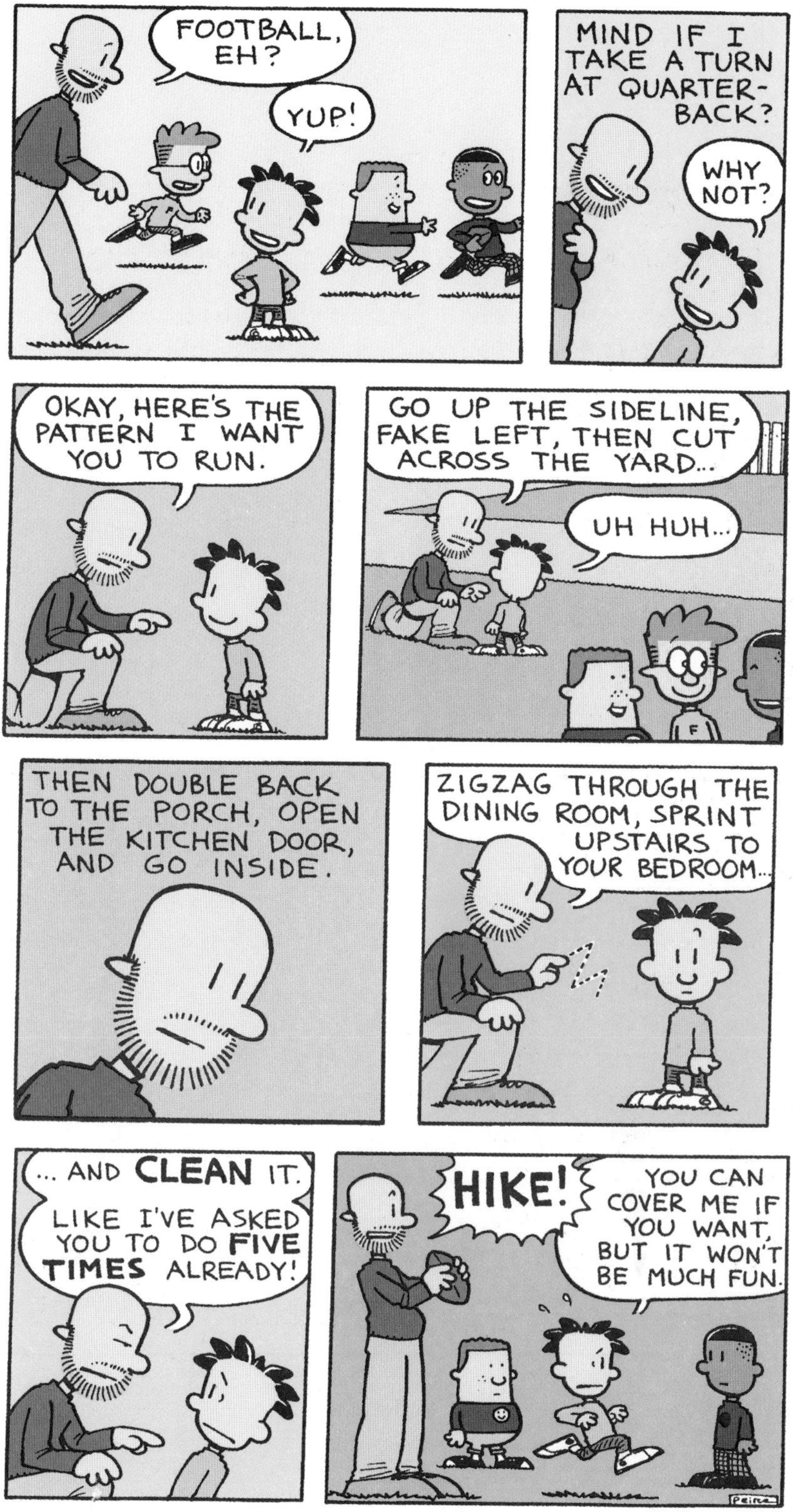
FOOTBALL, EH?
YUP!
MIND IF I TAKE A TURN AT QUARTER-BACK?
WHY NOT?
OKAY, HERE'S THE PATTERN I WANT YOU TO RUN.
GO UP THE SIDELINE, FAKE LEFT, THEN CUT ACROSS THE YARD...
UH HUH...
THEN DOUBLE BACK TO THE PORCH, OPEN THE KITCHEN DOOR, AND GO INSIDE.
ZIGZAG THROUGH THE DINING ROOM, SPRINT UPSTAIRS TO YOUR BEDROOM...
... AND CLEAN IT.
LIKE I'VE ASKED YOU TO DO FIVE TIMES ALREADY!
HIKE!
YOU CAN COVER ME IF YOU WANT, BUT IT WON'T BE MUCH FUN.
PEIRCE

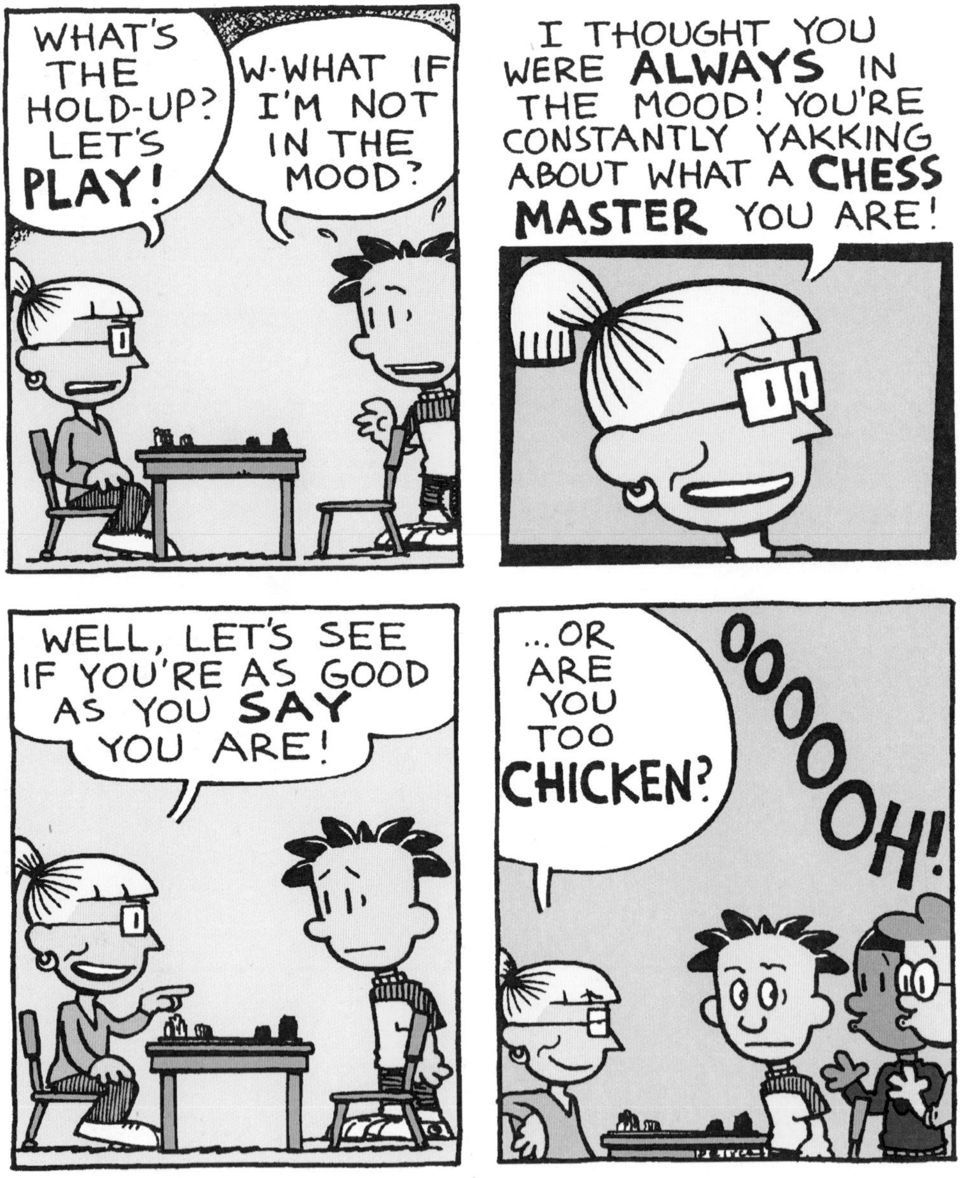
WHAT'S THE HOLD-UP? LET'S PLAY!
W-WHAT IF I'M NOT IN THE MOOD?
I THOUGHT YOU WERE ALWAYS IN THE MOOD! YOU'RE CONSTANTLY YAKKING ABOUT WHAT A CHESS MASTER YOU ARE!
WELL, LET'S SEE IF YOU'RE AS GOOD AS YOU SAY YOU ARE!
...OR ARE YOU TOO CHICKEN?
OOOOOOH!

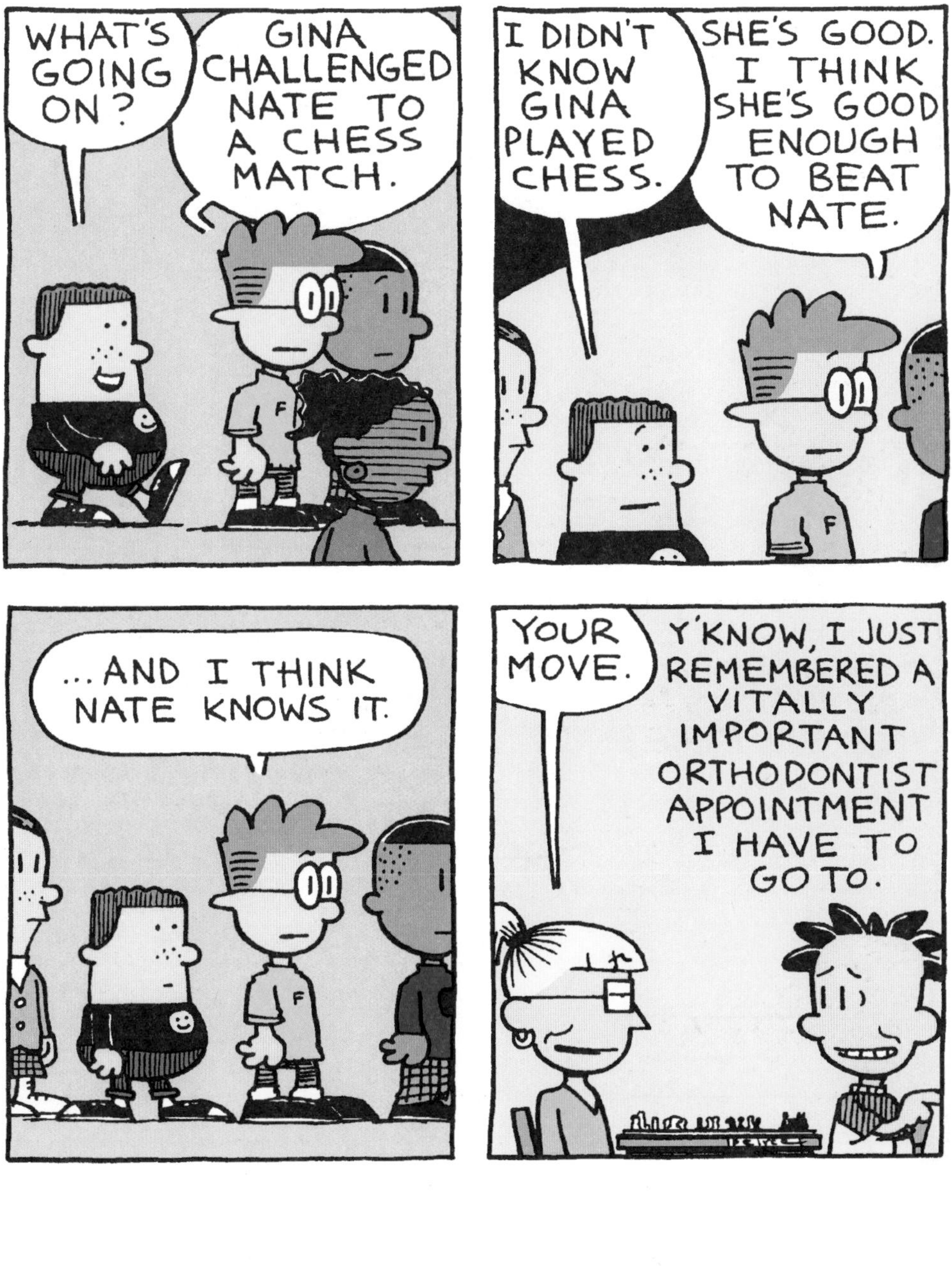
WHAT'S GOING ON?
GINA CHALLENGED NATE TO A CHESS MATCH.
I DIDN'T KNOW GINA PLAYED CHESS.
SHE'S GOOD. I THINK SHE'S GOOD ENOUGH TO BEAT NATE.
...AND I THINK NATE KNOWS IT.
YOUR MOVE.
Y'KNOW, I JUST REMEMBERED A VITALLY IMPORTANT ORTHODONTIST APPOINTMENT I HAVE TO GO TO.

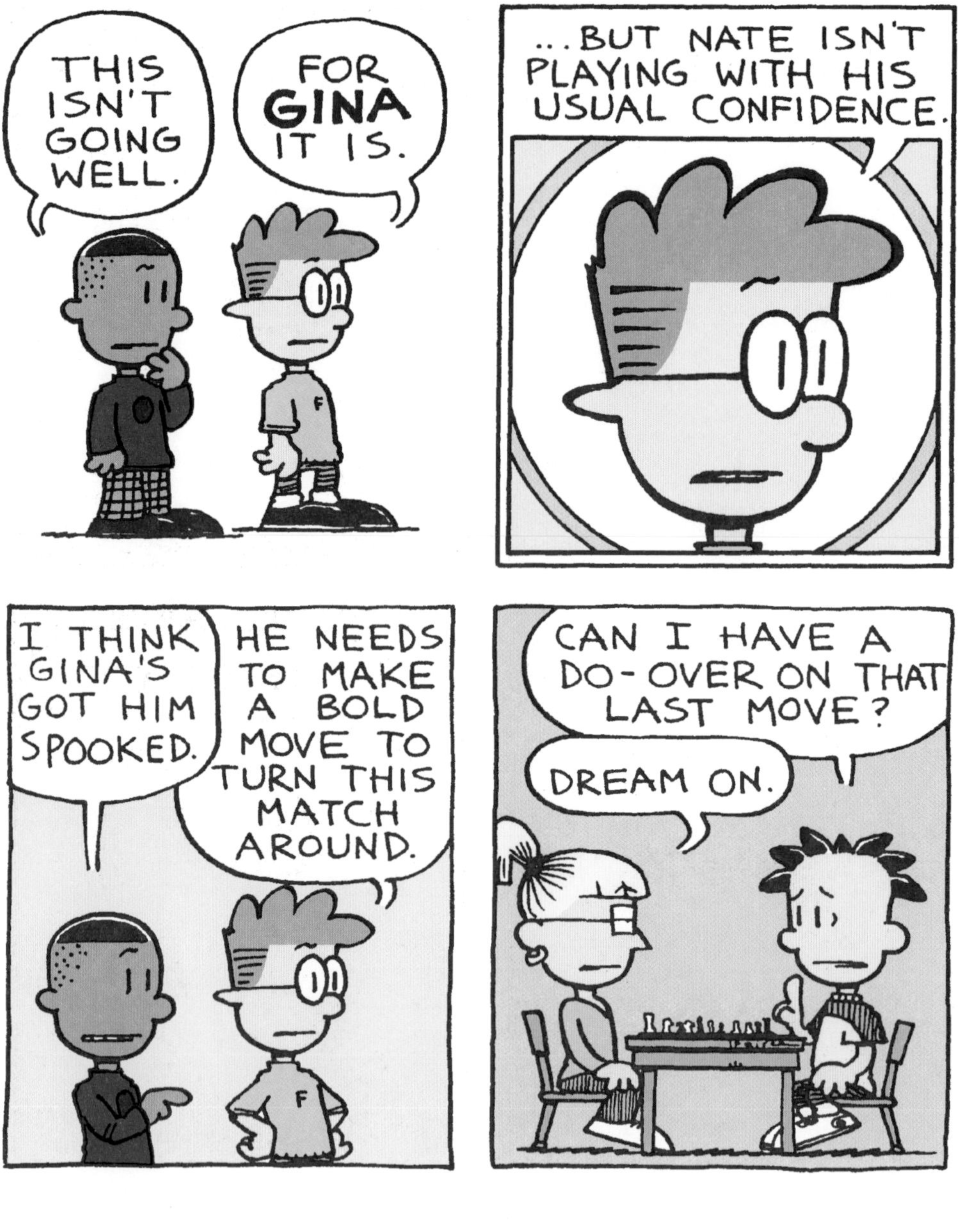
THIS ISN'T GOING WELL.
FOR GINA IT IS.
...BUT NATE ISN'T PLAYING WITH HIS USUAL CONFIDENCE.
I THINK GINA'S GOT HIM SPOOKED.
HE NEEDS TO MAKE A BOLD MOVE TO TURN THIS MATCH AROUND.
CAN I HAVE A DO-OVER ON THAT LAST MOVE?
DREAM ON.

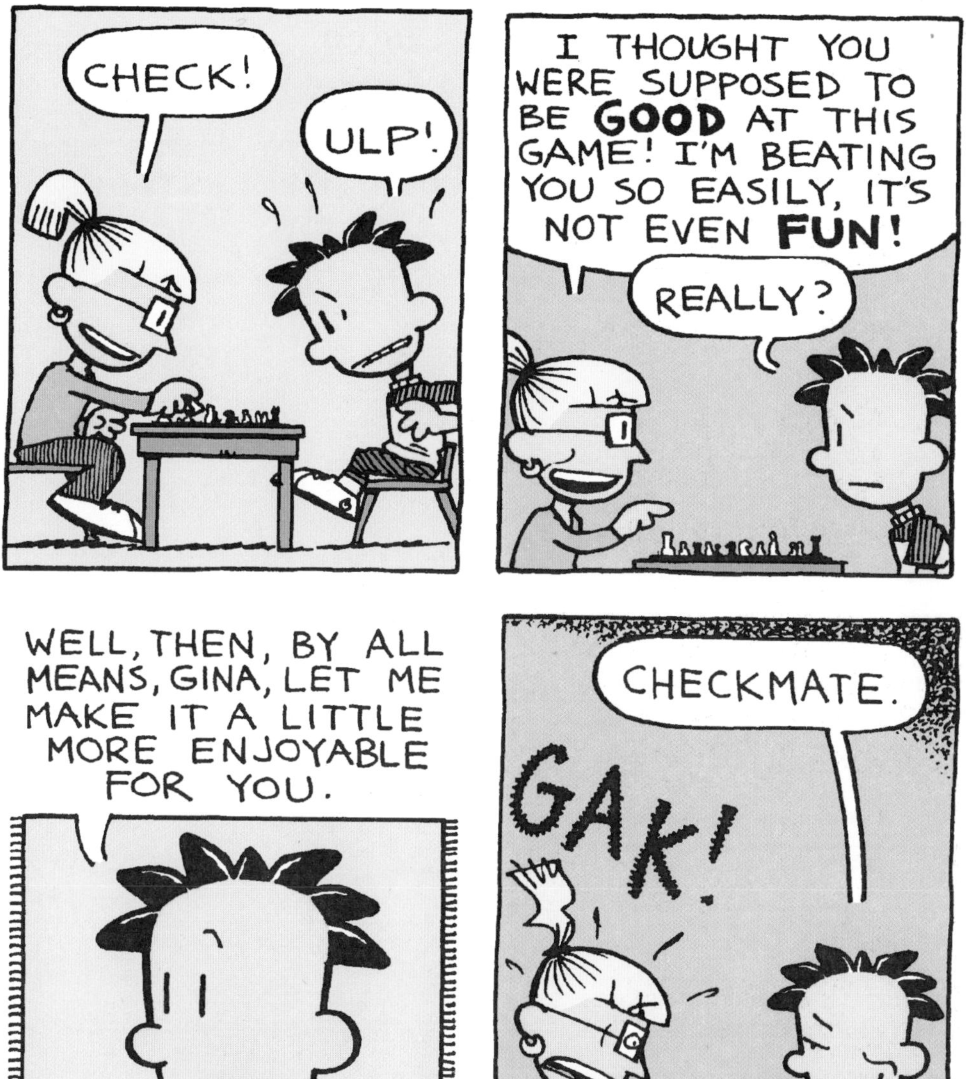
CHECK!
ULP!
I THOUGHT YOU WERE SUPPOSED TO BE **GOOD** AT THIS GAME! I'M BEATING YOU SO EASILY, IT'S NOT EVEN **FUN**!
REALLY?
WELL, THEN, BY ALL MEANS, GINA, LET ME MAKE IT A LITTLE MORE ENJOYABLE FOR YOU.
CHECKMATE.
GAK!

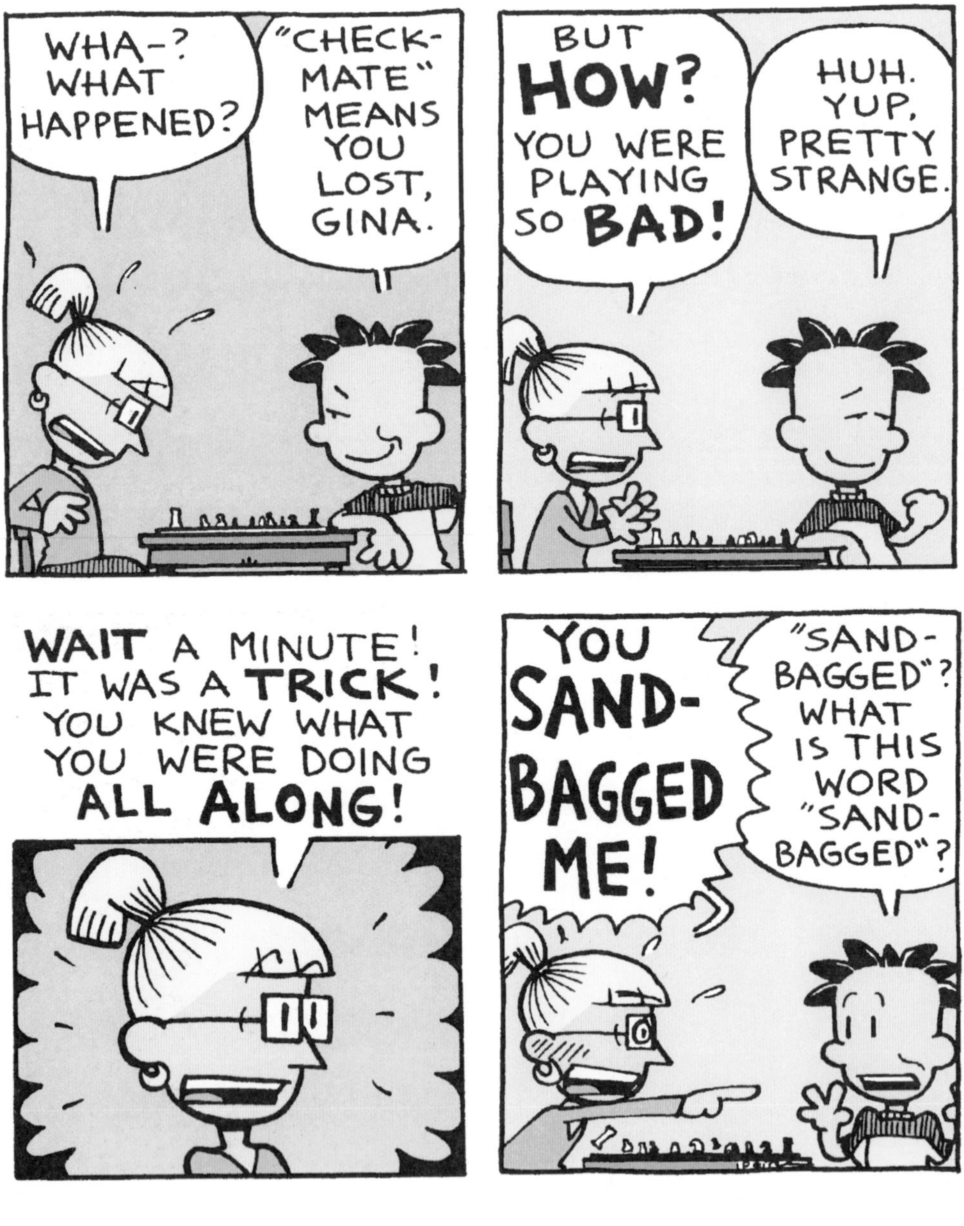

WHA-? WHAT HAPPENED?
"CHECK-MATE" MEANS YOU LOST, GINA.
BUT HOW? YOU WERE PLAYING SO BAD!
HUH. YUP, PRETTY STRANGE.
WAIT A MINUTE! IT WAS A TRICK! YOU KNEW WHAT YOU WERE DOING ALL ALONG!
YOU SAND-BAGGED ME!
"SAND-BAGGED"? WHAT IS THIS WORD "SAND-BAGGED"?

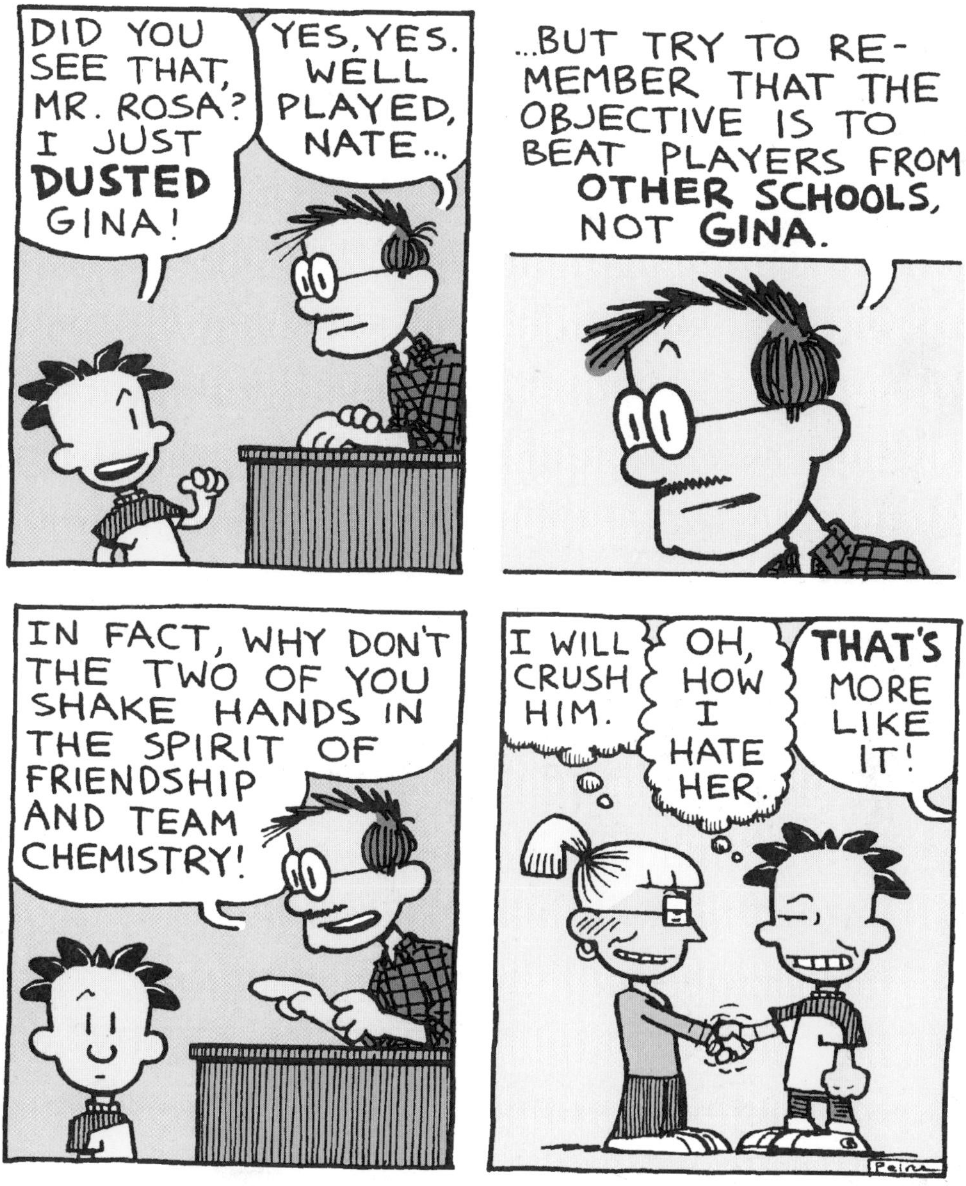
DID YOU SEE THAT, MR. ROSA? I JUST **DUSTED** GINA!
YES, YES. WELL PLAYED, NATE...
...BUT TRY TO RE-MEMBER THAT THE OBJECTIVE IS TO BEAT PLAYERS FROM **OTHER SCHOOLS**, NOT **GINA**.
IN FACT, WHY DON'T THE TWO OF YOU SHAKE HANDS IN THE SPIRIT OF FRIENDSHIP AND TEAM CHEMISTRY!
I WILL CRUSH HIM.
OH, HOW I HATE HER.
THAT'S MORE LIKE IT!
Peirce

Big Nate is distributed internationally by Universal Uclick.

Big Nate: Revenge of the Cream Puffs copyright © 2016 by United Feature Syndicate, Inc. All rights reserved. Printed in China. No part of this book may be used or reproduced in any manner whatsoever without written permission except in the case of reprints in the context of reviews.

Andrews McMeel Publishing
a division of Andrews McMeel Universal
1130 Walnut Street, Kansas City, Missouri 64106

www.andrewsmcmeel.com

17 18 19 20 21 SDB 10 9 8 7 6 5 4

ISBN: 978-1-4494-6228-4

Library of Congress Control Number: 2016930933

Made by:
Shenzhen Donnelley Printing Company Ltd.
Address and location of manufacturer:
No. 47, Wuhe Nan Road, Bantian Ind. Zone,
Shenzhen China, 518129
4th Printing—2/20/17

These strips appeared in newspapers from April 22, 2012, through October 13, 2012.

Big Nate can be viewed on the Internet at www.gocomics.com/big_nate

ATTENTION: SCHOOLS AND BUSINESSES
Andrews McMeel books are available at quantity discounts with bulk purchase for educational, business, or sales promotional use. For information, please e-mail the Andrews McMeel Publishing Special Sales Department:
specialsales@amuniversal.com

THE Epic Collection for Every *Big Nate* Fan

- How *Big Nate* got started

- *Diary of a Wimpy Kid* author Jeff Kinney's interview with Lincoln Peirce

- TONS of cartoons

AND MUCH, MUCH MORE!

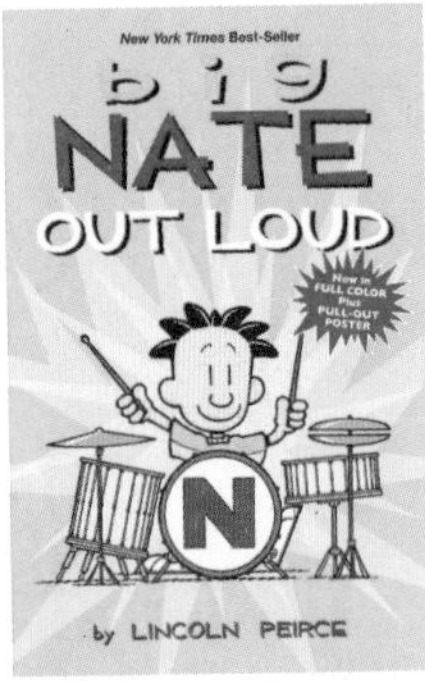

New York Times Best-Seller
big NATE
OUT LOUD
by LINCOLN PEIRCE

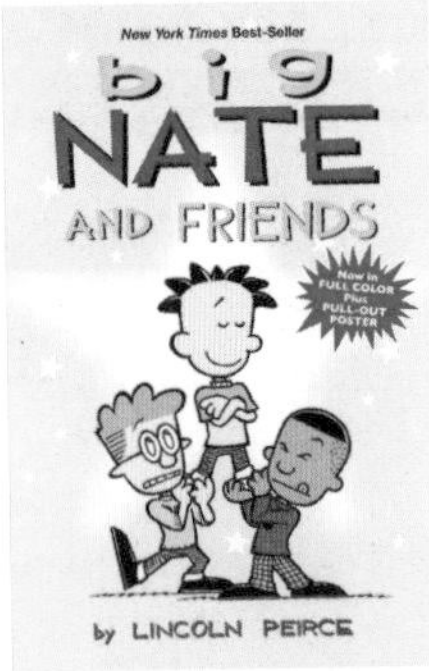

New York Times Best-Seller
big NATE
AND FRIENDS
by LINCOLN PEIRCE

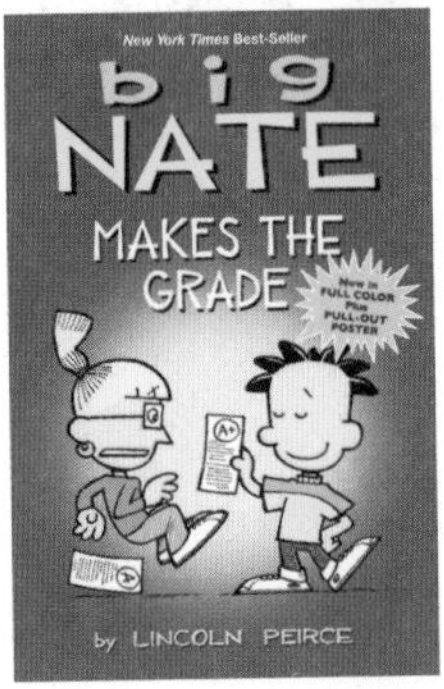

New York Times Best-Seller
big NATE
MAKES THE GRADE
by LINCOLN PEIRCE

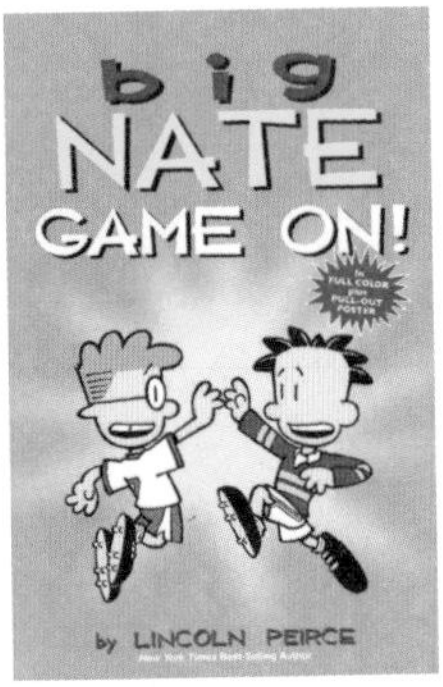

big NATE
GAME ON!
by LINCOLN PEIRCE

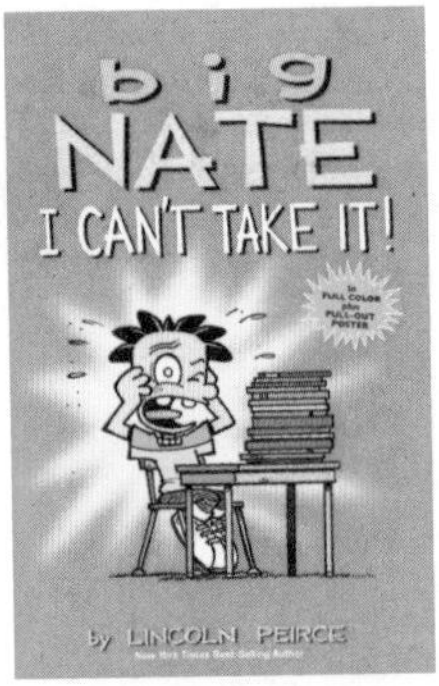

big NATE
I CAN'T TAKE IT!
by LINCOLN PEIRCE

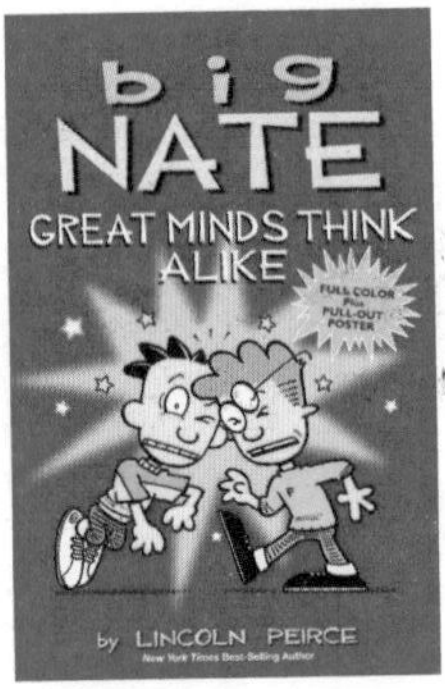

big NATE
GREAT MINDS THINK ALIKE
by LINCOLN PEIRCE

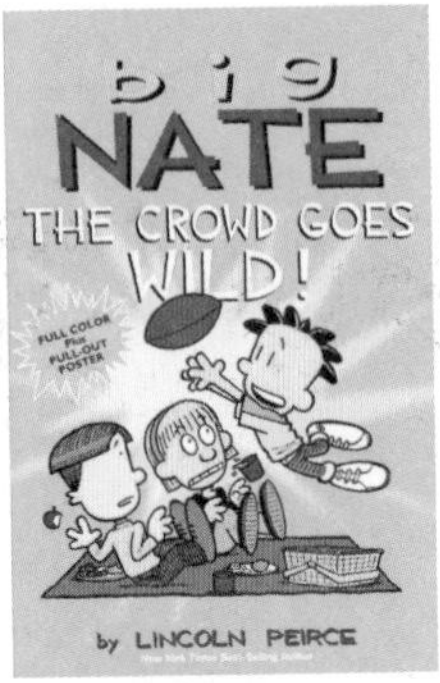

big NATE
THE CROWD GOES WILD!
by LINCOLN PEIRCE

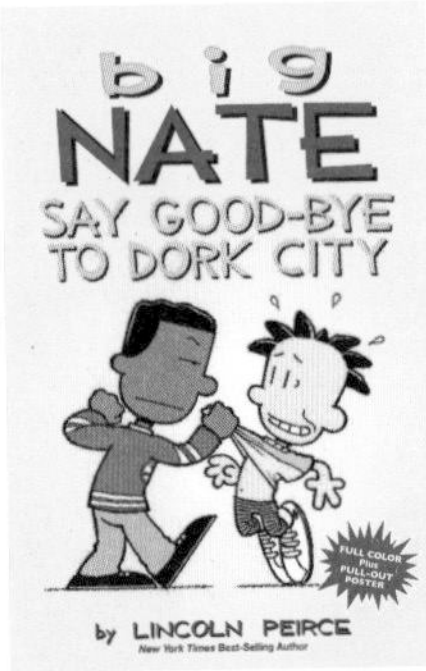

big NATE
SAY GOOD-BYE TO DORK CITY
by LINCOLN PEIRCE

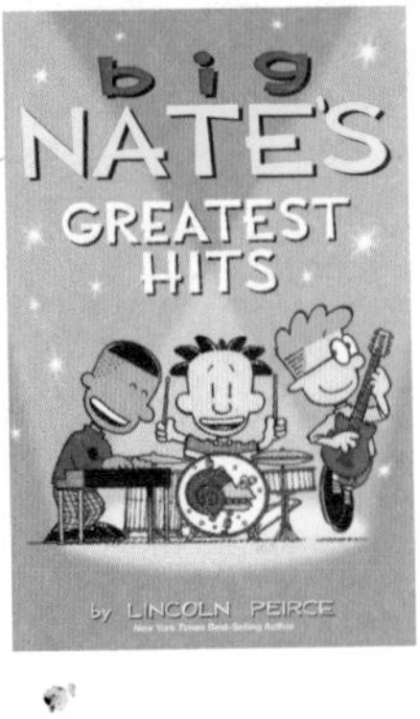

big NATE'S
GREATEST HITS
by LINCOLN PEIRCE

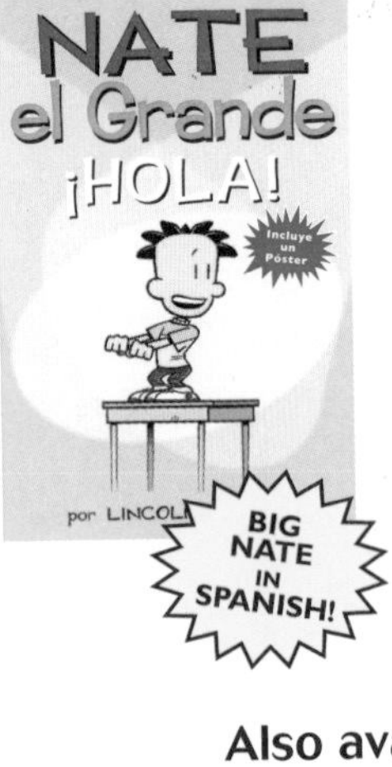

NATE el Grande
¡HOLA!
BIG NATE IN SPANISH!

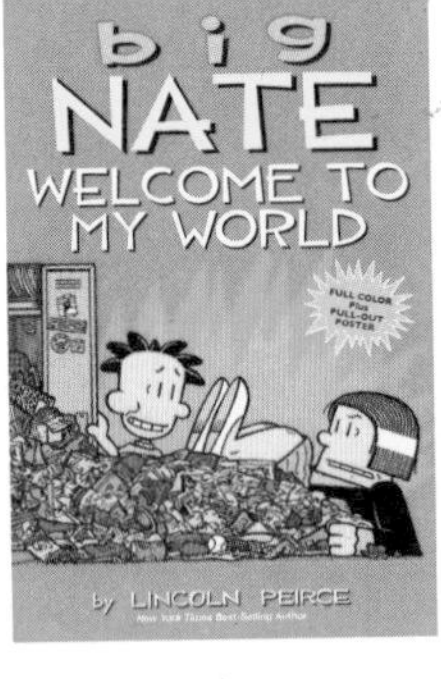

big NATE
WELCOME TO MY WORLD
by LINCOLN PEIRCE

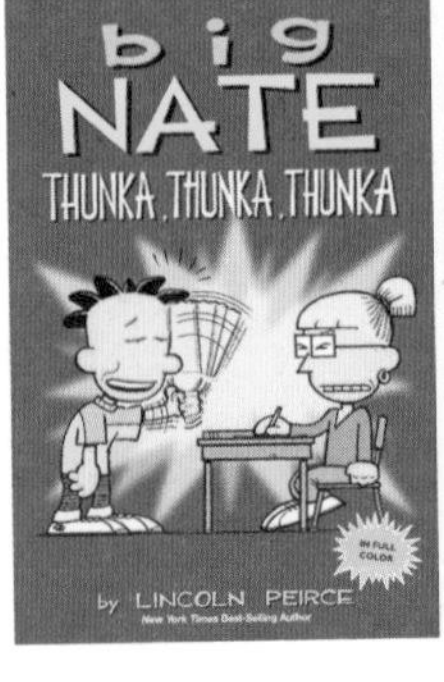

big NATE
THUNKA, THUNKA, THUNKA
by LINCOLN PEIRCE

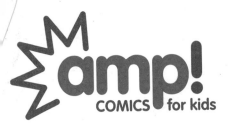